R

David Cliffe spent nearly five decades working as a journalist on newspapers, magazines and in public relations.

Born in North Staffordshire, he has a strong bond with Leek and the Moorlands, having lived in the town for many years. He is a former editor of several publications, including the *Leek Post & Times*. A local history enthusiast, David has a particular interest in Victorian and Edwardian photography and has published two books on the subject.

The Buried Secret, published in 2021, was his first work of fiction and proved an immediate success, its many local references being particularly popular with readers. An audio version has been recorded by the Staffordshire Moorlands Talking Newspaper. A musical work, based on scenes from the book, is planned to receive its premiere in 2026.

Images of Revenge, the second in the *Old Leek Mystery* series, has been similarly successful and was runner-up for the Arnold Bennett Book Prize 2025.

The Chilled Affair once again follows the exploits of the book's main characters in Leek and the Staffordshire Moorlands in Edwardian times.

Also by David Cliffe

Fiction

The Buried Secret: Old Leek Mystery N°1
A tale of death, deceit and detection in Edwardian Leek

Images of Revenge: Old Leek Mystery N°2
Tragedy strikes when a theatre comes to Leek
Runner-up, Arnold Bennett Book Prize 2025

Non-fiction

A Moorland Album: Leek, Cheadle and neighbouring villages in Edwardian times from the photographs of W.H. Nithsdale

Victorian Views: Leek & District's first photographers

For more information or to purchase any of the above titles, email moorlandalbum@gmail.com

THE CHILLED AFFAIR

DAVID CLIFFE

A WINTER OF FEAR
AND SUSPICION
IN THE MOORLANDS

First published November 2025

ISBN 978-1-83688-605-1

Typeset and designed by David Cliffe
moorlandalbum@gmail.com

Published by Independent Publishing Network

Printed by Biddles Books Ltd, King's Lynn

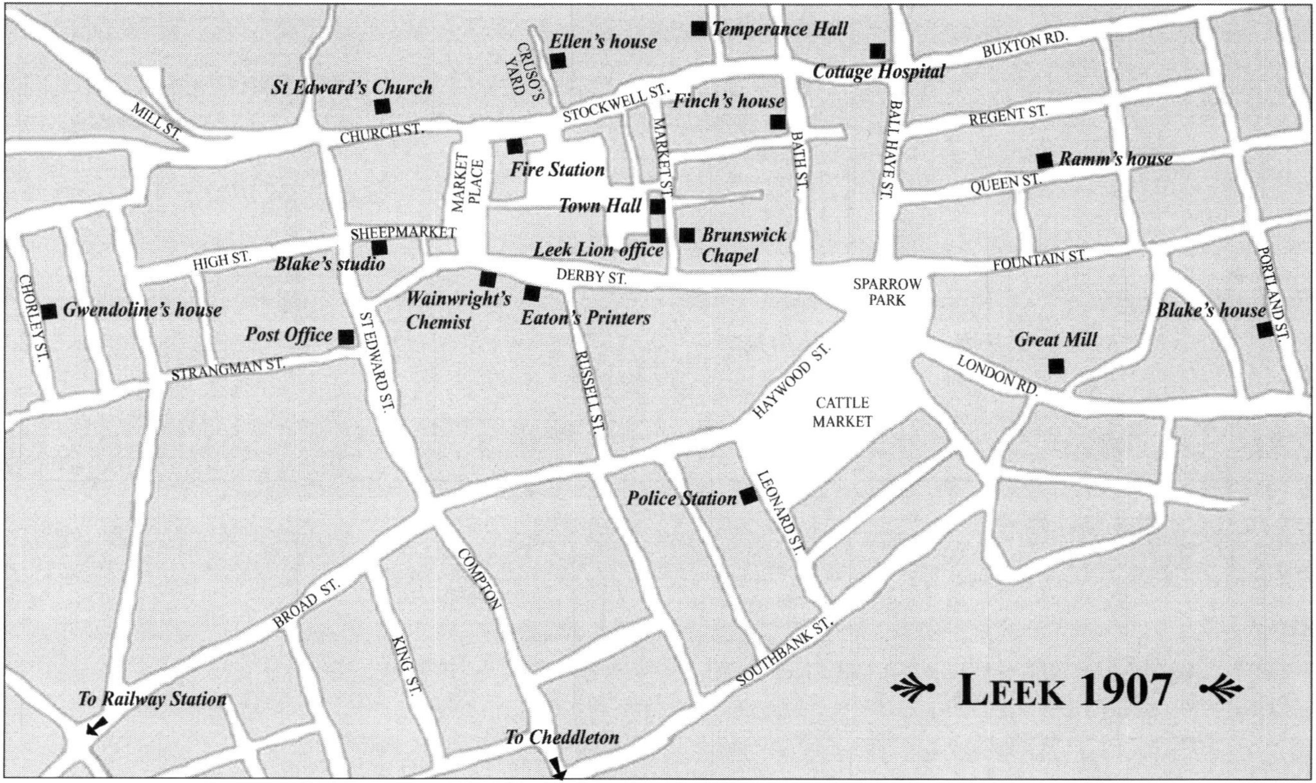
LEEK 1907
Temperance Hall
Ellen's house
Cottage Hospital
BUXTON RD.
CRUSO'S YARD
St Edward's Church
STOCKWELL ST.
Finch's house
MILL ST.
CHURCH ST.
MARKET ST.
BATH ST.
BALL HAYE ST.
REGENT ST.
Fire Station
Ramm's house
MARKET PLACE
QUEEN ST.
Town Hall
Brunswick Chapel
SHEEPMARKET
Leek Lion office
HIGH ST.
Blake's studio
FOUNTAIN ST.
DERBY ST.
PORTLAND ST.
SPARROW PARK
CHORLEY ST.
Gwendoline's house
Wainwright's Chemist
Eaton's Printers
Blake's house
Post Office
ST EDWARD ST.
Great Mill
HAYWOOD ST.
LONDON RD.
STRANGMAN ST.
RUSSELL ST.
CATTLE MARKET
Police Station
LEONARD ST.
COMPTON
BROAD ST.
KING ST.
SOUTHBANK ST.
To Railway Station
To Cheddleton

A Word of Thanks

The Chilled Affair would not have been possible without the wise words and eagle eyes of my wife Delia and my friend David Butler. I would also like to thank Leek artist Gavin Bowyer ASGFA who has again provided a fine drawing for the front cover.

The encouragement and enthusiasm of my readers from across the Staffordshire Moorlands and beyond has not only been humbling, but has been the motivation for me to complete this third *Old Leek Mystery*.

David Cliffe, Leek, November 2025

Prologue

He clicked open his pocket watch. Half past seven. He had plenty of time, but he would have to take care – it was treacherous out there.

He put on his tweed coat and stepped out into the night. He didn't need to check the brass thermometer on the wall to know that it was well below freezing now.

He glanced up and saw the great tower rising up against an inky black sky, pinpricked by sparkling stars.

Through the fence, the snow covered field was glowing a ghostly blue in the moonlight. As he walked down the familiar path, he thought again about the curious message he had received that morning. What was so urgent? He would soon find out.

The snow was deeper in the valley bottom, but he marched on with long strides. When he finally reached the canal he saw silvery ice was starting to form on its surface. The temperature was still plunging. By midnight the canal would be frozen solid, he thought.

He waited in silence, his breath billowing white in the chilled air. Towards Leek, a barge was moored, smoke drifting up from its stovepipe. On the path beside it, a strange black shape was moving and his heart beat a little faster. He relaxed when he realised it was a draft horse, draped in a blanket for the night.

Suddenly something dark shifted amongst the frosted branches by his side. Had he disturbed a bird? Or was someone hiding there?

"Hello?" he called out. "Who's there? Is that you?"

Things happened quickly after that. The peace of the night was shattered by his cry of pain and the sound of thin ice on the canal being cracked into pieces. Then came the heart stopping shock of the freezing water.

He made a final desperate struggle, but couldn't stop himself sinking below the surface.

The stars dimmed and blackness descended.

Chapter One

January 1907

Cora had feared this day might not go well, but she had no inkling what really lay ahead: a chain of events that would change her life for ever.

It was Thursday the sixth of January. The year was not yet a week old and the moorlands were gripped by the harshest winter in memory. For Cora Blake and her stepfather, Nathaniel, the journey from Leek had been arduous, deep ruts of snow and frozen mud making the road almost impassable. Progress became easier when their trap turned off the highway and they joined a long winding driveway, swept clear of snow. On their right, a large sign announced their destination – Cheddleton County Pauper Lunatic Asylum.

On the hilltop ahead, a great tower loomed ominously and sent a shiver down Cora's spine. It was an awesome sight and she could not help thinking about the gossip she had heard, that people were locked inside it.

As they drew closer, her stomach churned as she took in the sheer size of the buildings. The huge asylum had become a landmark on the edge of the village of Cheddleton, some three miles south of Leek. At its centre, the huge red brick tower had been built to hold thousands of gallons of water, not asylum patients as some local folk had said. It stood eight storeys tall, a conical slate roof piercing the grey January sky.

Cora had never imagined she would see inside the asylum, but today she would. She was going to there to work.

For five years, Cora had assisted her father who was Leek's leading photographer. Developing hundreds of his glass negatives, printing thousands of his picture postcards and greeting countless customers at his studio. Now, at the age of twenty, she was at last going behind the camera on her first photographic assignment. She would be helping Nathaniel to make a complete record of the asylum, currently being extended to become one of the largest in the country.

She was filled with a mixture of excitement and trepidation as they approached the grand main entrance and gripped the side of the trap with her mittened hand. When her father had told her of the project, she knew it was a step towards becoming a photographer in her own right. However this would be no ordinary place to work and she had spent hours imagining what it was like inside this refuge, a place of protection for a thousand ailing people, closed off from the outside world.

Nathaniel sensed her unease. "There's nothing to fear, my dear. I am sure that everything will go splendidly," he reassured his daughter, giving her arm a friendly squeeze through her winter coat. "I have every confidence in you, Cora. You have mastered the art and the science of photography. This is your chance to show your creativity behind the camera. I expect the staff here will be most helpful."

"But what about the people who are being kept here?" Cora had asked the same question many times in recent days, but still sought his reassurance.

"I doubt we will see many. A lot of them will be safely in their wards, as I understand it," Blake replied. "And in any case, the folk are here to be cared for and, hopefully, to become well again. You need have no worries."

Cora said nothing. Since the County Asylum had come to the moorlands there had been lurid stories about what went on here, the sort of thing gossiped about in pubs, shops and tea rooms.

They climbed down from the trap and unloaded their leather cases of cameras, photographic plates and tripods. Blake glanced up at the clock tower which rose high above the entrance and saw it was just past one o'clock. He asked the driver to collect them in three hours. That would be sufficient for their first visit, he decided, and in any case the light would be fading by then. He knew they would need to make several more visits before their assignment was complete.

Blake reached forward and pressed a brass button at the side of the great double doors. From within came the faint sound of an electric bell followed by a key being turned in a lock. One of the heavy doors swung open to reveal a male member of staff in an immaculate dark uniform. He looked first at Nathaniel, then at Cora and finally at their baggage before beckoning them into a wide entrance hall.

The man returned to his post behind a high desk on the right which bore a nameplate stating 'Hall Porter'. He pressed a button on the desk and soon afterwards a nurse appeared from a side door. She wore a dark blue uniform with a starched white apron that stretched almost to her feet. A white headdress draped onto her shoulders and reminded Blake of a nun's habit.

"I take it that you are Mr Blake. We have been expecting you," she announced with some authority. "My name is Ellis and I am the Matron here at the County Asylum. I will show you where you may take your..." she glanced down suspiciously at the leather cases, "your accoutrements so that you may begin your work."

Before Nathaniel could reply, she continued in a disciplined tone. "Senior Medical Assistant Gibson is in charge at the moment. Dr Menzies, our Medical Superintendent, is away on important business. Dr Gibson is a very busy man, so he will not have the time to see you today. However, he has asked me to ensure that you have everything you need."

Cora looked around a little uncertainly. There were mahogany doors on either side of the hallway, one had a brass plaque stating 'Medical Superintendent' and the other 'Committee Room'. In front of her stretched a corridor so long she could barely make out the far end. Its green linoleum floor was highly polished and many doors led off on either side. She was surprised to see there were no gas mantles on the walls, instead electric light bulbs hung from the ceiling every few feet.

She saw a uniformed nurse emerge from a door far down the corridor, many yards from where they stood. The woman immediately turned and locked the door behind her before hurrying away.

There was silence apart from what Cora thought was the occasional shout from somewhere deep inside the building. What struck her the most was the heat. She had never been in a building that was so warm in the depths of winter and imagined the large cast iron radiators must be almost glowing.

Blake surveyed his surroundings enthusiastically, eager to explore the impressive building and record it for posterity. Seeing his interest, the Matron said: "This is one of the most modern and best equipped asylums in the kingdom. The County Lunacy Committee is proud of the facilities we have here."

Blake nodded briskly. "We are very much looking forward to working here."

The Matron cast a glance at Cora, who was slightly built and looked younger than her age. "And you are Mr Blake's helper?" she asked, obviously expecting this young woman to be tasked with carrying the photographer's bags.

"This is my daughter, Cora. She will be taking some of the photographs," Blake announced proudly.

"Indeed?" said the Matron, apparently surprised to hear the young woman would be capable of operating a camera.

"If you are ready to begin, I will show you the way," she continued brusquely. "I gather it is intended you should start in the kitchens and the main hall. The inmates have finished their meal in the hall and have all returned to the wards or the workshops. The ward doors are kept locked and you are not allowed to enter any secure part of the asylum without prior arrangement with a member of staff. An attendant will accompany you at all times."

Nathaniel and Cora gathered up their cases and followed Matron Ellis as she led the way down the corridor. Cora knew there was no turning back now. She needed to put from her mind all thoughts of the people in the wards and concentrate on what she saw through the camera lens.

A quarter of an hour later, Blake was gazing up at the hammer beam roof of the main hall. He shook his head in amazement. "This is bigger than Leek Town Hall!" he mused.

The great hall was where many hundreds of meals were served three times a day and was laid out with long tables covered with white tablecloths. On other occasions it was used for dances, concerts and theatrical entertainments – a huge stage and orchestra pit were built into the far end. A few days previously its cavernous roof space had been filled with flags, bunting and streamers for a grand New Year's Ball. Blake had been asked to come back in two weeks' time to photograph another important social event in the hall, the Annual Soirée, which was laid on for the better class patients.

The size of the hall was in keeping with the scale of the rest of the asylum. Blake already knew much about the huge project thanks to his friend FJ Finch, Editor of the *Leek Lion*, the town's weekly newspaper. Like any good journalist, Finch could supply endless facts and figures. He had told Blake how five hundred men had been involved in the construction, laying 18 million bricks, many supplied by the nearby works at Wall Grange. When the asylum had opened seven years' earlier, it accommodated 618 people, but the County Lunacy Committee had quickly realised it was not large enough. The current extensions would mean its wards would hold 1,038, an equal number of men and women, many drawn from far beyond the county.

The buildings were equipped with central heating and there were electric lights throughout, powered by the asylum's own generators. An electric tramway linked the asylum to the North Staffordshire Railway at Leekbrook. It was used to bring in visitors once a week, as well as hundreds of tons of coal for the mighty boilers which heated the radiators and provided steam for the generators. Water was supplied by a private borehole in the valley below which was piped into a tank in the top of the huge tower. Another modern innovation was the installation of flushing toilets throughout the building.

Blake had set up his camera of polished mahogany and brass in the hall after leaving Cora to begin photographing the adjoining kitchens with another camera. The cooking facilities were equally impressive, equipped with the latest steam ovens and great cauldrons that were used to heat gallons of tea and soup.

A uniformed male attendant watched with curiosity as Blake dipped his head under his black cloth hood and peered into the back of his camera before adjusting the focus of the lens and inserting a glass photographic plate. After taking several images, he was about to move his tripod to a new position when he saw Cora appear in a doorway at the far end of the hall, a female attendant standing behind her.

“Father! You need to come!” Cora called.

Fearing some mishap, Blake dashed across. He could see she was upset. There had been times in the past when his headstrong stepdaughter had seemed to attract trouble. She had been in mortal jeopardy on more than one occasion. Surely it could not be happening again?

“Whatever is the matter, my dear?”

“It is not me, Father. There is something amiss outside,” she said. “A fellow has just rushed in and said that someone is trapped in the ice on the canal. He said they need people with spades or something.”

As a responsible member of the community, Blake was always prepared to lend a hand in an emergency. But as a photographer, he also realised this might be the sort of incident he should capture with his camera. He was used to being confronted by dramatic events. He had worked with the town’s police force for some years, recording the scenes of crime and, on occasion, his pictures helping to identify culprits.

“Did they say whereabouts on the canal?” he asked urgently.

“It must be nearby, Father. Somewhere behind the asylum, I think,” Cora replied, turning to point behind her. The attendant nodded in agreement. “He came in through the yard at the back,” the woman said.

Blake knew the Leek Arm of the Caldon Canal ran near to the rear of the asylum grounds and he should be able to reach it in a matter of minutes.

“You stay here, while I go to see what is going on,” he told Cora before taking a smaller portable camera from his case.

Pulling on his coat, he hurried through the kitchen and into a large store room where he spotted an external door stood ajar. Once outside, he ran across a cobbled yard and, with the great water tower in the background, finally found a gap in the boundary fence.

He looked across the snow covered valley. He could make out

the dark shapes of a group of people on the canal towing path a couple of hundred yards away.

Although the route across the field appeared well used, the snow and ice still made the going treacherous. Blake slithered and stumbled down a slope, crossed the railway line and then a footbridge over the ice-filled River Churnet. The drifts were deeper as he trudged onward across open ground and lumps of snow were clinging to his trousers and the hem of his coat by the time he clambered up a steep embankment to reach the towing path.

Four men in overalls were bent forward, looking at the silvery mass of the frozen canal. Two were pointing and another was poking at the solid ice with a garden hoe to little effect. Each seemed to be telling the others what to do.

Blake edged forward and peered down into the opaque ice. At first he could see nothing unusual. Its rippled surface was dotted with leaves and twigs from nearby trees and there was a scattering of snowflakes, but no sign of a person.

Then he focused more closely and was shocked to perceive a face staring back at him through the ice. No, not looking back, he realised. There was no life in those eyes. This was the face of a dead man.

Chapter Two

By the time Inspector Albert Ramm, senior officer of Leek Police, arrived at the scene, the light was beginning to fade. He had made his way across the snowy field from the asylum and now stood on the towing path surveying the frozen surface of the canal.

His expression was grim, not only because of the nature of the incident, but because he was chilled to the bone despite his heavy winter cape. He was stamping his feet, beating his hands at his sides and could taste frost on the fringe of his moustache.

Beside him two workmen had been chipping at the ice with long handled spades. Another wielded a long iron bar and had managed to poke a hole in the ice, which appeared to be several inches thick. Through the hole, the black shape of the victim's coat could be seen just beneath the surface of the water.

"Hit the ice harder," Ramm ordered with an exasperated tone. "We need to crack it and make a much bigger hole if we're ever going to haul him out. Constable Knowles, give them a hand, otherwise we'll still be here in the morning."

With the assistance of the constable, who had accompanied Ramm from the Leek station, the men set about their task with renewed vigour. Finally they managed to break the ice into jagged slabs and cleared a space large enough to reveal the body, or rather the head, shoulders and upper torso.

The task of pulling the man from the water was to prove equally difficult. First, the rescuers used their tools to try to snag the sodden clothing and pull the body closer to the canal bank. Next, they knelt on the snow covered ground and leaned as far forward as they dared so as to get a grip on the dead man's coat.

One of the workmen yelled out as he slipped headlong towards the ice, saving himself with outstretched arms. His mates hauled him back onto the towing path. "Thought I were going in the cut next," said the man as he shook frost and snow from his overalls. He looked unhappily at his cap which now lay some feet away on the frozen surface.

The efforts resumed with the added muscle of the Cheddleton village constable, a police boxing champion named Hawkins and a useful man to have around in such circumstances.

Finally the body, weighed down by freezing water, was dragged out of the canal and onto the towing path. A greenish brown mess of weed and rotting leaves was smeared over the man's clothes. His skin was as white as the snow on the ground around them.

The Inspector stooped closer to get a better look at the man and noted that his features were not as bloated and discoloured as other drowning victims he had seen fished out of local canals and lakes in the past. This made him wonder if the man had been in the water a relatively short length of time. Ramm could see they were dealing with a very tall man who, in life, may have been decidedly slim. His face was notable for an aquiline nose and a beard that was closely cropped.

"A tragic affair and no mistake," said Ramm. "The fellow may have slipped on the towing path and fallen in, but if that was the case, it must have been days ago before the canal froze solid. Or he might have stepped on the ice and it cracked," he said. "Or," he paused and looked back towards the mass of buildings on the hill behind him, "he could have come from the asylum and thrown himself in. It wouldn't be the first time something like that has happened."

Ramm knew that since the County Asylum opened there had been a number of incidents where inmates had lost their lives.

Several had been found in the stretches of canal which bordered the grounds on two sides and one had even been knocked down by the electric tram that ran up the incline from Leekbrook.

"Shall we take him up to the asylum, Sir? Might be easier. They have their own mortuary, don't they?" suggested Constable Knowles.

Ramm considered for a moment, but decided he did not want asylum staff involved, at least not until he knew who and what they were dealing with.

"No, put him in the cart and I will join you directly. Let's get the body to the Cottage Hospital as soon as possible so that Dr Handbridge can take a look at him. And Knowles, check the fellow's pockets to see if there is anything to identify him."

The body was carried off on a stretcher brought from the asylum while Ramm lingered to assess the scene in what was left of the daylight. Any evidence of what might have gone on had probably been covered by the recent snowfalls and then trampled in the efforts to recover the body, he thought. There were dark brown patches in the snow which he took to be mud. He looked along the canal towards Leek and saw a barge was moored, stuck fast in the ice. Thin spirals of smoke rose from its narrow chimney and a hefty draft horse was tethered close by.

Beside the barge stood a heavily built figure whom Ramm took to be the boatman, marooned until the canal thawed or an ice breaker was brought along. Despite the cold, the man was wearing only a singlet above his moleskin trousers. He had been watching the desperate operation to release the body and now, hands on hips, he continued to gaze towards Ramm.

It would be worth speaking to the bargee in case he had seen an incident on the path, the Inspector thought. However, the barge folk would have to wait. First he wanted to check with the asylum management. There was a chance the matter might be cleared up quickly.

Ramm was about to descend the steep embankment from the canal when Nathaniel Blake approached. The two men had come to know each other well through the photographer's work for the police. In the past, Blake had been caught up in some of Ramm's most curious cases. So had his daughter.

"Cora and I had just started to take photographs at the asylum – the buildings and such like – when I heard something was going on down here," Blake explained. He patted his camera. "I took pictures of the poor fellow in the ice and also when the men got him onto the towing path. I can let you have some prints tomorrow, Inspector."

"Thank you, Mr Blake. Your timely presence may be of help to us, once more. But to be honest, I think this is probably a straightforward affair. Most likely an unfortunate accident. The man wouldn't have lasted long in the water in temperatures such as this," Ramm replied.

There was a hint of frustration in his tone. If this death was an accident, he thought, then his own freezing excursion to Cheddleton had most likely been a waste of his valuable time. He would be glad to get back to the station, slip off his galoshes and revive himself in front of his office fire. However, he also knew it was wise not to jump to conclusions. There had been cases in the past – including at least one involving Blake and his daughter – that had seemed routine at first, but had turned out very much to the contrary.

The two began to make their way across the fields away from the canal before climbing the slope into the asylum grounds.

"What a mighty establishment this has grown into," said Ramm as he surveyed the buildings stretching across the hilltop. "I wonder at the location, though. So exposed on this hill, you can see it for miles."

"The authorities wanted a site where those in their care can get plenty of fresh air. It is all part of the treatment, apparently,"

Blake replied, quoting more information supplied by his friend Finch. "I think they plan to plant quite a lot of trees eventually, so one day much of it will be masked by greenery."

When they reached the rear yard, Ramm said: "I intend to have a word with the Medical Superintendent before I leave. The asylum may well be connected with this affair."

"Dr Menzies is away at some conference in France, or so I've been told. There is someone by the name of Gibson in charge at the moment, his deputy. The office is next to the main door," Blake explained. "For myself, I need to find out where Cora has got to. She insisted on following me after I went down to the canal, but I sent her back inside. It was no place for her to be. I don't think she was up to taking any more photographs, though."

Seeing no sign of Cora in the kitchen or the main hall, Blake asked an attendant and was told his daughter had been taken to the nurses' sitting room on the female side of the asylum. He was led through a succession of doors and corridors to what turned out to be a homely room furnished with a dining table, potted plants and even a piano. Cora, who was seated in one of the comfortable chairs with a teacup in her hand, looked up anxiously as he entered.

"I know you said not to follow, Father, but I just had to come out to find you. I simply could not rest until I knew what was going on," she said. "It looked so… so horrible."

"Well, I would prefer you not to see such things. The man had been in the water for some time, days probably, so there was nothing anyone could do for him. It's now just a case for the police to find out what happened."

There was an awkward silence between them as they both thought about the grim scene on the canal. Nathaniel had come face to face with gruesome death all too often in recent years, but coped by focusing on the photographic process rather than the reality of what was before him. His camera was almost a shield.

It was only later – usually in the middle of the night – when the full horror would return to him.

Blake shook his head to clear his thoughts and beckoned to his daughter. "Come Cora, we need to gather our things and make our way home. Our trap will be waiting outside."

With the help of a male attendant who unlocked various doors, Inspector Ramm found his way to the Superintendent's office. After knocking on the door, he went inside without waiting to be summoned. The room was lined with shelves crammed with leather bound books. Behind a large mahogany desk, far grander than the one in Ramm's own humble office, sat a balding man in a grey tweed suit and oval rimless spectacles.

"Dr Gibson? Inspector Ramm, Leek Constabulary. May I have a word?"

The man looked up from the hefty ledger in which he had been writing, closed it with a thud, put down his fountain pen and gestured to a chair facing the desk. He seemed unhappy to have been disturbed.

"And what can I do for you, Inspector, er… Ramm, was it?"

The Inspector took an immediate dislike to Dr Gibson's officious tone. Did the man not realise who he was talking to?

"There has been an incident on the canal. A man has been found drowned. It probably occurred in the last few days."

"Really? I was unaware of it. I have been occupied with our record books all afternoon. But I doubt this has anything to do with the asylum, Inspector," said Gibson shortly.

"Is there no possibility of him being one of your people?"

"None are missing, I can assure you. We take a daily roll call and, as of eight o'clock this morning, no male inmate was absent."

"But there have been deaths in the past, have there not?"

Gibson took a sharp intake of breath, obviously uncomfortable being reminded of such matters.

"We aim to provide the utmost care and protection for our inmates, Inspector. Security is also very important to us. Doors are kept locked, inmates are supervised when they are out of the wards or in the grounds."

"In the grounds?"

"Three quarters of our people engage in regular useful work. It occupies the mind, gives them a sense of purpose and they can earn extra rations," Gibson went on.

"Some of the men help to maintain the buildings, others go to the workshops for carpentry, brushmaking, upholstery, shoe-making, joinery and so on. Women work in the kitchens, the bakery and the laundry. And of course we have a farm and vegetable gardens to look after. Although, in this weather few of the patients are working outside, except those who are keeping the driveways, paths and yards clear."

He paused before adding: "Fresh air is important for peace of mind, Inspector, so we also have supervised areas where inmates can spend time out of doors."

Mention of the vegetable gardens reminded Ramm of when he passed the asylum in the previous summer. He had seen row upon row of crops being tended by teams of men, their backs bent tilling the soil or wheeling wooden barrows loaded with produce. At the time he had thought they must be gardeners employed by the asylum, now he realised they were patients working for their own good – and for extra rations.

The Inspector waited to see if Gibson would say anything about deaths at the institution.

"Sadly, we do lose some poor souls through illness and…" Gibson cleared his throat, "on rare occasion, through accident. But that could not be the case today. What sort of clothes was this unfortunate person wearing?"

"His clothing was in a poor state, as you can appreciate, after being in the canal, but it looked like he had a tweed overcoat and a decent suit," Ramm replied.

"There we have it then. He is very unlikely to have been one of ours. Most of them have simple work outfits which we make in our own tailor's shop. Only a small number of private patients are allowed to wear clothes that they bring with them. And I know for a fact that none of those people are missing." Gibson fell silent, satisfied that he had proved his point.

When the conversation was over, Ramm rejoined Constable Knowles in the cart outside the main door. The corpse had been laid in the back and, for decency's sake, covered with a sheet.

"I've had a quick look in his pockets, Sir, but it's rather awkward as he's in such a state. There was no pocketbook or keys. In fact nothing apart from this," said Knowles, holding up what looked like a sodden postcard. The writing on the back was indecipherable. It almost fell apart as he handed it to Ramm.

"Take care, Constable, this might be important," said Ramm as he wrapped his handkerchief delicately around the card and placed in an inside pocket. "We will need to make a proper search when he's dried out." He blew out his cheeks. If the man had been robbed, perhaps this death was not the straightforward accident he had at first thought.

That Thursday evening, most of the folk of Leek were at home, trying to keep warm. Even the town's many public houses were doing scant trade. In hundreds of terraced houses, fuel of any sort was being fed into the grates and kitchen stoves. Some of the poorest families had received a free bucket of coal from a welfare committee run by the town's better off. Others had sent children out to scour fields and nearby woods for twigs, branches and even fence posts. Many would go to bed early that night, fully dressed.

Keeping water running was another problem in these temperatures. Although many houses now had the luxury of a tap in the scullery, it was a challenge to stop it freezing solid. Similarly, the cisterns of the backyard toilets had to be wrapped up against the frost, as were the communal water pumps which were relied on by folk in the humblest cottages.

At the Blake home in Portland Street, a terraced house that was bigger and more comfortably equipped than most, Cora was sitting near to the coal fired range, her hands knotted in her lap. She was looking blankly at the red quarry tiles on the kitchen floor, lost in thought.

After supper, her father had put work before family duties and returned to his studio. He intended to develop the negatives from that afternoon, most of which were of the incident on the canal rather than views of the asylum.

That death on the canal filled Cora's thoughts now. She had been confronted by tragedy in the past and today it had happened again. The poor man! Oh, why had no one been able to save him? she wondered.

Her thoughts were disturbed by the sound of coughing from upstairs. Her brother William, who was ten years old, was suffering from whooping cough. He seemed to settle again and Cora heard the murmur of her mother's voice. Soon afterwards Edith Blake came into the kitchen, her face lined with worry.

Whooping cough was sweeping the town that winter and was striking fear into many parents, especially those who had seen children die in other epidemics. The Blakes had lost their youngest, little Emily, in the scarlet fever epidemic of three years before.

"William's no better and there are dozens at his school with that cough," said Edith. "I've tried him with tar, but tomorrow I might take him to the gas works."

Although there seemed to be no cure for the cough, many

children were coaxed to inhale vapours from a bowl of tar to ease their breathing. Every day a queue formed at the Town Gas Works on Newcastle Road where the managers were allowing parents to hold their children near the coke ovens so they could breathe in the fumes and hopefully cough a little less.

"I do hope he's better soon," said Cora with a shaking voice that showed she was on the edge of tears. Edith knew there was more troubling her daughter than young William's cough.

"It must have been awful for you this afternoon," said Edith reaching for her daughter's hand.

"I was so hoping that today would turn out well, Mother, and in the end, it was just the opposite. That poor man must have had a terrible death in the canal. The water was absolutely freezing."

"It was a pity that you were there today Cora, but by the sound of it, there was nothing that you, nor anyone else, could have done. It may well have been over very quickly for the poor chap." Edith knew that most winters brought similar tragedy when someone went through the ice on the canal or a pond.

Cora was glad of her mother's sympathy, but there was someone else she wished she could talk to tonight – Oliver Finch.

She had known Oliver for more than four years and their friendship had grown closer by the month. He had supported her through difficult times in the past and encouraged her ambitions to be a photographer. He had even understood her fervour for the Votes for Women campaign, although he worried that she might land herself into trouble. Friendship had grown into love and Cora had started to dream of what their future together might hold.

But Oliver's compulsion for his work, just as like her father's, could get in the way of their time together. He was five years older than Cora and worked for his father as a reporter on the *Leek Lion*. It was an absorbing job that put him at the heart of goings-on in the town, but also occupied much of his time. That evening he was reporting on a meeting of Leek Urban District Council. Afterwards he would most likely return to the *Lion* office and be typing up his stories until late, ready for the next edition, which came out on Saturday. Cora knew there would be no chance to see him tonight.

"I suppose you would really like to see Oliver and tell him about it," said Edith. It wasn't difficult for her to read her daughter's thoughts. She had realised some time ago that the young man held the key to Cora's happiness.

"Yes Mother, but I shall just have to wait."

Cora's gaze returned to the quarry tiles and once again she began to picture the scene after she had followed her father to the frozen canal. The workmen's desperate efforts to break the ice, the dark shape glimpsed beneath the surface. She gave a deep sigh. What a way to die, she thought.

Chapter Three

"Will that stove turn up any higher?" Oliver Finch looked accusingly at the paraffin stove in the corner of the office he shared with his father in the *Leek Lion* building in Market Street. It was Friday morning, a time for Oliver and FJ Finch to type up their final reports, check final proofs and consider what space was left in the newspaper's eight pages before it went to press that evening.

Their desks were piled with notebooks, letters and shorthand jottings on odd pieces of paper. The office itself was crammed with random documents, well-thumbed directories and bound files of yellowing past editions, not to mention stocks of books which FJ had published long ago and was still hoping to sell.

However all this paper appeared to do nothing to insulate the low ceilinged room on a bitterly cold morning such as this. They were on the top floor of a three storey building which had no regular form of heating. FJ had been fortunate to get his hands on a paraffin stove the previous week – it was the last one in Skinner's ironmongers shop in Derby Street. But its modest, fume laden heat did not encourage the Finches to shed their overcoats and Oliver wore fingerless gloves as he hit the keys of his gleaming Imperial typewriter.

"Farmers up around Longnor are suffering far worse than this, young man. It's something we have to bear – this is the moorlands of Staffordshire, not the south of France, you know," said FJ, trying to make light of the matter. Since coming to Leek to establish the *Lion* two decades earlier, he had indeed seen how harsh the winters could be.

"What about some more heating? A boiler even?" asked Oliver.

"In the current state of affairs, there is no question of making any unnecessary expenditure on comfort. Don't forget, we might be fighting for our future." FJ's tone had turned stonily serious.

The 'state of affairs' was the appearance of a rival weekly newspaper, the *Moorland Argus*. Although there were other well established and larger newspapers in the county, such as the *Staffordshire Sentinel*, Finch's *Lion* had enjoyed a virtual monopoly on the news – and advertising revenue – in Leek and the moorlands. Until two months ago, that is, when a local printing business had surprised Finch and the rest of the town with the launch of the *Argus*.

The timing was crucial. The *Argus* had aimed to capture some of the increased advertising income that the *Lion* enjoyed in the weeks before Christmas. Finch was sceptical about the venture which hc was sure was driven by a disagreement he had had with the printer over the price of a book contract. The editor of the new paper was a young journalist from Manchester. "Stirring things up, making a name for himself. Then he will move on to bigger things," said Finch bitterly.

Despite his doubts, Finch knew he had to take the competition seriously and had become even more obsessive about the *Lion*'s content in keeping with its motto '*We Roar The Truth*', as proclaimed on the banner on the wall behind his desk. He dragged his hand through his unruly red hair as he pored over the morning's post, checking whether there was anything important enough to warrant inclusion in that week's edition at this late stage, or whether there were any new advertisements which would bring in extra income.

"There was some juicy argument at last night's council meeting. The debate over the new sewage works became quite heated," said Oliver. "It makes good copy," he added, passing to his father a sheaf of typed sheets, the result of his late night session in the office.

"Excellent, excellent. We want our readers entertained as well as informed. Some of those councillors should be on the stage at the Town Hall…" FJ began, but he stopped as his attention was drawn to a piece of blue notepaper which had arrived that morning.

"Another one!" he blurted out.

Oliver swivelled in his office chair to see what his father was talking about. "What, from that woman?" he guessed.

"Yes. It appears she's more worried than ever."

The *Lion* had now received three letters from a woman who claimed she was being followed in the street and spied on at home. "I am being stalked like a beast," she had written. The letters were written in a meticulous, flowing hand, but bore no signature or address.

FJ was concerned about the claims and recognised there could be a good story in this. However he was in a quandary. He would normally avoid printing an anonymous letter unless the writer had given their name in confidence or Finch had guessed who the correspondent was, often not too difficult in a small town like Leek. In this case he had published a cryptic appeal for the writer of "a certain letter" to contact him confidentially so that the *Lion* could pursue the matter. No identification had been forthcoming, but today had brought another troubling letter.

"This raises the stakes somewhat," he said as he passed the note to his son. Oliver scanned through it quickly.

> *"My life has become a nightmare. I feel I am being observed and trailed in the street. At night I am sure there is a figure in the shadows across the way, watching my window.*
>
> *Now my fears have been justified. I have received a note making suggestions that I am too ashamed to repeat.*
>
> *Are others in Leek suffering like this? Is this man trying to intrude on the lives of other innocent women? Something needs to be done to stop this insidious behaviour. Who can help me?*
>
> *I am not certain I know the person who is to blame, but I have my suspicions. I appeal to him to desist and let my life return to normal. Otherwise I may be forced to name the person I suspect and let others decide what his punishment should be."*

"Father, we really must do something," said Oliver after reading the letter a second time. "This sounds like a woman – I'm sure it's a young woman – with no one to protect her. She could be in real danger! Shouldn't we tell the police? Or publish the letter and see what happens? It might flush out the culprit, shame him into stopping. If we do nothing, who knows how this might end?"

FJ was struck by his son's passion. The young man had shown strong feelings, outrage even, about other topics in the past, especially when he thought the *Lion*'s influence could be put to good use.

However the editor was not keen on the idea of approaching the police. Although they had good relations with the town force – either Oliver or himself called at the station most days – he could not see what would be gained by approaching Inspector

Ramm just yet. They had no idea who the correspondent was, so what could the police do about it? He was not even sure that any law had been broken.

No, it was clear they needed to pursue the matter through the *Lion*. As well as assisting the woman, they would most likely rake up a story to intrigue their readers. Just the sort of thing they needed to keep the rival *Argus* at bay.

Then FJ had second thoughts. He leaned across his desk and began to fire questions at his son. "What if she's imagining it all? What if she's deranged? What if it's all a hoax to make fools of us? Why write to us in the first place, rather than the police?"

"Well, not everyone is comfortable opening their hearts to some burly policeman who might tell them to go away and stop being excitable," Oliver retorted. "And what can we lose by printing it? It will make excellent copy and we might help to put right a real wrong. For all we know, this man may be following other women in the town."

"All right, all right," FJ conceded. "Let us have it set into type and we will put it amongst the readers' letters. I might even make some comment in my editorial column." He turned his attention to other papers on his desk. "Now, there is plenty more to get on with. Do we have the latest from those lads who are on their way to the Antipodes?"

A number of young men from the moorlands had decided to try their luck in Australia and New Zealand after advertisements with tempting offers of work and land had appeared the *Lion*. Finch had been printing excerpts from a diary which one of them had written during their long voyage across the oceans to a new life.

"Oh… yes. I was about to read it. Actually Father, I wanted to speak to you about that subject."

"Can we talk about it later? There is much to do before deadline. First, I need to check if the police have anything for us." With that, FJ stood up, donned his new style trilby and started down the stairs.

"Later then," Oliver said to himself and began to type again.

When FJ Finch arrived at the police station in Leonard Street, just across from the cattle market, he was shown into Ramm's office to find the Inspector deep in thought, ruminating on the case of the man hauled from the canal.

On reaching the Cottage Hospital with the body the previous afternoon, Constable Knowles had made another thorough search of the dead man's clothing and found nothing in the pockets of his tweed coat or his three-piece suit – neither papers, keys, wallet nor cash. The only possible clue was a label in the suit jacket which showed it had been made by a tailor in Carlisle.

The absence of personal items prompted Ramm to wonder again if the man had come from the County Asylum and had somehow managed to change out of the overalls which were issued to the patients. Of course, this theory ran contrary to Dr Gibson's assertion that no one was absent, but Ramm believed the doctor had been a little too anxious to deny any connection with the death. With Medical Superintendent Menzies away, his deputy no doubt wanted to avoid any embarrassing incident while he was in charge.

While Ramm did not wish to expend too much effort investigating a death which might well turn out to be accidental, he thought it was probably worth sending an officer to speak to whoever was on the barge near the scene, just in case they had seen anything. He also wanted a statement from the man who had been the first to spot the victim beneath the ice.

However, the arrival of the *Leek Lion* editor presented another avenue for him to pursue. Ramm came straight to the point. "Mr Finch, we have a body we wish to identify and I believe an appeal in your newspaper would be most useful."

Finch sat forward, immediately alert to a promising story. He produced his notebook and pencil in readiness.

"Yesterday afternoon, the body of a man was extracted from the Leek Arm of the Caldon Canal, approximately a quarter of a mile beyond the Leek Tunnel. We are anxious to confirm his identity and therefore we wish to hear from anyone with a relative or acquaintance who may have gone missing in the past week."

"Drowned, I take it."

"I believe so, but the body is being examined this morning."

"And you have no idea who he is? What sort of age was he, what did he look like?" asked Finch.

"It appeared there was nothing to identify him by. It was difficult to tell his age, bearing in mind the time he must have spent in the water. But I might be able to tell you more later today."

Finch made rapid shorthand notes, then frowned as he considered the sparse details.

"The far side of the tunnel? A fair distance from town, then. Had he fallen off a barge, perhaps? And surely, that would not be far from the lunatic asylum. Do you think there could be any connection with that establishment?"

Ramm kept his expression non-committal. "At present, your guess is as good as mine, Mr Finch, but please do not print that. This is why we need to appeal to your readers for help. Someone must be aware that this fellow is missing."

Finch nodded vigorously before Ramm added: "Incidentally, you may wish to refer to the gallant work of a group of men – including two of my constables – to liberate the body from the frozen canal in most difficult conditions. Your friend Mr Blake saw it all."

Before Finch could ask any more, Sergeant Reynolds, Ramm's second in command, hurried into the office. There was an urgent telephone call, he said. Ramm left Reynolds to brief Finch on minor incidents which had occurred the previous day and went to the reception counter where the station's sole telephone apparatus was installed.

The call was from Leek Memorial Hospital – the Cottage Hospital as most townsfolk called it – which had recently been equipped with its own telephone. Ramm waited while the town's Medical Officer, Dr Handbridge, was put through by the operator at the exchange. His tone conveyed a degree of urgency that was unusual for the medical man.

"Inspector? Handbridge here. I have begun examining the body you fished out of the canal. What a puzzle! I still have to finish the procedure, but I thought I should call you at once."

Ramm was intrigued. "I take it you have managed to confirm he was drowned – or was the fellow frozen to death?"

"Far from it, Inspector. He was stabbed in the neck."

"What?" Ramm blurted out in surprise. "But it looked for all the world like a drowning! I've seen plenty of bodies like that when they have been pulled from the water."

"Certainly immersion may have had some effect on the body, Inspector, that is probably why no one noticed the neck wound," Dr Handbridge replied. "And this was no rough swipe of a blade. It looks to me to have been a precise incision into the carotid artery with a very sharp instrument. It could have been a matter of chance, but on the other hand, I rather think the perpetrator must have known exactly what they were doing. This was surgically exact, straight into the artery in the neck. The poor fellow would have bled to death in a minute or two."

"So you are suggesting the attacker could be a medical man?" he asked.

"Either that or someone with a good understanding of human physiology. Or, as I said, perhaps it was simply a fortunate strike with the right sort of blade."

"Have you any idea when the time of death occurred? Looking at the state of him, I surmised it could be relatively recent."

"Difficult to tell, Inspector. The chilling effect of the freezing water would have prevented the man's flesh from decomposing at its normal rate, almost as if the poor fellow had been stored in an ice house. Surprising as it seems, I think it could be anything up to a week since he died."

Dr Handbridge promised to inform the Inspector of any further developments, as and when he had the information, and then rang off to continue his examination of the body.

Ramm slowly replaced the heavy handset in the telephone's cradle as he came to terms with this surprising new twist in the case. The body in the canal was not the result of an unfortunate accident, or even suicide. It looked like the man had been murdered. As Ramm steadied himself against the reception counter, FJ Finch passed by on his way out of the station.

"I shall check with you again this afternoon, Inspector, before we go to press," said Finch.

"Yes, yes, of course," Ramm replied, lost in thought. It was far too soon to tell the newspaperman of this state of affairs. However, he knew that the investigation now had to begin in earnest and his first act would be to return to the canal.

Light snow had begun to fall as Inspector Ramm and Constable Knowles reached the towing path on the Leek Arm. As on the previous day, they had approached from the grounds of the County Asylum. The stables near to the police station in Leonard Street had again provided a horse and trap and Ramm had told the driver to go around the rear of the complex of buildings. They went past the asylum church and the place where the private tram line ended, so that they could alight near to the boundary fence.

The two officers had still faced a challenging walk, picking their way across the fields covered in snow. They were about to cross the railway tracks when a whistle warned them of a train steaming down the line towards Stoke on Trent. Its trucks looked to be filled with limestone from the quarries at Cauldon Lowe which had only recently been connected directly to the railway network. The thick black smoke pouring from the locomotive's chimney was a stark contrast to the white of the landscape. After it had passed, they pressed onward, next crossing the frozen River Churnet. Ramm went sprawling when he slipped on the canal embankment and, cursing the weather, had to be helped to his feet by Knowles.

They finally gained the towpath at the point where the body had been recovered. Now he knew the victim had been stabbed, Ramm paid much closer attention to the scene although yesterday's frantic activity had disturbed most of the area. He scuffed the fresh covering of snow with his rubber galosh to reveal dark patches on the frozen ground. Yesterday he had thought this was mud, now he surmised it was more likely to be the dead man's blood.

Ramm tried to picture what might have happened at this lonely spot. The victim had been stabbed in the neck and his blood had gushed onto the ground. Could his attacker have emptied the man's pockets before pitching him into the freezing waters of the canal? It was as brutal as it was baffling. A violent quarrel? A chance robbery? A clinical murder? And the case was doubly mysterious because they knew the identity of neither the culprit nor the victim.

The Inspector turned to his officer. "Have a look around on the ground and see if you can find anything. I know it's unlikely, but perhaps something fell out of the man's pockets or, if we're very fortunate, there is a blade lying somewhere close by." Seeing Knowles' doubtful expression, Ramm added: "Down to it then, Constable."

While Knowles crouched down and began to scrabble about in the snow, Ramm surveyed the frozen canal in either direction. Ice had formed again over the hole gouged the previous afternoon, its uneven surface the only sign of yesterday's struggles. On the opposite bank, the ground rose up steeply with golden fronds of bracken poking through the blanket of snow. The bare branches of an oak tree stood out like a black skeleton against the grey sky. Apart from the occasional crow, nothing moved. It was a peaceful scene which Ramm could have found appealing if not for the gruesome events that had unfolded there.

In the direction of Wall Grange he could see a column of dark smoke rising through the snow-flecked air. He assumed this was coming from the chimney of the pumping station which fed fresh water from the valley to Stoke on Trent. Looking back towards Leek, once again he saw there were wisps of smoke coming from the barge stuck in the ice. With a determined stride he set off towards the boat.

As Ramm approached the barge, the tethered horse looked up. Small clouds of mist billowed from its nose in the frigid air. At the same moment the burly boatman emerged from the cabin and stepped onto the towing path, standing with his feet apart. Ramm guessed the man had been watching him.

"A good day to ye, Officer," announced the bargee. The man was aged about sixty, his head completely bald, his ruddy face framed by thick grey sideburns. His stained singlet revealed broad shoulders and thickly muscled arms which were covered with tattoos stretching up to his neck.

"Good day., my man. I expect you saw what was going on yesterday – a body in the canal. You haven't happened to see anything else, something suspicious perhaps?" Ramm asked.

"Ye better come aboard," the boatman said, adding: "Turnock is the name, Silas Turnock."

Ramm stepped onto the barge and followed him through a

narrow hatch and down two steps into the living quarters. The small cabin was lined with cupboards and shelves of gleaming varnished wood, almost every flat surface crowded with brightly painted trinkets. An iron stove pot stood in the centre of the floor, its straight chimney piercing the roof, and a small bed had been built into the woodwork at the far end of the cabin. On it sat a woman almost as broad in the beam as the boatman. An embroidered apron was stretched across her girth and she wore a bonnet to match. She acknowledged Ramm with a nod.

Ramm knew that cargo barges such as this were often crewed by married couples, the wives being expected to shoulder as many of the tasks – operating locks, loading and unloading cargo – as their husbands. It was a hard life and boatpeople were fiercely independent.

"Hardly seen a soul since we got stuck 'ere at start o' the week," Turnock began. "We were on our way from Leek loaded with iron from the foundry. It were getting dark and the cut were freezing over so we thought we'd get through the tunnel and then moor up for the night. We stop 'ere regular."

"By morning it was froze solid. I knew we should've carried on!" the wife interjected, obviously unhappy with the enforced delay. Turnock shot her a glance to keep quiet.

"So have you seen anything suspicious?" asked Ramm, hoping to focus the conversation on the matter in hand.

"Not in particular. Might've 'eard summat though," Turnock replied, then paused as if considering whether to get involved in the affair. "That first night I 'eard some sort o' shouting. More than one voice probably. Wondered if they were shouting a dog or summat. Sounded a bit peculiar, y'might say."

"Peculiar?"

"Not normal like. After the shouting it was more like a scream."

"Go on."

"Couple o' minutes later there were a great splash as if summat jumped in the cut. That's when I thought it must've been a dog. Nobody in their right minds would've gone in the water that night."

"Did you go out and take a look?"

"No we didn't. It were pitch black and freezing cold."

"So that's it? You heard unusual voices, then a splash, but sat here and did nothing?" Ramm was exasperated to think a man had lost his life just yards away as these people sat in their barge.

"You get all sorts of things happenin' on the cut, Officer. But we minds our own business," Turnock replied heatedly.

His wife shifted uneasily on the bed and then leaned forward as if about to say something. Her husband shot her another threatening look and she sat back again. Ramm noticed the exchange and waited to see if the Turnocks would say any more, but they remained silent.

Ramm thanked the boatman for his help and climbed back out of the cabin. He made a mental note of the name painted elaborately on the bow of the boat, *The Esperance*, and returned to where Knowles was still on his hands and knees in the snow. The constable looked up and shook his head.

"Come on. Let's get back to the station and warm up," said Ramm as he began to step warily down the embankment. There was much to discover about what had gone on here and he suspected the barge folk knew more than they were telling.

Nathaniel Blake had spent the morning in his darkroom on the upper floor of his studio in Sheepmarket, making prints from the negatives he had processed the previous evening. Most of the pictures he had taken beside the canal were either of the frozen surface or the group of men bent in the laborious task of breaking the ice and hauling out the body.

However he had a macabre photograph of the victim as he had first seen him, apparently staring through the ice, and another when the body was lying on the towing path. Looking at these prints now, Nathaniel was once again confronted with the horror of the incident. There was something else, too. Although the face was bloated and discoloured, he felt a twinge of recognition. It might have been the man's nose – thin and aquiline – or the shape of his neat beard, but there was something familiar about him.

Surely this poor fellow can't be someone I'm acquainted with? Blake asked himself. More likely it was someone he had photographed before. And because of the sheer number of pictures he took, that could be one of many hundreds of people.

Blake slipped the prints into a packet, ready to take them to the police station. He thought it best not to let Cora see them. This morning, dark patches under her eyes betrayed her sleepless night and she had barely spoken as they walked to the studio together. Going to Cheddleton again would be difficult for her, but equally he believed that focusing on her task at the asylum – and making a success of it – would be the best way of moving on from what had happened yesterday. He planned to arrange another visit as soon as possible.

He also picked up the copies of the photographs Cora had taken at the asylum, and he handed them to her as he walked through the showroom downstairs.

"These have come out well, my dear. You can be very satisfied with them," he said encouragingly. "The light from those skylights in the kitchen is very effective and you have captured some fine detail of that gleaming equipment."

Cora took the prints, but her expression barely changed. Her eyes were on the other packet her father held. She knew what was inside.

"I'm just going to drop these others off for the Inspector," Nathaniel said rather awkwardly, reaching his overcoat from a peg by the door. "Later I shall call in at the Poultry Market. They will be getting ready for the Poor Children's Dinner and I think it might make an interesting picture."

Cora simply nodded. When her father had left she finally examined the photographs he had handed to her. She had to admit that, despite all her misgivings about visiting the County Asylum, she had made a professional job of those pictures. How she would feel when they went back there was another matter entirely.

A cacophony of young voices greeted Nathaniel Blake as he entered the Poultry Market. The hall adjoined the Buttermarket building off the Market Place and since it opened nine years previously had been used for a variety of events other than trading.

Rows of long trestle tables and wooden benches had been laid out and these were now filling rapidly with children who were laughing, talking, shouting and squabbling excitedly. Others were jostling as they queued at the door, brandishing the paper tickets to show they were entitled to a free dinner.

From that week until the end of winter, children from Leek's poorest families were to be treated to a midday meal on Tuesdays and Fridays, paid for by funds raised by the Poor Children's Dinner Committee. In a winter such as this, the hot meat and potato pie was more welcome than ever. Not every family was happy to accept charity, however, and most of the children were turned out in their best clothes to keep up appearances. The parents' misgivings were not shared by their offspring and the dinner was one of the highlights of the week for young people such as this.

Blake had collected his camera and tripod from the studio, which was only a short walk away. He was about to set up to take a general view of the crowded hall when he noticed Oliver Finch come in through the door from the Red Lion yard, notebook in hand. The reporter first went to interview one of the organisers, then came over to the photographer.

"Good day, Mr Blake. It appears we were both of the same mind. Father felt this charitable effort deserves recognition, especially in this weather, and he sent me round to take a few notes. Mr Tomlinson, the Committee Secretary, tells me they served over five thousand dinners last winter. He has asked me to appeal to our readers for donations because they are running very low on funds. Apparently they can provide seven dinners for just a shilling."

Oliver paused and looked about the hall. "This is quite a gathering – there must be well over a hundred children in here, do you think?" he added.

"I would say it is nearer a hundred and fifty," Nathaniel replied as he surveyed the throng crammed onto the benches. He ducked under his camera's hood and pressed the shutter lever. "There is so much going on I expect half of children will be blurred. But I can't very well ask them to sit still!" he said.

"Actually Mr Blake, I intended to call at your studio afterwards. Father said you may have seen something of this awful drowning in the canal yesterday and I wanted to check some of the details with you," Oliver continued. "Cora was with you at the asylum, was she not?" he added, revealing his more pressing reason to visit the studio might be to see how she was coping.

"Certainly, let us walk back together when we're finished here," Blake replied.

Cora's heart leapt when, thirty minutes later, Oliver arrived at the studio. She had to restrain herself from rushing over, putting her arms around him and burying her face into his chest.

Nathaniel coughed with embarrassment as he saw the look

exchanged between his daughter and Oliver. "I will go upstairs and leave you two for a little while," he said.

"Oliver! I am so glad to see you. Yesterday was… was so upsetting," said Cora, managing to choke back her tears.

"But surely, you weren't involved in what happened on the canal?"

"There was a hue and cry and it was I who told Father about it. After he left, I couldn't stop myself running down to find out what was going on. I thought someone was being rescued, but… it was all too late!"

"Cora, I so wish you had not been there. And I'm sorry I didn't see you last night, my darling, but I knew nothing about this accident."

They embraced briefly and then broke off when they heard the creak of floorboards as Nathaniel moved about upstairs.

"Did you manage to take any photographs? Inside the asylum, I mean. I know you were worried about your first proper assignment."

"Yes, I took some and they turned out all right. I think Father's happy with them, at least. But after all this, I don't know if I can face going back there."

"Cora, you must," said Oliver, grasping both her hands and looking earnestly into her eyes. He knew it was important to give her encouragement as well as sympathy. He believed she was capable of so much.

"Yes, yes, of course," Cora replied, somehow gaining strength from the power of his gaze.

"I must speak to your father now about… about the accident," Oliver went on. "But first I wanted to ask you about tomorrow. I know the weather is little better, but I really think we should go down to Rudyard Lake and see what's going on there. It might take your mind off things."

He was obviously anxious to lighten Cora's mood. "There are

no football matches to report on, so I am free for the whole afternoon. It's not fit to walk, so I think we should catch the train after lunch," he added.

Cora hesitated but then agreed. If nothing else, she would welcome more time with Oliver.

That Friday evening, Albert Ramm sank wearily into his armchair in the parlour in Queen Street. The fire was lit, his slippers were comfortable and he could have easily nodded off to sleep, had it not been for the thoughts and theories swirling around in his head.

He was feeling tired and old. For two days in a row, he had been left cold and wet after the uncomfortable journey to the lunatic asylum over ice-bound roads followed by a trudge through the snow to the canal bank. He was nearly sixty years old and wondered how long he would be doing this job. It had been his life since leaving the army twenty years earlier, but now his mind was turning towards retirement. He and his wife Edna would have to manage on a small pension, but they were lucky. Most people did not receive even that and had to work until they dropped.

He would have felt better if the day's efforts had been more rewarding. Instead, he seemed to be no closer to the facts. He picked up the packet of Blake's photographs which he had brought home to study: the frozen canal, the body, the workmen's efforts.

The Medical Officer had telephoned again that afternoon and confirmed that the victim had ingested little water. The stab in the neck had undoubtedly been the cause of death, the man had probably been breathing his last as he went into the icy canal.

When Ramm had asked him about the possible weapon, Dr Handbridge said it could have been a scalpel or certainly something narrow and very sharp. Once again he emphasised the precision of the wound to the man's artery.

Ramm had dealt with many attacks in the past, but the implications of this one disturbed him anew. Medical knowledge of where to strike, a surgical instrument for the weapon? Could a doctor or a surgeon really be responsible for such a violent crime? Surely they signed an oath to safeguard life, not destroy it?

Neither was he any nearer to discovering who the victim was. His appeal through the *Leek Lion* might yield some information, he hoped. He had given Finch some more details that afternoon, but had not revealed that they were now investigating a murder in case the attacker saw the story. He wanted the culprit to believe they had got away with it for a little while longer.

To add to his worries, Ramm's confidence as an investigator was being shaken. Although his position as head of Leek Police had not been questioned, his superiors at Stafford had made it plain that a dedicated detective would very soon be a permanent member of the force in the town. Ramm knew that this case may be the last of its kind that he, a uniformed officer with a desk full of other duties, would have the chance to solve. No matter what the difficulties, pride would drive him to complete it.

Once again he went over the scene of the attack in his mind. From what Turnock, the bargee, had said, the crime may have occurred in the dark on Monday. It would certainly be a lonely spot on a winter's evening. Ideal for an attack, but why would the victim be there? And Ramm still could not forget the presence of the lunatic asylum and the hundreds of people held there, just across the fields from the canal. Was that really a coincidence?

His thoughts were interrupted when Edna came in with a slice of freshly baked fruit cake which she was sure would improve her husband's spirits. "Have you thought any more about the concert tomorrow night?" she asked.

"Concert?"

"The one I told you about the other day. The Moorland Philharmonia are performing at the Town Hall. According to the advertisement, they are playing pieces by Mendelssohn, and Gilbert & Sullivan, and several more. I'm so looking forward to it," Edna explained. As well as practising on the piano, she had become something of a musical enthusiast in recent years.

"Not really my cup of tea, dear," Ramm replied doubtfully. "And won't it be freezing in the Town Hall? I heard the boiler was out of order."

"Someone says it's been mended and the concert is definitely going to take place. If those good people are prepared to turn out and play their music in weather like this, then I think we should support them." Edna was obviously in no mood to be dissuaded, but her husband was equally firm in his view.

"Well, Edna, don't let me stop you from attending. Your sister will be going, I take it? As for myself, I shall stay at home, by the fire."

With that, Ramm put aside Blake's photographs, picked up his slice of cake and sank a little deeper into his chair.

Chapter Four

The Leek Lion

SATURDAY, JANUARY 11TH 1907

MYSTERY DEATH IN CANAL

Leek Constabulary are anxious to establish the identity of a man found dead in the Leek Arm of the Caldon Canal on Thursday of this week.

Inspector Albert Ramm said that the victim had been found beneath the frozen surface approximately one quarter mile on the Wall Grange side of the Leek Tunnel. It is thought the man, who is believed to be aged in his middle years, may have been dead for some days. A post mortem examination was being carried out yesterday (Friday).

"As yet, we do not know how this unfortunate fellow came to be in the water. There was no obvious means of identification and therefore we are appealing to the public to contact us if a relative or an acquaintance has gone missing during the past week," said Insp. Ramm.

The body was recovered from the canal after considerable effort by a party of men which included workers from the nearby Cheddleton County Asylum and police officers. The Leek photographer, Mr. Nathaniel Blake, witnessed the recovery work and afterwards praised the dedication of those involved. "As to be expected in this weather, the conditions were very poor, but the men stuck to their task. Nothing could have been done for the unfortunate fellow," said Mr. Blake.

As reported in last week's *Leek Lion*, a general warning has been issued to people of all ages, but particularly children, to take care when venturing onto frozen bodies of water following a number of unfortunate accidents.

PROTECTING OUR WOMENFOLK

A most disturbing letter has been received this week and can be seen in our Correspondence Column on Page 5. It is a plea from a local woman who complains that she is being watched, intimidated and pestered by an unknown man.

According to the correspondent, the culprit keeps himself in the shadows, but is constantly prying into this innocent woman's affairs. If this is correct, then this odious person is breaking a moral code if not the law of the land.

Let it be known that the *Lion* would support this lady's intention to unmask the wrongdoer and to force him to desist his activities. Equally, he should know that his days as a spy on our womenfolk are numbered. We appeal to the complainant to contact us in strict confidentiality so that we may print the fullest information in our next edition.

TOWN HALL CONCERT GOES AHEAD

The Moorland Philharmonia, under the baton of their Conductor, Mr. Jeremiah Alsop, are delighted to announce that their New Year Concert at Leek Town Hall will go ahead tonight (Saturday). The event, which was originally to have taken place last week, was postponed after frozen pipework brought about the failure of the heating system at the Town Hall. Engineers from Leek Urban District Council have now resolved the problem, allowing the much anticipated musical evening to take place.

The Philharmonia promise a variety of enjoyable and stimulating pieces from the classical and popular repertoires. The programme will include the First Movement of Haydn's Symphony No.2, followed by Mozart's ever popular Overture to The Marriage of Figaro and Edward German's Gypsy Suite.

The second half of the programme begins with Mendelssohn's Capriccio Brilliant for Pianoforte and Orchestra, with the renowned local pianist, Miss Jemima Beddington, as soloist. This will be followed by a selection of favourites from the operettas of Gilbert & Sullivan.

The Concert will commence at 7.30p.m. with carriages at 10.15p.m. Tickets cost 3/- and 1/6 reserved, with general admission priced at 1/- and 6d. (limited availability). Tickets can be bought in advance from W.H. Eaton, Booksellers, of Derby Street, and at the Town Hall entrance prior to the start.

TEMPERANCE HALL, UNION STREET, LEEK

THURSDAY, JANUARY 16TH, 1907

FOR ONE NIGHT ONLY

Important Visit of the International

BIOSCOPE

Company

Presenting a Magnificent Series of the Very Latest

ANIMATED PHOTOGRAPHS

A CRUISER IN A STORM, THE LATEST AND MOST EXCITING PICTURES EVER SHOWN

THE BLACKSMITH'S DAUGHTER, A BRILLIANT NOVEL IN A NUTSHELL

MILL WORKERS OF LEEK, A UNIQUE RECORD OF CROWDS AT THE WORKPLACE ENTRANCE

FROM FOAL TO FAVOURITE, OR THE LIFE OF A RACEHORSE

LAUNCH OF RMS MAURETANIA, THE WORLD'S LARGEST SHIP

THE DEADLY EARTHQUAKE, NEW IMAGES OF DISASTER IN CHILE

Show to commence at 7p.m.
Interlude with entertainment.

Reserved seats, 2s. Second seats, 1s. Back seats, 6d.

OPPORTUNITY AWAITS!

Farmers, Farm Labourers, Vignerons, Orchardists, Market Gardeners and Domestic Servants.
Assisted Passages to the Crown Colony of New Zealand on offer from £5 to £7. 10s.
Free grants of land up to 160 acres.

NEW ZEALAND

A land of opportunity and excellent climate which will further benefit from its elevation to a Dominion of the British Empire in 1907.

In addition to workers in the Agricultural and Domestic fields, Settlers are sought with a complete range of Professional Skills to assist New Zealand to prosper and achieve its full potential.

For illustrated pamphlets and further particulars apply to: The High Commissioner for New Zealand, 13 Victoria Street, London, S.W.

It was a weekly ritual for FJ and Oliver to pore over the latest edition of the *Leek Lion* on a Saturday morning. Although Finch Senior scrutinised the pages as they came off the press the previous evening, it was the following morning when he and his son took a considered look at what they had achieved that week.

This morning was different, however, as FJ had the *Moorland Argus* in his hands instead. The *Lion*'s new rival was published the same day and Finch was anxiously scanning its six pages to see what stories – and advertisements – he may have missed. Just as in the *Lion*, many of its tightly-packed columns were filled with stories that had no connection with the Leek Moorlands – salacious court cases, shocking crimes, natural disasters, instalments of a romantic novel. Finch quickly passed over such content and focused on the page that carried the local news.

"No report of the canal death. Ha, they've missed that! I don't think the *Argus* man called at the police station yesterday," he commented. "And it appears that our damsel in distress has not contacted them either. That's a relief."

Finch fell silent as he continued to study the news items, then took a sharp intake of breath. "That young editor is doing his best to stir up trouble. According to this," he stabbed at the page, "the mill workers are expected to strike at any moment over the new working hours the owners are trying to introduce. It's all nonsense, of course! The mill folk would be mad to walk out in the middle of winter. How are they going to survive?"

"Father…" Oliver tried to intervene as he saw FJ becoming more agitated.

"This madcap scheme for another newspaper will damage the town, spoil our business, drag the good name of local newspapers through the mud, mark my words. And just look at how many of our customers have bought advertisements!" The *Argus* crumpled in his fists.

"Father, please calm down," Oliver managed to interject. "I know you are concerned, but remember, you have served this community for twenty years. People respect the *Lion*, they will carry on supporting us."

FJ was about to resume his rant, but Oliver was not finished. "And sometimes I wonder whether there's more to life than the *Lion*," he said, trying to avoid the look on his father's face.

Finch stared at his son in surprise. "What do you mean by that? What could be more important than our work? You said so yourself, we're serving the community."

"I know, I know," said Oliver, wondering if he should take a step back to pacify his father. "I love my work, but there are other things ...people... which are important to me. And..."

"Oh, I see. This is about Cora," Finch interrupted, calming down a little. "Well, Oliver, it's perfectly possible to take a wife and settle down and to continue working on a newspaper. Look at your mother and myself? We have managed, haven't we? If you're worried about the money, I'm sure we can come to some arrangement, when the time is right – especially if we get rid of this damned *Argus*. And, of course, one day the *Lion* will be yours, my boy."

Finch was now leaning earnestly across his desk towards his son to ensure he fully understood. Oliver sighed and nodded. "Yes, Father, I know what is planned and I appreciate it," he said. There was much more he wanted to say, but seeing his father's agitation his courage had drained away.

Inspector Ramm had begun the day determined to make some progress with the mystery of the murder on the towing path. He was now convinced the attack was no chance affair. The lonely location, the deadly accuracy of the stabbing, the emptying of the victim's pockets – it all signified a carefully planned attack.

However, he desperately needed more information and knew that sitting at his desk would get him nowhere. He felt drawn back to the scene and to the couple on the barge whom he was sure had been keeping something from him.

And so the Inspector forsook the warmth of his office fire and boarded a trap. This time he decided to approach the case from literally a new angle. They left the town via Ladderedge, although the trap driver was not particularly happy at being asked to scale the steep hill in such slippery conditions. To Ramm's relief they made it to the top without incident.

On reaching Longsdon, they turned off the main road and onto Sutherland Road between the Waterworks Inn and the village post office. The road was fronted by substantial houses which had been built in recent years. Many belonged to wealthy people, pottery owners from Stoke on Trent and the like, who had been attracted to the village by the convenience of Wall Grange railway station at bottom of the road. The growing wealth of neighbourhood had not gone unnoticed by the criminal fraternity and Ramm had dealt with an increasing number of burglaries in the area. Could someone from one of these houses have been the victim in the canal? he wondered.

After descending the hill towards the valley bottom, they reached a bridge over the canal, Horse Bridge as it was called. Ramm got down and told the trap driver to wait for him there. He then set off along the towing path towards Leek and the scene of the attack. On a normal day, he would have had to stand aside each time he encountered a heavy horse pulling a barge, but the canal was still frozen solid and he saw no one on the path ahead.

Once out of earshot of the steam pumps inside the tall buildings of Wall Grange Water Works, he felt enveloped in the eerie peace of the snow blanketed countryside. It helped to concentrate his mind as he tried to imagine the victim and his attacker meeting in this place.

The draft horse's ears twitched at the sound of Ramm's footsteps in the frozen snow as he approached *The Esperance*, still fast in the ice. Silas Turnock was nowhere to be seen, so the Inspector stepped aboard the barge and rapped on the cabin door. Turnock opened it and looked dismayed when he saw Ramm.

"Officer?" said the boatman, with no invitation for Ramm to enter.

"Mr Turnock. I would like to speak to you again about the incident. May I come in?" Ramm, not waiting for a response, stepped down into the cabin. Once again he was impressed by how expertly the woodwork had been crafted to fill the small space with shelves and cupboards, the claustrophobia relieved by colourful ornaments and painted tinwork.

Turnock went back to a small stool beside the stove and his wife was once more perched on the edge of the raised bed. There was nowhere for Ramm to sit, but that suited him. Standing over the Turnocks at such close quarters somehow signalled his authority over the barge folk. He was not there for a friendly chat.

"So, have either of you any more recollection of what went on earlier this week?" Ramm began. "I find it hard to believe that someone lost their life a matter of yards away and yet you knew so little about it. Are you sure you saw nothing?"

The Turnocks exchanged the sort of look that Ramm had spotted the previous day.

"Tell 'im, Silas," said the woman firmly.

Turnock rubbed his unshaven jowls with the back of his hand and was silent for a moment. "Well, I was watching yer men pull that fella out o' the water. Tall thin chap, was he?"

"That is likely," Ramm confirmed.

"Well, we're up and down this cut all the time and, like I told you yesterday, this is where we tie up regular. If it's the chap I think it might be, we've seen 'im on the path a few times since summer," Turnock continued. "He were usually hanging around just about the same place you fished the body out. Tall fella, smartly dressed, not a workman or anything."

"On his own or was he with someone else?"

"Sometimes on 'is own, waiting like. Other times there'd be somebody with 'im."

"And what was he like, the other man?" Ramm breathed a little quicker at the prospect of his first real clue to the culprit.

"Not a man, Officer. Usually it were a woman. And there were a few different ladies over the months, I recollect."

Ramm was taken aback. This was a new scenario to consider.

Was a woman mixed up in this murder? He pressed the Turnocks for a description of any of the women, but they could offer little more information other than the women were invariably young and well dressed. The fact that there was more than one made Ramm wonder if this was where the man met up with local prostitutes. There were a number who worked near the pubs in Leek, but would such women venture this far out of town?

"Were these women of ill repute, do you think?"

"How would I know?" Turnock replied with a shrug and a slightly guilty glance at his wife.

"And you never saw him meeting anyone else?"

"I think there was a man once. I say 'think' 'cause he were such a little fella and standing next to that other chap, 'e looked more like a young-un wearing grown-up's clothes. Had a big cap on 'im."

Ramm took out his notebook and went over the details again, making a careful note of it all. Satisfied the Turnocks had no more to tell him, he was turning to climb out of the cabin when the wife muttered something to her husband, then called out: "Hang on, Officer, there's summat else."

Silas sighed, opened a drawer and took out a small object. Rather sheepishly he handed it to Ramm. "I found this on the path, would be Tuesday morning when it came light. It were lying in the snow," he said.

It was a gold pocket watch. Ramm clicked open the hinged case and saw that the initials "J.J." elaborately engraved inside the lid. Ramm wondered if the boatman originally intended hanging on to his valuable find, but had changed his mind because the police were now involved, or because his wife had urged him to do so. Or had this rough character been the attacker? Had he stolen the watch from the victim before pushing him into the canal?

"Was there anything else?" the Inspector asked. Turnock shook his head.

“This may be important evidence and I shall have to take charge of it,” said Ramm. “I also require you both to stay here until you are told otherwise.” When Turnock began to remonstrate, the Inspector put up his hand to silence him. “This is a serious matter and I must ask you to co-operate. In any case, until this ice clears, you won’t be going anywhere.”

As he walked back along the towing path, the Inspector mulled over what this new evidence might mean for the case. Was the boatman telling the truth about having seen a man meeting women on the path, or was he trying to cover his tracks? But if Turnock had carried out the attack, why would he incriminate himself by producing the pocket watch? The fact that the tall man – probably the victim – had been on the towing path more than once could also be important. Where had he come from? Leek, Longsdon, a nearby farm? Ramm stopped and looked across the valley at the great buildings of the County Asylum. Perhaps that place held the answer, he thought.

CHAPTER FIVE

The platform at Leek Station was crowded as Cora and Oliver boarded the train for Rudyard that afternoon. Even in the depths of winter, Rudyard Lake was a popular destination for a weekend visit, especially now the lake was frozen hard.

In past years, Cora and her friends had gone skating on a fish pond at the bottom of the slope behind St Edward's Church in Leek, the Old Church as people called it. The pond was in the grounds of Ball Haye Hall, but the mill owner who lived in the mansion didn't seem to mind folk using it for winter fun. However for Cora, today's outing was as much about spending time with Oliver as sliding about on the ice.

Minutes after leaving Leek, the train halted at Rudyard Station and they joined a crowd of passengers on the short walk to the lakeside. When they reached the reservoir, they found its usually dark waters had been transformed into a solid expanse, glinting white against the bright blue sky now that the clouds had cleared.

There were dozens of people out on the ice. Some were walking unsteadily in winter boots, couples were clinging onto each other and laughing. Others were gliding more assuredly on skates they had hired from a wooden hut that provided parasols to visitors on warmer days. Two or three men had even wheeled their bicycles onto the frozen surface – perhaps as a dare – and were perilously close to collapse as they tried to balance on the slippery surface.

The sound of cheers floated from the distance. Cora looked down the lake and saw that a group of men were moving swiftly across the ice, holding sticks in their hands and leaning forward to pick up speed.

"What's going on across there?" she asked.

"It looks like they're playing hockey on the ice! Can you believe it?" Oliver laughed.

Cora knew her father would like to photograph that. Postcards of scenes on the frozen lake sold well at their shop and he often came here in winter. In harsh weather some years previously he had taken pictures of Leek Fire Brigade standing proudly on the frozen lake with their gleaming fire engine. A couple of days before that, the firemen had crossed the ice to tackle a blaze at a boathouse that was known as The Lady of the Lake.

Cora stared at the ice and, despite the fun going on around her, her mind spun back to the frozen canal she had seen on Thursday and the body beneath. Oliver interrupted her thoughts. "Shall we skate?" he said, giving her hand a squeeze as she huddled next to him.

"Oh no! I couldn't face being on the ice. Not after… after what happened," she replied. It was hard for her to put that terrible scene into words.

Oliver grimaced, realising he should have guessed her reaction. He had wanted to lighten the mood, but it appeared he had done just the opposite. This outing with Cora was not going the way he had planned. "Of course! I'm sorry," he said. "Well, perhaps we should have a warm drink? I see the tea room is open. We might be more comfortable in there."

There was a wooden chalet which served lunches and afternoon teas all year round. It had a coal stove in the corner, so Cora was able to slip off her woollen hat and mittens after they sat down. Oliver poured tea from a china pot, they each ate half of their scone and sat quietly for several minutes. Cora sensed he was preoccupied. “Is something wrong?” she asked.

He took a deep breath, then began hurriedly: “No, not at all. It’s just that I have something important to talk to you about.”

He reached across and grasped her hand. “I have been doing a lot of thinking… about the future. Our future,” he went on. “I love Leek, it’s the only home I’ve known, but there’s a whole world out there and I want to see something of it.”

Cora sat very still, her eyes fixed on Oliver. There was bad news coming, she was sure of it.

“I want to leave Leek, I want to go abroad,” he blurted out, relieved to be finally telling someone what he had been planning in secret for months.

Cora opened her mouth to speak, but was too shocked. “What… not live here any longer?” she stuttered.

“That’s right.”

“Where will you go?” Cora’s voice was weak. She had torn her hand away from his and was twisting her mittens into a knot.

“New Zealand,” Oliver said cautiously.

Although the tea room was bustling with the sound of conversation and the chink of cups and saucers, a gulf of silence opened up between the two young people.

“But that’s… the other side of the world,” Cora finally stammered. She began to feel sick at the thought of perhaps never seeing Oliver again.

“It’s 12,000 nautical miles, actually, depending on which route you take. I know it’s far away, but I have found out lots about it. There is work and there are good places to live,” Oliver replied excitedly. He then became serious and stared straight into her eyes.

"And I want you to go with me."

Cora gasped. "Go with you? Do you mean..."

"Yes, I love you, Cora. I want us to marry and start a new life together – over there."

"So, is this a proposal, Oliver?"

"Yes, it is. Will you be my wife?"

"Oliver, I don't know what to say." There were tears in her eyes now. A proposal of marriage, across the table in a tea room, was not what she had expected of today. Yes, she had dreamed of spending her life with him, but did she really want to go to the opposite end of the earth? It was too much to take in.

Seeing Cora hesitate, Oliver went on. "Of course, I shall speak to your father and ask his permission."

"But who will you know there? How will you find somewhere to live? Where will you work?"

"Their Government will help, they are appealing for new settlers all the time. And there are people from Leek already living in New Zealand, they support each other."

"What does your father say about all this? About you leaving Leek and not working for the *Lion*?" she asked.

"Well, I haven't actually told him yet. I intended to, but there has not been the right moment. I know it will be hard on him, and on Mother, too. But I wanted to speak to you first. I don't think I could go there without you, Cora."

Later, Cora could not remember the rest of the afternoon at Rudyard or the journey home. Her mind was too full of what Oliver had said for her to take in anything else. After walking up from Leek Station, they had stolen a kiss before they parted in Portland Street. She was not concerned who might see them embracing in the street, propriety did not seem so important now.

Cora told Oliver she would need time to think about his proposal. She knew that both their futures depended on her decision.

Although the boiler was supposed to be working again, the temperature in the Town Hall that Saturday evening was not particularly comfortable as the Moorland Philharmonia gathered on the stage an hour before their concert. Most of the musicians planned to keep their hats, coats and fingerless gloves on until the last minute.

The atmosphere was made even more chilly by the tone of the conductor, Jeremiah Alsop, when he saw that some players were absent.

"Dear, dear, this is not good enough," he tutted as he peered disapprovingly over his pince-nez spectacles at the empty seats. A retired schoolmaster, he ruled his musicians with a rod, or rather a baton, of iron. Indeed, many of them felt as if they were back in school.

"No first violins? No second clarinet? Only one cello? Where are they all? Do they not know we have a concert tonight?"

A horn player dared to speak up. "There's a lot of influenza about, Mr Alsop. And this cold is playing havoc with our instruments." Other players nodded and exchanged knowing glances, but said nothing.

"It's simply not good enough, Horn Two. Musicianship counts for nothing without discipline and punctuality," Alsop replied, sweeping his hand through his flowing white hair. As usual he referred to his musicians by their place in the orchestra, rather than by name.

"One of the violins is sick, his wife told me this afternoon. And the other is away somewhere, I think," said the solitary cellist.

"I will be glad when this concert is done with," a wind player whispered. Her neighbour, a young woman with a flute, simply nodded nervously.

A violinist in the second row raised his bow. "I could move up to First Desk, if that helps, Mr Alsop," he suggested. The man was taking his opportunity to lead the violin section. He cast his eyes around his fellow players, especially the women sitting opposite, apparently looking for their approval.

"Well… I suppose you will have to, in the circumstances," the conductor accepted with ill grace. "The rest of you will just have to do as best you can. This concert is an important occasion, it's our first of the year and I need your complete concentration. No excuses."

There was a shuffling of sheet music and a scraping of chairs on the floorboards as Alsop called on the principal oboe to play a note for the rest of the orchestra to tune with. Many adjustments and trial notes followed, particularly by string players whose instruments had been more affected by the cold. The conductor cast increasingly impatient looks across his company, then finally raised his baton to signal the start of a brief rehearsal before the audience started to arrive.

"Let us start with the Mozart. And remember, presto! Presto!" Alsop called out. He began to beat time vigorously with both hands before spearing his baton towards the sparse violins as they began the familiar flurry of notes at the opening of the *Figaro* overture.

The orchestra had worked its way through short excerpts of half a dozen pieces when, through the heavy velvet curtains across the stage, they could hear the audience starting to arrive. The sound of voices and the tramp of winter boots were heard as folk made their way up the grand staircase with its tiled walls. In the ballroom itself, on the Town Hall's upper floor, there was a murmur of conversation as people found their seats and started to look at their programmes.

"It appears that is all we will have time for," said the conductor, laying down his baton on his music stand. "Let us hope it all goes a little better in the actual performance. Everyone, back in your seats by twenty minutes past," he added before stalking off stage.

The players relaxed and quietly exchanged comments about the music and the temperature in the hall. Someone noticed that the young woman playing the flute had tears in her eyes. Old Alsop was a tough taskmaster, one of them thought, but surely he had gone too far this time?

Despite Jeremiah Alsop's misgivings, the concert turned out to be a success and at the end of the evening the players were rewarded with rousing applause from an audience which included Edna Ramm. Half an hour later she delivered a full review to her husband when she got back to their house in Queen Street. Inspector Ramm, it appeared, had spent the evening in peace, sifting through police reports.

"You should have been there, Albert. You need to have a rest from work sometimes, find something different to think about," Edna told him, although she could see he did not necessarily appreciate her advice. "There were plenty of people there who you would have known."

"Well, in my position I do tend to know a lot of people in town. Not all of them on a friendly basis though, Edna," Ramm replied.

He had spent much of the evening puzzling over the canal attack once again. In particular, he mused on what he had learned about the tall man's visits to the towing path and what kind of incident could have led to his death.

He was still baffled as to whether it was significant that the weapon could be a scalpel. Where had it come from? he wondered. The asylum perhaps? Or had the attacker simply bought one? If so, where would one obtain such a thing? There was a chemist in Derby Street, a man called Walter Wainwright, whom Ramm had known for years. He decided it was worth having a word with him about how easy it was to buy a scalpel. He thought he could trust him to keep the matter private. His first priority on Monday, however, would be to speak to Dr Gibson at the County Asylum again.

That night, Cora's mind was in turmoil as she lay in bed. Her attic bedroom was freezing cold and frost had spread icy fronds across the panes of her window. She pulled her eiderdown up to her chin and gazed at the ceiling in the glow of her oil lamp.

At supper she had not known how to answer when Mother asked what she and Oliver had done at Rudyard Lake. Afterwards she had made an excuse to come upstairs as soon as possible, leaving her parents to think she was still upset about the incident on the canal.

She had imagined that Oliver's proposal of marriage, if it ever happened, would be one of the happiest days of her life. She had often wondered what their life together would be like, but she had always pictured it in Leek. Oliver working at the *Lion*, her mother around the corner, children at a town school… Now those dreams had been upended by his plan for a great adventure.

Unlike some of the young women she knew, Cora's horizons had already stretched beyond the moorlands. Only this week, her friend Beatrice, a women's campaigner, had written to her about a protest march planned for the following month. Although it was to take place in London, Cora had decided she wanted to go to it. She had joined in Votes for Women protests before and even organised one of her own. She was happy that some people might think of her as a Suffragette. A few months ago, a *Daily Mail* reporter had coined the name to mock the campaigners and now the women protestors had adopted it with pride.

But it seemed that Oliver's ambitions were far bigger. Spending weeks on a steamship – how many miles did he say it was? – then starting a new life in a country on the other side of the world. Worst of all, saying goodbye to her parents, to her brother William and her friends, not knowing when or if ever she would speak to any of them again.

It was a heartrending choice. To be with Oliver, she might have to give up everything else, including her ambitions for a career of her own, perhaps. But if she wouldn't go to New Zealand, then his dreams would be shattered.

Instead of dwelling on the sadness, she resolved to focus on the happiness that Oliver promised, the excitement of life in a new country. Before she gave him her decision, she wanted to know more about this faraway place. On Monday, she would go to the Lending Library and see what she could find out about New Zealand for herself.

In a street not far from the middle of town, a man watched as a young woman arrived and opened the front door of a terraced house. He saw an oil lamp flicker into life in the parlour. His feet were freezing as he stood motionless on the icy pavement in his usual place, well away from the street lamp. His breath condensed into a chilled wetness on the woollen wrapped around his face.

His only movement was a tilt of the head when he saw the light was now glowing behind an upstairs curtain. He knew she had gone up to her bedroom. She was undressing, he thought. He had imagined that scene so often. Her taking off her day clothes one by one, folding them neatly then giving a shiver as she slipped into her long white nightgown, her dark hair untied and cascading onto her shoulders. One day, he hoped, he would be in the room with her.

The window went dark as the lamp was extinguished. He nodded with resignation. That was the end of his enjoyment for another day.

His beloved had been at the Town Hall and he had stolen tantalising glimpses of her all evening. How still she sat when she was concentrating, her beautiful forehead crinkled by a small frown. He had nearly spoken to her, but then someone had interrupted and the moment was lost. He had been so preoccupied with watching her that he was almost deaf to what the orchestra was playing. Let's face it, he thought with a smile, the music was only an excuse to be near to her. When the concert was over, he had followed her home, hanging back a few yards and keeping to the shadows in case someone recognised him.

He had wanted her for so long, but had never spoken to her of his desires. That other rogue had tried to win her over and she had nearly fallen for his philandering. How could she have been so weak!

The man ground his teeth. Why didn't she recognise his devotion? How could she so misunderstand him? Had he been too hasty when he put that note through her door? he wondered. A little too forward in what he suggested, perhaps? But how else was he to tell her what he felt, what he craved?

It had been a shock when he saw that morning's *Leek Lion*, though. He had felt a chill as icy as the winter wind. There was a letter, complaining and threatening. Could his loved one have written that? And that fool Finch was getting hot under the collar. Whatever the *Lion* might say, he had as much right to be on the street as the next man. Love was not against the law, was it?

This nonsense in the newspaper would have to stop, though. There could be no more letters like that. He would have to watch his beloved even more closely.

The man trudged off along the deserted street, his mind full of the woman he had observed all evening. One day, he thought, she will see me as the only man in her life.

Chapter Six

The frozen pavements were flecked with soot from the mill chimneys as Inspector Ramm made his way to the police station the following Monday morning. The boilers in Leek's mills had been lit for hours, providing the steam to drive machinery for the many hundreds of workers whose shifts had started at half-past six. It was barely an hour later and just coming light when Ramm walked through the town, but there was already plenty of activity.

The town lamplighters were doing their morning rounds, turning off the gas street lamps and shopkeepers were out clearing snow from in front of their stores. In the side streets, householders had scattered ashes and cinders out of their front doors to make patches of pavement safe to walk on. At Sparrow Park, the open space at the bottom of the main street, Derby Street, he saw a young man had been given the job of sweeping snow from the paving stones with a broom. Nearby, a council workman was urging a pair of horses to pull a wooden snow plough along Haywood Street.

With snow clinging to the conical roofs of its twin turrets, the imposing police station in Leonard Street looked even more like a baronial lodge transplanted from the highlands of Scotland. When the Inspector arrived he gathered together the half dozen of his men who were on duty.

It was his routine to begin the week by reviewing the most recent crimes and incidents with his team. He was in the process of explaining what progress he had made with the canal murder, when he was called to the telephone. It was Dr Gibson from the County Asylum.

"Yes, Ramm speaking," he barked into the handset. He found

Gibson's tone was quite changed from their conversation after the body had been recovered from the canal on Thursday.

"Inspector, I hope I am not interrupting your other important duties, but I thought I should speak to you as soon as possible this morning," Gibson began smoothly.

"Do you have some information for us, Dr Gibson?"

"Well, it appears that we have someone who is unaccounted for. Not an inmate, I can assure you of that. However, a member of staff appears to be – how shall I put it – missing."

"Missing, you say?" Ramm was immediately on alert.

"One of our Medical Assistants, Dr Jervis. He went on leave at the start of last week and was due back by the weekend, but he has not returned," Gibson explained. "His quarters were checked, just to be sure, and apparently all his belongings are still there. It seems that either he took nothing with him when he left or… something else may have happened."

"Touch nothing in his room. I shall be there within the hour."

"James Jervis joined us last summer," said Dr Gibson. "He is one of the new members of staff we appointed to cope with the increasing number of inmates. And a very capable young doctor he is, too."

Gibson looked somewhat nervously at Inspector Ramm across his desk at the asylum.

"When was Dr Jervis last seen?" asked Ramm.

"It would be sometime during last Monday afternoon. He had been on duty throughout the Christmas and New Year period and was due to begin his leave that evening. He had said he was going to visit his parents, they live in Cumberland, I think," Gibson explained.

"He was expected to be back on duty on Saturday, but when he didn't return in time we thought his train had perhaps been delayed by the weather. We had not heard anything from him yesterday and so one of his colleagues inspected his room and realised that something may be amiss. We sent a telegram to his family and last night they replied that they had not seen or heard anything of him. They thought he had been too busy to make the journey back home."

He added hurriedly: "Obviously, I would be very surprised if there is a connection with that unfortunate incident on the canal, but in view of your inquiries last week, I thought it only proper to inform you."

Ramm guessed that, as much as helping the police, the doctor wanted to ensure his own conduct would stand up to scrutiny when his superior, Dr Menzies, eventually returned from abroad.

The Inspector considered the sequence of events. It appeared that Jervis had not been seen since Monday. That night the canal had frozen over and the boatman, Silas Turnock, had heard voices on the towing path. The doctor could indeed be the victim. Particularly as his initials matched those engraved on the pocket watch Turnock had found in the snow. "What does Dr Jervis look like?" he asked.

Dr Gibson frowned as he recalled the missing man. "In his early thirties, tall with dark hair. He's a very amiable chap and something of an athlete, a runner I believe, so he carries no weight."

"I don't suppose you have a photograph of him?"

"Unfortunately, we do not keep photographs in our records. Perhaps we should," Gibson replied. He picked up a pencil and wrote a reminder to himself to ask Nathaniel Blake to take portrait photographs of senior members of staff.

"Perhaps I could examine the doctor's room now," Ramm continued, then added, almost as an aside: "By the way, he wasn't involved in any sort of dispute, was he? With a colleague or one of the people he was looking after, perhaps?" He had decided not to tell Gibson that the dead man had been attacked. After Gibson's defensiveness the previous week, the Inspector did not want to put the management, or anyone else at the asylum, on their guard too soon.

Gibson looked puzzled, then answered: "I have heard of nothing untoward. In fact, his conduct has been exemplary as far as I'm concerned. As for his personal life, well, that is not something I have any knowledge of. I believe Dr Forbes is his closest colleague, so he may know something. I will ask him to take you to their quarters."

Some minutes later, Arthur Forbes led Ramm through the asylum towards where Medical Assistants lodged. "This place is something of a maze," the young doctor explained as they made their way along corridors and through a succession of locked doors. "But it's actually quite logical. The main building is divided into two matching halves, one side for male inmates, the other for the females."

Ramm was surprised by the amount of bustling activity in the corridors. He saw parties of men and women heading off in different directions, all in the simple work clothing that he had been told patients wore. Each group was accompanied by a uniformed attendant, keeping a watchful eye to make sure the patients went in the right direction. Seeing Ramm's curiosity, Forbes said that the people were going to and from their places of work – the men to various workshops and many of the women to the laundry, the sewing room or the kitchens.

"The laundry is busy six days a week. You can imagine the amount of bedding and clothing that has to be washed," Forbes explained. As if to confirm it, a side door swung open, letting a cloud of steam into the corridor. Ramm caught a glimpse of a scene of great activity. Women were feeding or emptying a line of huge cylindrical washing machines. He could see that in an adjoining room there were ironing machines and many white sheets hung from lines across the high ceiling.

"The kitchen will be just as busy at this time of day. As well as making hundreds of meals, there are cookery classes so that female patients can better themselves. It might help them lead a more normal life as and when they go back out into the outside world, just like the men who are learning a trade in the workshops or maintaining the buildings," Forbes added.

Eventually he unlocked an outer door and led Ramm into the cobbled yard at the rear of the main block of buildings. They walked past the asylum church and towards a row of substantial semi-detached villas on the edge of the grounds.

Ramm realised that this was close to where the path led down towards the meandering river and the canal where the body had been found. Forbes showed the way into one of the villas and strode straight up the stairs. "There are two of us doctors lodging in the house and this is James's room," he said, opening a door on the first floor.

The bedroom was simply furnished; there was a narrow iron bed – Ramm wondered if it was the same as those which inmates slept on – a small desk, a chair, a chest of drawers and a single wardrobe. The desk was littered with documents and personal items. In the corner of the room there was a suitcase and, on top of that, a smaller black case of some sort.

"I had a quick look around here yesterday after James didn't return from his journey," Forbes explained. "I thought there was something wrong when I saw his suitcase was still here. Then I noticed there were things which he would have taken with him, like his shaving kit and especially that parcel," he pointed to a brown paper package on the desk. "He'd told me that was a gift for his mother."

"Do you know Dr Jervis well?" Ramm asked. He had noticed that not only did Forbes call Jervis by his first name, but there was a marked air of informality in the way he talked about him.

"Well, we are of a similar age and we both came to Cheddleton around the same time last summer, so we have been working alongside each other from the outset." Forbes fell silent, apparently thinking about his missing colleague. When he began to speak again there was a deep concern in his voice. "I don't know where he's got to, but he simply couldn't be the poor chap who was found in the canal. It just doesn't make any sense that he should fall in. Have you found out what happened down there?"

"We are still investigating," Ramm replied, then changed the subject. "This must be a challenging place to work. I expect some of the people can be difficult to handle. And aggressive sometimes, no doubt," he said.

He was wondering if anyone from the asylum could be involved in this affair, but tried to keep his tone conversational. In the past, he had been stickler for paperwork, making sure everything a witness said was written down. More recently, however, he had discovered that he could gain more by putting people at their ease and seeing what surfaced as the conversation progressed.

"Our patients have all sorts of problems, but certainly we have our work cut out with some of them. And with around one thousand people in here, there are bound to be one or two bad apples. Some are sent here by the courts, as I'm sure you are aware, Inspector."

Ramm was struck by the comment. The asylum had grown into one of the biggest communities in the moorlands, its population larger than most of the villages. He knew only too well what problems could arise amongst that number of people, regardless of the reasons why some of them were there.

To his dismay, he realised that his officers played little part in the affairs of the asylum. The local police – including himself – had virtually no idea what was going on behind the locked doors of this vast complex. He decided to pump Forbes for more information.

"Dr Gibson tells me that the folk here are kept inside the wards and workplaces or, if they are allowed outside, they are supervised at all times. Surely, some of them manage to sneak away at times?"

"Well…" Forbes paused, choosing his words carefully. "Yes, it does happen on occasion, but an inmate is not absent for long before one of the staff realises. We sound an alarm, send out search parties and it's usually sorted out quite quickly."

"And what about weapons? Could someone get hold of a knife, perhaps?"

"Weapons? What has this got to do with James?" Forbes asked, wary of where the conversation was leading.

"Apologies, Dr Forbes, it is purely professional curiosity. I realise there is so much I do not know about this institution."

Somewhat reassured, Forbes decided to answer. "Well, it would be virtually impossible for them to get hold of a knife. Every item is checked and counted. At mealtimes, there are boxes on all the tables where the cutlery is put when it's finished with. The knives and forks are specially designed to prevent a patient doing any harm to themselves. Although we did have an unfortunate incident recently when someone on the female wards swallowed a spoon, but that sort of thing is very rare."

Ramm began to sift through the papers on the desk while he continued talking to Forbes, hoping to build a picture of Jervis. If the missing doctor was indeed the person recovered from the canal, finding out more about his character and behaviour could help to discover a motive for the attack.

"What sort of person is your friend James?" he asked casually.

"Oh, he's quite a character. An enthusiast for so many things, music, sport. He makes friends easily, especially amongst the ladies." There seemed to be a touch of envy in Forbes' tone.

"Indeed? Anyone in particular? Might he be with one of those friends now, do you think?"

"I'm simply aware he has friends on the outside, so to speak, but I wouldn't really know their names or where they live. When he's free James is often out and about, he's not one for sitting in the common room of an evening. Occasionally he goes to the Black Lion down in the village and into Leek quite regularly, when he can slip away," he added.

"Slip away? Would that be through the back fence?"

Forbes looked a little uncomfortable. "Well, staff should really have the Superintendent's permission before they leave the grounds. However I know that James does go that way on occasion. That's why I was so worried when I heard someone had been found in the canal. But honestly, I can't believe it could have been him."

"Might he have a friend he meets out of the asylum, on the towing path, perhaps?"

"As I said, he's a friendly sort of chap," Forbes replied, then added quickly: "But I wouldn't know who he meets when he's out and about. Myself, I don't venture out much."

Ramm picked up something from the desk and looked at it closely. A colourful postcard of the sort that lovers would send. It was embroidered with a spray of flowers and the words "Sealed with a kiss". On the back, the words '*To the Dashing Doctor*' were written. Jervis obviously had an admirer somewhere, he thought.

Next he saw a small notebook with a red cover. He opened it, hoping to find a diary which might reveal more about the man, who he was involved with, perhaps even a note about the previous Monday. Instead, Ramm saw that each page bore a list of names, dates and sums of money. He read a page at random:

October 19th, Plumpton, Lord Schonberg. £1 2s 6d.

October 23rd, Liverpool, Young Challenger. 10s.

November 4th, Doncaster, Duke of Melton. Nil.

It took a moment before he fathomed what the notes meant, then he realised it looked like a record of winnings – and losses – on horse races. The lists went on for page after page and the sums represented a considerable amount. As if to confirm it, Ramm noticed there was a page of a newspaper on the desk. It was torn from *The Sporting Life* and had various runners and riders underlined in ink.

Ramm was aware that Forbes was watching him closely. "Is this one of the things he was enthusiastic about?" the Inspector asked, holding up the newspaper for the doctor to see.

"Oh, the horses? Well, yes, James does partake in the odd wager," Forbes replied, doing his best to make light of the subject.

"This appears to be more than the odd wager."

Ramm wondered if James Jervis's gambling could be connected with the attack on the towing path? How did that fit with an attacker who had some sort of medical knowledge? Also, who had sent the amorous floral postcard? Jervis's personal items prompted more questions than they answered, but Ramm knew that first he had to confirm the missing doctor was in fact the victim.

He felt in his pocket for the watch the bargee said he had found by the canal. He handed it to Forbes. "Do you recognise this?"

Forbes flipped it open and saw the initials engraved inside and gasped in surprise. "Yes, I'm sure this belongs to James! He's very proud of it. His father gave it to him when he qualified. But where did you get it?" he said.

"I'm not at liberty to say at the moment," Ramm replied. "However, I would like you to come with me to the Memorial Hospital and take a look at the poor fellow we brought out of the canal last week. I am hoping you may be able to confirm whether or not it is Dr Jervis."

"It is the least I can do, Inspector, and I'm sure Dr Gibson won't object. But I still sincerely hope it is not poor old James." Forbes seemed genuinely shaken after seeing the pocket watch.

"Before we leave, is Dr Jervis in that photograph?" Ramm nodded towards a framed picture on the wall beside the bed, a group of young men in striped blazers.

"That's from his college days. The athletics team. James is

standing on the far left," said Forbes with a smile as he pointed at the picture.

Ramm took the photograph from the wall and sighed as he looked at the tall fellow on the edge of the group. James Jervis, relaxed and in the peak of health, so different to the remains he had seen dragged out of the ice. He turned and picked up Jervis's notebook and the embroidered postcard. "I shall need to retain these for our enquiries," he said, "and I would like this room to be kept locked."

Arthur Forbes accompanied Inspector Ramm back to Leek and fulfilled his promise to view the dead man in the hospital mortuary. He gave an involuntary cry as the sheet was drawn back to reveal the body and then staggered sideways, so much so that Ramm reached for Forbes' elbow to steady him.

"Oh poor James! I can barely recognise him, but yes, it is him. However did this happen to you, old fellow? That tow path must have been treacherous," he said, his eyes fixed on the body and his own face now deathly pale. Then Forbes reached forward and touched the bare arm on the mortuary slab. Ramm, thinking that Forbes' medical training would have steeled him for such a sight, was surprised at the depth of the man's reaction.

Ramm asked Forbes to make a formal statement. Could he be involved in this affair? the Inspector wondered. After all, he was a medical man, he might have access to a suitable weapon and he certainly knew the victim. He also admitted being aware that Jervis went down to the canal on occasion.

After they had walked to the police station, Ramm ordered mugs of tea for himself and Forbes. The man had not spoken since they had left the hospital and looked like he would benefit from a hot drink. As soon as they were seated in his office, the Inspector wasted no time in setting out the seriousness of the situation.

“Dr Forbes, I am sorry to say that the person you have identified as Dr James Jervis was not the victim of an accident.” He saw the doctor’s features suddenly tense. “It is our belief that he was attacked on the towing path near to where his body was found. In other words, just a short distance from the County Asylum where you work.”

Forbes’ hand right shook violently, spilling tea from his mug onto the parquet floor. He reached forward to place the mug unsteadily on the corner of the desk before slumping back in his chair and letting out a gasp as if he had been punched in the stomach.

“This is beyond belief!” he exclaimed. “Who would do such a thing to James?”

“That is exactly what I intend to find out,” said Ramm icily. He could not be sure whether Forbes’ reaction was genuine, or if he was covering his tracks with an extremely effective act. “It appears you knew Dr Jervis probably as well as anyone else did at the asylum. Tell me, are you aware of any arguments he may have had there?”

“Arguments? No. The occasional professional disagreement, but certainly nothing serious enough to lead to… something like this!”

“Let me be the judge of that, Dr Forbes. So there were disagreements? With other members of staff? And what about the people he was looking after?”

“Like the rest of us, he had difficulties with one or two inmates, but there is a strict rule that no patient is abused in any way. And James got along well with nearly everyone on the staff, especially the nurses. He was that type.”

“What about yourself? Did you ever argue with him?”

“Me? As I told you, James and I were friends. I didn’t necessarily agree with all his activities – the horses, the ladies, perhaps – but that was his business. It was not my place to interfere.”

"As regards these *activities*, are you sure you cannot tell me anything more? Did he ever mention any names?"

Forbes took a deep breath, as if considering whether he should breach a confidence. "Well, I think sometimes he went to the Black Lion to meet someone. Something to do with horse racing, I suspect."

Ramm made a note. "And what about women?"

Forbes flushed and shook his head vigorously. "James is, er, was very discreet about that. From time to time he would become – how shall I put it? – rather more attached to someone, but I have no idea who they were."

Once the interview was over, Ramm arranged for the doctor to be taken back to the County Asylum, then sat thinking what his next move should be. In one of his favourite Sherlock Holmes novels, he had read how the supreme detective had organised his thoughts to focus on a culprit. He took a sheet of paper and began to write.

Arthur Forbes.
Motive: Professional rivalry? Jealousy over a woman? Dispute over money?
Means: Medical knowledge for stabbing. Access to weapon from asylum?
Opportunity: Knew Jervis's movements. Knew victim would not be missed for days.

Ramm sat back and looked at the list. There were enough reasons to keep a careful eye on Forbes. His comments, and his reaction on seeing the body, had somehow revealed a relationship that went much deeper than that between mere professional colleagues. It was not unknown for someone who claimed to be a man's friend to turn out to be his enemy, he thought.

Nathaniel Blake had been in his darkroom developing negatives from the wedding of a mill owner's son – only the well-off could afford a photographer for such occasions – when Constable Phillips arrived. He handed Blake a brown paper parcel which contained the framed photograph Ramm had taken from Jervis's room.

"The Inspector has asked if you can print some photographs of this chap. It's the man from the canal," said Phillips pointing to a tall man on the left of the photograph. "The Inspector wants six copies as soon as possible."

Blake looked at the figure behind the glass that Phillips pointed out. The man was young and in the full vigour of life, far different from the grim corpse Blake had first seen through the ice and then being dragged from the canal. But seeing the new picture he again felt he had seen the man before. He must have appeared in one of his photographs in the last few months, he thought.

"So the Inspector has made some progress with that awful accident, then," said Nathaniel.

"I don't know about progress, Mr Blake, but it was no accident. We're investigating it as a murder now. He was a doctor at the lunatic asylum, apparently," the constable replied.

Cora, who was standing in the background, gave a gasp. "This is a bad business, for all concerned," said Nathaniel, casting a worried look towards his daughter.

After Philips left, Nathaniel dismantled the picture frame and mounted the college photograph on an easel. He focused his camera on the man the constable had indicated. Seeing the face appear in the tray of developing fluid in his darkroom, he tried to remember where he had seen his features before, but still he could not be certain. There was only one thing for it, he decided. He would have to search through his files. It would take time, but if this man had been the victim of a murder, a photograph showing him somewhere else in the town might assist Inspector Ramm.

Meanwhile, Cora had said she wanted to go out and Nathaniel

had readily agreed. He wished she had not heard about the murder and thought it would do her good to be out in the fresh air, cold as it was.

Indeed, Cora did feel that a walk would help clear her mind of images of the canal death, a scene which horrified her anew now that she knew it was no accident. But her real motive was to visit the Lending Library in the town's Nicholson Institute to see if she could discover anything about New Zealand. She had spent most of Sunday thinking about Oliver's proposal and the dramatic change it would bring to her life if she accepted, and she knew she would have to give him her answer soon.

As she reached the Institute she saw that the copper dome on its impressive entrance tower was almost lost in a blanket of freezing fog which had descended over the town during the morning. She went up the stone steps, through the arched doorway and turned left to the counter where a library assistant was waiting to deal with requests for books. Members of the public were not allowed to browse books on the shelves in case they put one back in the wrong place and upset the meticulous filing system.

"I would like to find out about New Zealand. I hope you can help," said Cora, presenting her borrower's ticket to the assistant. The woman at first frowned in thought, then she picked up a ledger which listed the stock of books.

"Let me see… we have *Captain Cook, His Voyages and Discoveries*. There's also *The Forest Flora of New Zealand* by Thomas Kirk," she said, running her finger down the page. "I believe that one has many beautiful plates," she added, giving Cora a rather patronising smile. No doubt she thought a young woman would be delighted with colourful illustrations of plants and leaves.

"Thank you, but I don't think that is quite what I'm looking for. Do you have anything that says what New Zealand is like for the people who live there?"

"Oh, in that case, we might have to look in the Reference

Section," said the assistant, somewhat disappointed her previous suggestions had been rejected. She scrutinised another ledger, then turned to the hatch behind her and whispered a reference number to another member of staff who was stationed there. The second woman walked off along the shelves laden with books and returned with a sizeable tome bound in black leather. "This is the *Colonial Office Year Book* for 1906. I believe there is a chapter on the colony of New Zealand," the assistant told Cora.

Cora accepted the heavy volume and carried it into the Reading Room with its tall windows of many small panes that stretched up to the high ceiling. After laying the book on one of the polished oak tables, she took off her coat, drew up a chair and found the chapter about what might be her future home.

She passed quickly over statistics about such things as population, the economy and agricultural production. The descriptions of the dramatic scenery and unusual wildlife were rather more interesting, but what really captured her attention was a reference to a new programme of incentives being offered to attract settlers from the United Kingdom. Then she read something that set her heart beating faster: the role of women in helping to forge the colony's future. Amazingly she saw that New Zealand had been the first country in the world to allow women the vote – nearly fourteen years ago! New excitement drove her curiosity and she started to read the whole chapter through again, this time trying to picture what life would really be like for herself and Oliver so far away.

Having left the police station in search of a meat pie for his luncheon, Inspector Ramm decided to call in at the Wainwright Chemist and Druggist's shop in Derby Street. Ramm regarded Wainwright more as an acquaintance than a friend. In fact, there were few people in the town he would call a real friend. Being a policeman brought with it a certain caution on both sides of a relationship. Nathaniel Blake was one of the few people he was prepared to be completely open with, especially when it came to discussing police matters.

However, Ramm believed Wainwright was a person he could trust. For the past ten years they had both been members of the Moorlands Lodge of Grand Order of Oddfellows. It was a men's society which prided itself on helping folk at unfortunate times in life, providing a means to save money towards the cost of illness, injury or death. They also engaged in worthy debates at their weekly meetings. Its members, who included some of Leek's prominent residents, called each other 'Brother', though Ramm disliked such affectation.

Wainwright's shop window displayed three huge and shapely glass carboys filled with red, green and amber liquid, but it was inside that Ramm was confronted by the full array of the chemist's stock. It was usual for many local shops to be crammed with tins, jars and packets, all neatly stacked and arranged, but the sheer orderliness of this place was on a different scale. On three sides, the walls were lined with dark wood cabinets, the lower halves fitted with numerous small drawers, each neatly labelled; the upper sections were shelves which held row upon row of porcelain jars bearing Latin inscriptions in gold leaf. Meticulous lines of brown, green and blue bottles containing various concoctions were arranged on the marble counters. Beside them were large ornamental jars filled with paper tubes of pills and glass phials of yet more medicaments.

Looking around the chemist's, the Inspector could not help being impressed. Wainwright kept it in immaculate order. He knew the chemist was married, but he had no idea what his home life was like. He suspected the man spent most of his time at the shop, because he was obviously a fanatic for his work.

A door into a back room was open and Ramm could see the

chemist at his workbench, surrounded by the tools of his trade – scrubbed white mortars, brass scales and polished steel devices for the making and sorting of pills. The man was methodically pouring a container of pink pills through a funnel and into a series of bottles. "I shall be with you in a moment," he called over his shoulder.

When the job was done, Wainwright came through into the shop and on seeing Ramm he hesitated slightly, then smiled. "Brother Albert? It is unusual to see you here. What can I do for you? Nothing amiss, I hope."

Ramm tried to hide his discomfort at the word 'Brother'. "Do not worry Walter, I'm not here for medicine. Edna and I are in rude health, although sometimes I think a tonic would do me good," he said.

"Well, in that case, I do happen to have something that's very good," Wainwright began, reaching for a bottle of *Paine's Celery Compound*.

Before he could say more, Ramm held up his hand and interrupted. "Actually, I wanted your opinion. In confidence, of course."

Wainwright dragged his thinning hair across his scalp and stared at the Inspector expectantly.

"Do you stock surgical scalpels or some such instruments?" Ramm asked.

Wainwright raised his bushy eyebrows, obviously intrigued. "If you require one, I shall certainly be able to oblige. Is this an official matter?" he replied.

"I wonder, have you sold any recently?"

"Well…" Wainwright seemed to be searching his memory. "I do not recall a recent sale, although Mary, that's my shop girl, she might remember otherwise. Unfortunately, she is off work today."

"Are they easy to obtain elsewhere? From another shop in Leek perhaps?"

"Cope's in Cawdry Buildings might have them, but of course, their stock of surgical supplies is nowhere near as extensive as mine. So, Albert, is this really part of some investigation?" said Wainwright, apparently struggling to contain his curiosity.

"It is an official matter, and as I said, at this stage it is confidential. However if you can find any record of a recent sale, I would be most obliged."

"I shall look in my ledgers, but it may take a little while to find out what was sold and when," Wainwright replied.

Ramm thanked the man and left. He was a little disappointed that Wainwright had been unable to give him chapter and verse on the sale of scalpels. He wondered if he had he got his reasoning wrong. Perhaps any number of people could have put their hands on a suitable weapon.

The chemist watched Ramm leave and walk past the front window, the policeman's image reflected in the columns of coloured liquid in the display. Wainwright appeared to be intrigued by the visit and dearly wished he could have discovered more. He turned back to his workbench and started bottling his pills again, but kept losing count. His mind was on what Inspector Ramm had asked him about.

Later that afternoon Ramm received another telephone call from Dr Gibson at the County Asylum.

"Dr Forbes has given me some most disturbing news and I am surprised you did not inform me directly," he said. "He tells me that not only was Dr Jervis the unfortunate fellow who was found in the canal, but that you believe he was murdered!"

The man was obviously in a state of high anxiety. Ramm could understand why: not only had Gibson lost a valuable member of staff, but to make matters worse, the unfortunate incident had occurred while he himself was in charge of the lunatic asylum.

“I am afraid the evidence points to a fatal attack on the towing path, Dr Gibson. We now need to investigate just why and by whom it was committed. That will include exploring any links with the asylum, other than the obvious fact that Dr Jervis worked there.”

“But surely we can have nothing to do with this awful crime, Inspector?” Gibson’s voice was rising in new horror at the implications. “It must have been some random attack, some criminal seizing the opportunity to rob poor Dr Jervis.”

“That may be the case, but I need to explore all possibilities. I must ask you again, Dr Gibson, were you aware of any dispute Dr Jervis may have had with another member of staff. Or with someone in his care, for that matter?”

Gibson’s indignant attitude from the previous week returned. “What exactly are you suggesting, Inspector? Do you honestly think that someone from this institution could have committed this horrible crime? It is totally out of the question.”

“So, you know of nothing that could have prompted this attack on your good doctor?”

“I am not aware of anything of that nature. Dr Jervis was a well-respected member of the staff who played a valuable part in the life of the County Asylum.”

“Depending on where my enquiries lead me, I may need to visit the asylum again and speak to other members of your staff. I take it you have no problem with that?”

“Of course, I shall seek to assist in whatever way I can,” Gibson replied rather grudgingly, then he drew a deep breath. “It seems I will have to telegraph our Medical Superintendent to inform him what has happened, although I doubt Dr Menzies will be able to return from his conference in France at such short notice. And I feel I should also notify the management committee. They will be most concerned.”

Now it was Inspector Ramm’s turn to take a sharp breath. There would be influential figures on the County Lunacy Committee who, when they learned of the murder, might contact the Chief Constable. And if the head of the County Constabulary started to take an interest in the case there would be added pressure on himself.

After the call ended, he leaned back in his chair and stroked his moustache, deep in thought. Finding the victim's identity had been an important step forward, but this case had all the makings of a complicated affair. If suspicions pointed to the County Asylum, it could involve conducting literally dozens of interviews. However there were other aspects of the victim's life which deserved scrutiny. He picked up the notebook he had brought back from Jervis's bedroom and began to study it, page by page. Perhaps this could hold a clue to the crime.

Chapter Seven

It was seven o'clock and Oliver Finch was the last person in the *Leek Lion* building that Monday evening. His father had gone to a council meeting and the two men and a boy who worked on the printing of the newspaper had departed an hour earlier. Oliver closed his notebook, extinguished the paraffin stove and left the office. On the ground floor he turned off the remaining gas mantles, plunging the room which held the printing press into darkness save for dim light from a street lamp filtering through the window. He opened the front door onto Market Street and almost cannoned into someone who was about to put something through the letterbox. It appeared to be a young woman wearing a long black coat and dark bonnet, the lower part of her face swathed in a scarf.

"Goodness!" the woman gasped, stepping back in alarm at Oliver's sudden appearance in the doorway. After a moment's hesitation, she handed him an envelope, then lowered her head and hurried away before he had chance to apologise.

Oliver watched the diminishing figure as she walked away quickly past the front of the Town Hall and towards Stockwell Street. Oliver had caught only a glimpse of the woman's face above her scarf, but there was something familiar about her dark eyes. As he turned back to the doorway, he thought he saw a movement in the porch of Brunswick Methodist Church on the opposite side of the street. He stared into the pool of darkness for several seconds, saw nothing more and decided he must have been mistaken.

He was still holding the envelope the woman had handed to him. After this curious encounter, he wanted to know what was inside and took a few steps towards the nearest street lamp to examine it more closely. By the light of the gas lamp, the paper appeared to be a greenish blue colour and he was sure he recognised the handwriting. He felt a jolt of anticipation. It must be another letter from the mystery correspondent who claimed she was being spied upon by a man. Oliver was intrigued to think she must be the woman he had just seen.

Normally, Oliver would leave the *Lion*'s correspondence for his father to deal with, but tonight he could not restrain himself. He hastily opened the envelope and, still standing under the street lamp, quickly read through the letter that was inside.

Dear Editor, I write to give my heartfelt thanks for publishing my last letter. Finally I feel someone may take my plight seriously and help to bring an end to my torment.

I am not prepared to furnish my name and address for fear my identity could become known publicly and would attract even more unwanted attention. I appreciate that by speaking to you directly I could best explain my predicament, but I doubt I have the courage to do so. Sadly, I must confine myself to correspondence.

Unfortunately my situation is no better than it has been these past months. I am sure that my 'shadow' was following me again on Saturday and Sunday. After receiving the note last week which made such distasteful suggestions, my greatest fear is that this man will no longer content himself to simply observe my comings and goings, but will take matters into his own hands. That is when I may be in real danger!

Once again, may I thank you for your support and for any effort you may make to protect my honour.

Yours in appreciation, A Frightened Woman

Oliver folded the letter back into its envelope and stood deep in thought for a moment. The young woman with dark eyes was in trouble and he felt more than ever that he had to do something about it.

Ten minutes later Oliver was at the Blake house in Portland Street. Since their conversation on Saturday, he had thought of little except Cora and how she would respond to his proposal. For weeks he had been building up to asking her to be his wife and to go with him on his great adventure, but now he thought it had been unrealistic to expect her to say 'Yes' so quickly. He told himself that he had to give her time to think about it. Sunday had seemed to drag on interminably and today he had tried to bury himself in his work.

Now, with still no word from Cora, Oliver decided he must speak to her again, if only to find out if she was still considering the matter.

Edith Blake answered the door and called up to Cora who was in her room. The three then went into the parlour.

"How is young William, Mrs Blake?" Oliver asked, hoping his politeness would hide his nerves.

"Oh, he is much improved, thank you, Oliver. His breathing is a lot easier since I took him to the gas works," Edith replied, "but there's still a lot in town with this awful cough."

"Yes, I myself saw quite a queue down at the gas works this afternoon," said Oliver. "Many of the folk had children with them, but I think others were hoping for a free bucket of coke. It will certainly be needed if this bitter weather goes on."

The conversation petered out and there was a moment of awkwardness. Ethel looked from Oliver to Cora and guessed that they were waiting for her to leave them alone. "Well, I shall get back to my kitchen then, while you two have a talk," she said.

As soon as the door closed, Cora threw her arms around Oliver and they kissed passionately.

"Have you thought about what I said?" Oliver whispered cautiously, although Cora's greeting had filled him with hope.

"I've been able to think of nothing else, Oliver," she said.

"Oh?"

"I also decided to find out more about this country you want us to go to, so I went round to the library today."

"And did that help?" Still Oliver dared not believe what her decision would be.

"Well, there are forests and mountains and waterfalls and many colourful birds. And, most importantly, did you know that the women of New Zealand have the vote?"

He realised Cora was toying with him, making him wait for an answer. "But what about… us?" he asked, hoping not to sound exasperated.

"Us? You mean your proposal?" Cora smiled. "My answer is yes, Oliver. Yes to marriage, yes to a long sea voyage, yes to life together."

Cora couldn't stop herself laughing with delight. All her worries – the shock at Oliver's grand plan, the uncertainty what the future might hold, the sadness at leaving Leek behind – had been swept away by excitement at the prospect of a life and an adventure to be shared with Oliver. His proposal had opened up new horizons for her in every sense. For this evening at least.

Oliver wrapped her in his arms, embracing her so tightly she felt the breath being squeezed from her. He kissed her long and hard, breaking off only to murmur "Thank you, Cora. Thank you. I shall not let you down."

Cora detached herself and adjusted strands of hair which had been pulled from their grips. Her cheeks were burning with emotion as she looked into her future husband's eyes. "Calm yourself, Oliver. Suppose Mother came back in?" she said playfully. Then her expression became more serious. "You know you simply must tell your father – and mine – as soon as possible. This might be a great adventure for us, but it is not going to be easy for our parents."

She took a deep breath. Seeing Oliver tonight she had put the heartache of saying goodbye to her family to the back of her mind. But she knew how hard it would be on the ones they left behind, especially her mother. She remembered the heartbreak after little Emily died. Her mother might feel she was losing another daughter.

"Now you have given me your answer I will speak to both of our fathers and we can begin to make our plans. There will be so much to do, not only for the wedding but the arrangements for our journey, where we are to live, where I am to work," Oliver replied excitedly.

"Where you will work? I thought it was just farmers and labourers they were looking for. And what about me?" said Cora, prodding Oliver's waistcoat playfully. "I presume they need photographers in this wonderful new country you wish us to go to?"

"Well, there are plenty of newspapers over there, so I'm sure to find employment. Of course, you will be a married woman by then, so it might not be appropriate for you to be working. And you may have plenty of other things to keep you occupied," he replied with a smile.

Cora knew he was referring to them starting a family. Once more she was struck by the enormity of their plan. Their child would be born in New Zealand and Cora's own mother would not be there to support her. The only time Mother will see her grandchildren will be in a photograph, she thought.

Oliver took his opportunity to launch into a stream of facts and ideas about life in New Zealand. Cora realised just how long he must have spent studying the topic. Typical of a reporter, she thought. But there was simply too much for her to take in tonight.

She interrupted him: "Wait, please! You're making my head spin."

"Oh, excuse me. It's just that I have spent so many hours thinking about this. Don't worry though, I have it all written down, so I can show you some other time."

Oliver left soon afterwards. After they exchanged a final kiss on the doorstep, Cora watched him go down the street with a lively stride despite the slippery surface.

She lingered a few moments hoping the frosty air would cool her cheeks before she went into the kitchen and had to act naturally in front of Mother. She knew it would be difficult to keep the momentous news to herself until Oliver had asked her father's permission for her hand and had told his own father what he planned.

As Oliver walked away his mind was racing. Proposing to Cora and then waiting for her response had been difficult enough. Now he had to summon up his courage to face the conversations with his parents and with Nathaniel Blake. There were huge changes ahead for them all. For the Blakes, their daughter would be leaving Leek and they might never see her again. A simple letter would take many weeks to arrive. For the Finches, Oliver was not only leaving the family home, but the family business too. Facing his father's reaction was going to be far from easy. He just hoped FJ would find it in his heart to forgive him.

By the time he reached home in Bath Street he had decided he could not possibly broach the subject with his parents that night. He needed to prepare his speech and choose his moment well.

Horse race betting was on Inspector Ramm's mind as he climbed the narrow sunken lane towards The Black Lion at Cheddleton. He did not expect the inn to be particularly busy on a Monday evening, but it was imperative that he should go there. Arthur Forbes had told him that James Jervis came here probably in connection with his betting and Ramm was anxious to find out more about that side of the victim's life.

The rapid growth in betting had become controversial in recent times. There was national concern – particularly amongst those who also campaigned against alcohol – about the risks it posed, especially to poorer people. A few months earlier, a new law had come into force to stop bookmakers operating on the street or in public places like inns. This was where the bookmakers would employ a runner to act as their go-between with the punters. Such men would give the odds on races, take the money being wagered and eventually pay out any winnings.

But despite the new law, it was still easy to find a bookmaker or their runner and many police – including Inspector Ramm – had turned a blind eye. As far as he was concerned, there were more important matters to deal with. However, his discoveries about the dead man's habits brought the subject to the front of his mind. He feared he might face some awkward questions from his superiors if it turned out that betting figured in this crime. The notebook he had found in Jervis's room was a meticulous record revealing that the doctor had wagered hefty sums and sometimes lost the lot. Were gambling debts the motive for the murder?

The Black Lion stood on a rough track off Hollow Lane, its bay windows looking towards the village church and graveyard on the other side of the track. The Inspector estimated it would have taken around twenty minutes for Jervis to walk there from the asylum. Ramm himself had had to make yet another frigid cart journey along the snow covered road from Leek. By the time he arrived, the church clock was striking eight and the landscape glowed white in the moonlight. He smirked as he spotted a rough stone bench built against the wall opposite the inn. It was the remains of the village stocks, a reminder of crime and retribution from times past.

Constable Hawkins was waiting for him outside the inn, stamping his boots in the snow to keep his feet warm. Ramm had told him to meet him there, hoping the village bobby might smooth the way with the locals. However, the sight of the two burly officers in full uniform chilled the atmosphere as effectively as the blast of cold night air when they opened the pub door. The dozen or so drinkers went quiet and all heads turned towards the policemen.

It was a small room with a stone floor and a low ceiling ribbed by heavy beams. At one end was a substantial stone fireplace containing an iron grate in which a couple of logs smouldered. Facing the entrance was the small bar made of varnished wood and behind it stood the innkeeper, a man who Ramm knew to be William Barber. Some years ago, following a series of rowdy incidents at the inn, the Inspector had objected to the renewal of Barber's licence by Leek Magistrates. However, Barber had kept his licence after a prominent landowner, who lived in a mansion on the far edge of the village, spoke up on his behalf. Ramm had been puzzled what the connection between the two very different men could be, but now he wondered if they had horse racing in common.

"Evening, Officer," said Barber, looking at Constable Hawkins suspiciously before turning his eyes to Ramm and giving a curt nod. It was obvious he still bore the Inspector a grudge.

Dispensing with any greeting, Ramm came straight to the point. "Mr Barber, we want to talk to you about someone we believe may have been one of your customers."

"What's this all about?" asked Barber with an uneasy tone.

"A recent death," Ramm replied.

"Ye mean 'im as was pulled out o' the cut?" The comment came from one of a group of ancient men huddled on stools by the fire.

Ramm swivelled to face the old fellow. "Why? Do you know something about that?"

"Well, why else is Bobby Hawkins and his big boss 'ere on a Monday night? Everybody in the village 'as 'eard about it, 'aven't they? None of us knows who it was, mind."

"Well, we believe it may have been someone who used to come in here on occasion. A doctor from the County Asylum by the name of Jervis," Ramm explained, loud enough for all to hear.

The canal death had been one of the chief topics of conversation in the inn over the weekend, together with progress on the Shaffalong coal mine which was being sunk on the edge of the village. Now several drinkers exchanged glances and muttered comments, pleased to discover who the drowned man had been.

"Doctor eh? Not a local, then. Might be that tall fella that's been comin' in 'ere," said another of the old men.

"What about you, Mr Barber? Do you recall him?" asked Ramm, turning to the publican.

"Might do. Might not. We gets one or two in here from that place on the hill – when they can get out, you might say," Barber replied and grinned at a customer leaning against the bar. He then focused his attention on pouring a pint of ale, ignoring the two officers.

"This man, Dr Jervis, did you see him meet anyone here?" Ramm asked him.

"How should I know? I'm busy enough serving customers. Are you saying there's been trouble or something? Because I can tell you, Inspector, we keep a good house here… and a good pint." Barber's final words drew chuckles from the locals who were watching the exchange with some interest.

"Mind your tone, Mr Barber," Constable Hawkins growled.

"What about placing bets?" Ramm's change of tack sent the gathering silent again. He guessed that if a bookies' runner operated there, all the regulars would know. His gaze went around the men in the room and settled on the old fellow who had been the first to speak. "You seem very interested in what's going on, so you will know all about that, I presume."

"Nowt wrong with the odd flutter, Officer, though there's some killjoys out there that seem to think different," the man said defiantly. His companions murmured their agreement.

"And there are plenty around here that like a wager, no doubt," Ramm went on, stepping nearer to the old fellow by the fire. "But it's Dr Jervis that I am interested in, not whether the law is being broken. Who is it that takes the bets?"

"You need to speak to Chalky. He's yer man."

"Chalky?"

"Aye, Chalky Davis. Comes in 'ere regular, as well as all th' other pubs in Chedd. If you want a bet on the 'orses, Chalky'll sort it out. You can rely on 'im."

"This Davis, does he live in the village?"

"A little place by the canal, far side o' the paper mill. Might be quicker if you look in the pubs, though." The old man's companions chuckled at his final comment.

Seeing that the Black Lion folk would yield no more information, Ramm left soon afterwards. Outside the inn, he turned to Hawkins. "I'm off back to Leek – I've had enough for one day. Tomorrow I want you to find this Davis fellow and bring him in to the station. If he's not at home, I expect one of the pubs will help. And don't say we are investigating a murder, just let him think it's about betting or something," he told the constable. "I know you can handle yourself, Hawkins, but take care. If Davis is mixed up with Jervis's death, there's no telling how he might react. Shall I send someone from the station to assist?"

"No need to worry, Inspector. I've seen this Chalky around the village. I don't think I'll have any problem with him," Hawkins replied with all the confidence of a boxer.

Ramm climbed into the cart which was waiting for him at the bottom of the hill where Hollow Lane joined the main road. Thankfully the driver had provided a blanket to wrap around his passenger's legs. As they jolted along towards Leek, Ramm wondered how many times he would visit the village before this case was solved.

Chapter Eight

Inspector Ramm hardly had chance to sit down at his desk the following morning before he was summoned back to the reception counter. The Chief Constable was on the telephone and he came straight to the point.

"Good morning Ramm. I have received a rather disturbing message from Lord Sowerby about the County Asylum at Cheddleton. He is the chairman of the Lunacy Committee, you know. Why wasn't I informed about this murder? His Lordship is concerned that it should not reflect badly on the asylum."

The Inspector hoped the telephone's rudimentary mouthpiece did not pick up his exasperated sigh. He had guessed the force commander would be contacted once Dr Gibson at the asylum had informed his own superiors.

"It is very early days, Sir, in fact it is only a matter of hours since we established the victim was a member of staff there. I planned to make a full report today when I was in possession of more information," he replied. "Naturally I have made enquiries at the asylum, but that is just one of several avenues I intend to pursue."

"Well, take care to do it as discreetly as possible. I know you have a finger on most of what happens in your neck of the woods, Ramm, but some very influential people have been involved in setting up that place." The senior officer paused to ensure the Inspector understood what he was getting at.

"I will do my best, Sir, but if our investigations lead there…"

"Of course, of course, justice must come first. All I ask is that you clear up this matter as quickly as possible. And if it turns out that no one at the asylum was involved, it will make life a little easier for all of us."

Ramm gave a wry smile as he paced back to his office. He had come under this sort of pressure from his headquarters before. Some years ago, a local bigwig had tried to influence a murder investigation by dropping a word in the Chief Constable's ear. Ramm had stuck to his guns on that occasion and eventually tracked down the culprit. He intended to do so again.

He had little opportunity to consider his next move because minutes later FJ Finch arrived on one of his regular visits.

"Any news on the man pulled from the canal?" he asked as soon as he took the seat opposite Ramm. The Inspector was pleased that details of the victim were not yet public knowledge, however he knew he could not keep the murder secret for much longer. At least he had four days to make progress on the case before the *Leek Lion* and its new competitor were published.

"There has been progress of sorts, Mr Finch. We have identified the deceased as Dr James Jervis who was employed as a Medical Assistant at the County Lunatic Asylum," Ramm replied.

"A doctor, eh? So there was a link with the asylum!" said Finch, pleased that one of his own theories had proved correct. "He went through the ice, no doubt. There have been so many accidents of that sort this winter."

"Not exactly. We believe that foul play was involved." Ramm did not intend to share the full facts as he needed to keep some details, such as the stabbing, confidential for use when he questioned suspects.

"So you are saying that he was pushed into the canal deliberately? That is certainly unusual, especially for a doctor. He wasn't in a fight with one of the folk from the asylum, was he?" Finch's mind was working quickly through the possible angles for his story and he knew that the more he could drag the County Asylum into the story, the more his readers would be interested.

"At the moment there are many unanswered questions, but I am looking at every possibility," Ramm replied, determined to be noncommittal, especially as he had no clear idea himself how the attack had unfolded.

"So you believe there was some sort of incident on the tow path, but no one knew anything of it until the body was found on Thursday? I presume you will be making an appeal for witnesses," Finch went on.

"Most likely. Before the end of the week I should be able to give you more details."

"Was this Dr Jervis a local man? I take it the asylum has been informed. No doubt they can give me something on his background."

"Contact them if you wish, Mr Finch. Dr Gibson is in charge at the moment – Superintendent Menzies is away, I gather – but I do not know if he will be willing to talk to you."

Finch nodded that he understood. He was used to dealing with people in authority who would often prefer to keep bad news out of his newspaper. However this was a murder and a most newsworthy one in fact.

By the time he arrived back at the *Lion* building, Finch was filled with excitement about the mysterious death on the canal. The asylum had been the subject of local speculation and gossip since it had opened, and this added to the story's value for his newspaper.

"Oliver, you cannot imagine what Inspector Ramm has just told me," he announced to his son as he walked into the top floor office, casting his overcoat onto a spare chair. He proceeded to recount all he had learned about the death.

"We need to make as much of this story as possible," he enthused. "I'm going to find out all I can. I shall question the asylum management, perhaps speak to Blake again – he's probably got a photograph from last Thursday we can use. I might even go down to the canal myself to get a feeling for where it all happened."

Oliver guessed that his father's keenness sprang not only from the fascination of the story, but from his professional pride. He was determined to outdo the rival *Argus*. But the reporter had an important story of his own. He handed his father the latest letter from the anonymous woman.

"How does it come to be opened?" asked FJ.

"Apologies Father, but I could not resist reading it when it arrived last night."

FJ's response was little more than a mumble as he concentrated on the contents of the note. "It looks like things are no better then," he said finally. "But I suspect she is coming round to the idea of an interview, otherwise why would she reply so soon after our last edition? I wonder who on earth it is?"

"I virtually bumped into her last night. I was about to leave and there she was, just about to put the letter through the front door."

"So you saw her? What was she like? Young, old, decent appearance?" Finch fixed a keen eye on his son, willing him to come up with more information. Shaping the story around a real person, someone they could describe to their readers in every distressed detail, would make the tale so much more arresting.

"Well, she was wrapped up against the cold, but from what I saw she was fairly young and, if I might say so, quite attractive." Oliver fell silent as he thought of the dark eyes and eyebrows he had glimpsed above the woman's scarf. He raked his memory for where he had seen her before.

"What is it? Did you recognise her?" his father asked.

"I'm sure I have seen her before somewhere, but I don't know her name," Oliver said. Then his recollection crystallised into an idea. "I think Cora might know, though. I'll speak to her later."

"Oh, I've no doubt you will, my boy," FJ said with some irony. It was no secret how attached Oliver and Cora had become and how frequently they met.

"I need to concentrate on this canal murder, so I shall leave it to you to pursue the mystery woman," he continued. "We really need to get more from her if we're going to capitalise on this murky affair in the next edition."

Oliver readily accepted his father's invitation to take on the story. He was more determined than ever to find the young woman and interview her for the *Lion*. It would be a chance to please his father before he broke the news about his plan for a life in another country with his new wife.

An hour later, Oliver took a respite from typing a particularly tedious report on prospects for the silk trade in the year ahead and went round to the Blake studio to see Cora. She looked up excitedly as he entered the shop.

"Have you come to speak to Father?" she asked, her eyes searching his face, full of joy at what they had decided the previous evening.

"Er, no," Oliver replied, rather sheepishly. "I haven't had chance to break the news to my own parents yet. There just wasn't the right moment last night and…"

"But you must do it soon, Oliver. We can't keep something like this a secret for long. It's too important for us, and for them." Now that she had accepted Oliver's proposal, she was eager their life together should become a reality, not just a wild plan.

"Of course, Cora. I shall speak to them and we can start to organise things," Oliver reassured her. "But actually, I popped round because I was hoping you could help me with something else. Do you remember that concert you took part in a couple of years ago at the Maude Church Institute, when you were having dance lessons?"

"How could I forget?" said Cora bitterly, her mood having suddenly changed. Her time at Signor Manfredi's School of Music and Dance had been blighted by tragedy. It was the last thing she wanted to be reminded of just when she was feeling so happy about the future. Apparently it was Oliver the newspaper reporter who had come to see her this morning, she thought ruefully, not Oliver the man who had proposed to her.

"Well, there was a woman in the concert, not one of the dancers, one of the musicians," Oliver went on. "She was playing the flute, I think. She had dark hair, dark eyebrows. Do you know her name?"

"Why do you want to know?" Cora asked, trying not to feel jealous at Oliver's sudden interest in someone else. She had guessed who he was referring to, a young woman who was both a fine musician and particularly attractive.

Seeing Cora's reaction, Oliver felt rather guilty about his frisson of excitement when he had encountered the woman last night. He realised it would be best not to reveal how much he wanted to find her. "Oh, don't concern yourself, Cora. It's just something for the *Lion*. Father's received a letter from someone who didn't give their name and we think it might be her," he said.

Cora studied the *Leek Lion* each week, partly out of loyalty to Oliver so she would know what he was talking about when he sounded forth on some local topic. She had been appalled when she saw the letter from the unknown woman who said she was being pursued by a stranger. "She's not the one who thinks she is being spied upon by some awful man, surely?" she said. From Oliver's reaction she knew she was right.

"Do you know her name, Cora, or where she lives? It might be important if we're going to try to help her."

"Gwendoline Cope is the one who plays the flute. I've seen her at other concerts, she's very good. She's five or six years older than me, so we're not school friends or anything like that. She lives with an aunt I think, somewhere in the west of town. It might be Chorley Street." Cora paused, then continued with concern in her voice: "But there must be a reason she wants to remain anonymous. Should you really be doing this?"

"If we can talk to her and find out more, then the story in the *Lion* will be bigger and we stand a better chance of stopping the person who is following her."

Cora could see the logic of what he said, but she feared he was being driven by the hunt for a story as much as desire to do the right thing and help the young woman in her hour of need.

"Promise me, Oliver, that if it does turn out to be Gwendoline, you and your father won't make a mockery of her in the *Lion*. It looks to me like she is suffering enough."

"Have no fear, Cora, I shall do the right thing," he said. After giving her a swift peck on the cheek, he hurried from the studio and out into the snowy Sheepmarket.

When Constable Hawkins showed Chalky Davis into Ramm's office that afternoon, the Inspector gave a gasp of recognition. He had not met the bookies' runner before, but he had certainly heard a brief description of him a few days' earlier. Less than five foot tall, baggy clothes and an oversized cap, Davis was a perfect match for the man that the bargee, Silas Turnock, said he had seen with James Jervis by the canal.

Ramm now realised why the village officer had been confident he could apprehend Davis on his own. “I take it you had no trouble, Constable,” he said.

“Came as quiet as a lamb, Inspector,” Hawkins replied, clapping Davis on the shoulder. “We were handy for Cheddleton station, so I brought him in on the train – thought it would be quicker, seeing as it’s an urgent case.”

Davis dragged off his cap and screwed it up in his hands, then gave Ramm an insolent look. “What’s this all about?” he asked.

“Sit down. I have some questions for you,” said Ramm.

Davis was evasive at first, saying only that he worked as a messenger and telling of his love of horses since his days as a stable lad for the Meakins, the pottery owners who lived at Westwood Manor in Wetley Rocks. His hopes of becoming a jockey had been dashed by a riding accident.

“Enough of the life story,” said Ramm, getting impatient. “It’s common knowledge that you work as a runner between the bookmakers and folk in Cheddleton who are betting on horses. I want to talk to you about a particular client, a man by the name of James Jervis.”

“Don’t mean nothing to me, Inspector. But it wouldn’t, ’cause I only know most of my punters by their nicknames, not proper names.”

“And why is that?”

“Well, gives ’em a bit of privacy, don’t it? ’Specially with all this fuss about betting. They puts their bets in an envelope and writes their name, a nom-de-whatsit, on it. I passes it on to the bookie. If they have any winnings it comes back in another envelope with their nickname on, and I hands it over next time I sees the punter.”

“I’m talking about someone you might have seen at The Black Lion. Tall fellow, not a local, worked as a doctor at the asylum.”

Davis’s hairless face creased in an impression of deep thought. “Let me think now… that might be Gentleman Jim, a bit of a regular. Been taking his bets for about six months, I should say."

"Have you ever met him anywhere else, other than the pub?"

"Funny you should say that, Inspector. A couple of times he's sent a message for me to go and meet him by the canal. Not the sort of thing I'd do usually, but, like I say, he's a good customer is the Gentleman."

"Where on the canal?"

"Along the Leek Arm. Bit of a walk, it was. Round the back of that loony place. I thought at the time that he might be working there."

Ramm nodded. This fitted with what the bargee had told him. "When you say a good customer, I take it you mean a fair amount of money has been changing hands," he continued.

"Well, Inspector, I can't divulge a punter's private business, can I? We runners have certain rules, you might say."

Ramm couldn't help laughing at the comment, then leaned forward and fixed Davis with a steely stare. "Rules or no rules, this is an investigation into a very serious matter. It is in your own interests to divulge whatever I ask you to. Otherwise I might suspect you have some devious motive. The consequences of that would be dire, I can assure you."

The little man gulped as realised this was not simply a case of the police making life uncomfortable for anyone involved in street betting. There must be real trouble afoot and his eyes darted from side to side as he tried to think what it might be.

"Well, Challky?" Ramm continued. "What can you tell me about the wagers placed by James Jervis, Gentleman Jim as you call him."

Self-preservation took over and Davis became talkative. "Keen as mustard is the Gentleman, but there's usually more money going out than comes back in, if you gets my meaning. If he loses, he bets even bigger next time to try to win it all back."

"And so then he might lose even more money?"

Davis nodded vigorously. "You've got to be really clever to get ahead of the bookies, Inspector. I heard some gossip that the Gentleman was borrowing a bob or two to tide him over until he was back on a winning streak."

"Borrowing? Who from?"

"That I wouldn't know. Just gossip, you know."

"Did you meet him last week? By the canal, perhaps?"

"By the canal in this weather? There's no chance of me walking there. In any case, there's hardly been any racing since New Year, been dead as a doornail. Haven't seen Gentleman Jim for two weeks or more."

"Have you heard that someone was pulled from the canal last Thursday?"

"Yes, I did..." Davis began, then his eyes opened wide in surprise. "You're not telling me that was Gentleman Jim? Good lord!"

"Are you sure you didn't meet him on the towing path last Monday night? Collecting his wager or chasing up some debt he owed? Perhaps you got into some sort of argument with him and he finished up in the canal. Look Chalky, it's better that you make a clean breast of it now, rather than us find out later that you've been lying. If it was an accident, it could make the difference between prison and being hanged."

The word 'hanged' knocked Davis back in his seat with a look of terror. "Honest to God, Inspector, I had nothing to do with it," he pleaded. "I ain't seen nothing of him for at least a fortnight and I certainly didn't meet him on the canal. Poor devil! Fancy, falling in the ice like that?"

"So where were you last Monday night, the sixth of January?"

Davis went quiet as he thought back to the previous week.

"Monday nights I'm usually at The Boat. It's the pub nearest to where I live with me Ma and on Mondays they always have dominoes. I loves me dominoes nearly as much as the horses. Ask

Mrs Robinson, the landlady, she'll tell you I was there all evening."

Ramm nodded at Hawkins, who still stood by the door, and the village constable knew he would have to check whether The Boat Inn landlady could confirm Davis's story.

Ramm ended the interview by telling Davis that if he gleaned any more gossip about who Jervis had borrowed from, he should contact the village constable. He then let the man return to Cheddleton accompanied by Hawkins.

Alone in his office again, the Inspector tried to imagine whether Davis could be responsible for the murder, even though the man claimed to have an alibi for the night in question. He pictured the short fellow reaching up to stab Jervis in the neck. Would he know where to aim the weapon, or was it simply a lucky blow in the dark? Was a scalpel the sort of thing he would carry? Was he strong enough to pitch his victim into canal? And what could have been his motive for killing Jervis? Robbery or some dispute over a bet?

He shook his head. The questions were mounting up and he had precious few answers.

Soon afterwards Inspector Ramm received an unexpected visitor. As Sergeant Reynolds ushered Walter Wainwright into the office, Ramm saw from the way the chemist was looking around the room and over the papers on his desk that the man was as inquisitive as the day before. However this time his attitude seemed to be mixed with an air of satisfaction. He was obviously enjoying being involved in a police inquiry, Ramm thought.

"Walter? Do you have something for me?" Ramm hoped the interruption was not going to be a waste of his valuable time.

"Well Albert, I believe I can be of use to your… investigation. After you called at the shop yesterday, I went through our sales ledger and I found that we did indeed sell some scalpels over the last few months," said Wainwright, producing a foolscap book from the leather document case he was carrying. He laid it open on Ramm's desk, leaned close and put his bony finger on one page and then on another. "One scalpel, one shilling and sixpence on the twenty-eighth of September. And then another two on the thirteenth of November."

He turned to the Inspector, looking earnestly as if seeking his approval. "Does that help, Albert?"

"Is there a note as to who the purchasers were?" Ramm was now very interested.

"Unfortunately not. Is that important, do you think?"

Ramm sighed and then reached for the ledger so that he could read the entries himself. He saw the sale of two scalpels in November and next to it was an item for a quantity of medicines marked 'Asylum, on account'.

"I see you sold goods to the County Asylum on the same day. Is it possible the scalpels went there, too?" asked Ramm.

"Er… it might have been. I simply can't remember. The asylum usually send some errand boy round for supplies, not that they purchase much from me. They have their own dispensary."

"Well, thank you for the information, Walter. That is most interesting. Can I keep this ledger for the time being?"

"Yes, of course, Albert. Whatever you need," Wainwright replied with a smile, apparently happy to have helped his Oddfellows friend in his investigation, whatever it may be about. He hesitated, perhaps hoping Ramm would reveal something about the case, but when the officer was not forthcoming the chemist took his leave. "Let me know if I can be of any further assistance," he added as he went through the door.

After the chemist had left, Ramm considered whether Wainwright's information was of any help. The scalpel sales could be a pure coincidence. However he still considered that Dr Jervis's attacker could have been someone he knew from the asylum, and that person may have had access to the right weapon. Tomorrow, he would go back to the institution and try to get to the truth.

The streets were deserted as a dark figure kept his lonely vigil outside the house of his beloved. That evening he had been able to observe her in the Church Hall for the best part of two hours. It had been more a case of stolen glances – he could not afford to make it too obvious. Then, as usual, he had followed her home at a safe distance.

He thought again about the problem with the *Leek Lion*. He had seen her take another letter there last night. What was she telling them? He thought he saw her say something to that fellow who worked there, Finch's son was it? Was that the sort of person she liked? Young, good looking, full of himself? The man shook the thought from his mind. Jealousy would get him nowhere.

What was he to do? Leave her another note, perhaps, a little more discreet than last time, telling her not to be alarmed? He meant no harm, quite the opposite in fact. He might even be brave enough to speak to her. How to begin, that was the problem.

Whatever he decided to do, he couldn't bear to think of any more stories appearing in the newspaper.

He saw the light go out in the house and he moved on.

CHAPTER NINE

Wednesday was market day in Leek and usually the busiest time in the town, but with a fresh fall of snow blanketing the district there was little activity. Folk who habitually came from across the Moorlands to buy and sell goods and beasts were unable or unwilling to make the journey along lanes choked by drifts. Rural families had been relying on food from their store cupboards since the New Year. With the weather showing no sign of improving they had decided to stretch their rations a little further.

Across the street from the police station, the Cattle Market was strangely quiet, livestock pens standing empty because farmers were unable to herd their cattle, sheep and pigs into town. Men who would normally have been busy coaxing animals in and out of the iron pens were today huddled close to the market manager's office, talking amongst themselves, a cloud of smoke rising from their cigarettes and pipes.

Despite the weather, Inspector Ramm knew he would have to make another visit to the County Asylum. However, before he could leave for Cheddleton, his morning would be occupied giving evidence at the town's Magistrates Court. Most of the cases were minor compared with the murder that was foremost in his mind – a selection of thefts, fighting and drunkenness – but as head of the town force it was his duty to deliver the police evidence. Today he was less well prepared than usual because he had not had chance to consult the necessary documents the previous afternoon, as was his routine.

Just before he left the station, there was yet another complication: the town's Coroner telephoned to say he wanted to hold an inquest into the canal victim as soon as possible. Such hearings normally took place within a few days of a death, however Ramm managed to secure a grudging delay after explaining how little he knew of the circumstances and how complicated the case might become.

As he made his way to the court sittings at the Town Hall, Ramm noticed that streets usually lined with carts on market day were virtually empty. In Sparrow Park, the public weighing machine used by farmers and feed merchants was out of operation, its iron mechanism frozen solid in the ground.

In the Market Place, the cherubs of the Challinor fountain were frosted over and the spouts of water were transformed into cascades of ice. However despite the weather, council workmen had dragged the heavy wooden stalls onto the cobbles. Hopeful traders peered out from under canvas roofs sagging under the morning's fresh snow. Only the dairy and vegetable stalls in the indoor Buttermarket seemed to be doing any trade.

At the Blake studio in nearby Sheepmarket, a portrait client had failed to turn up and so Nathaniel found himself with time to search through his files to find a photograph which might include the canal victim. He pulled out the folders for November and December 1906, bulging with pictures taken at annual dinners, church sales, retirement presentations and Christmas dances. He scrutinised every group, sometimes snatching up his magnifying glass to examine the faces in a large gathering.

He was about to start on the folder for October when he heard the sound of the shop door bell. Cora shouted from below to say that Mr Finch was there to see him.

Finch came upstairs and, after a few pleasantries, got down to business. Now the police were treating the canal death as foul play he wanted as much information as possible from Blake about the day the body was found.

"Ramm asked me to copy a photograph of the man in his younger days. The officer who brought it round mentioned that it was now a murder case," Nathaniel explained.

"Murder? That was the word he used? So there was nothing said about a fight that went wrong or some such?" asked Finch.

"He didn't go into details, FJ. I wasn't even told a name," said Nathaniel, handing him a spare copy of the college portrait. "Be sure to ask Ramm before you use it in the *Lion*," he added.

"Ramm told me that the victim was a Medical Assistant at the asylum, a doctor by the name of James Jervis," Finch explained. "I have telephoned the fellow who's in charge at the asylum at the moment, Dr Gibson. I would have liked to talk to a few people face to face, but Gibson was most unhelpful. He said flatly that I would not be allowed through the door. To be honest, he seemed surprised that I knew about Dr Jervis in the first place. It was almost as if he wanted the whole thing covered up, but that might be just my newspaperman's suspicious mind at work."

Nathaniel did not respond. He was wary of talking about the asylum management, even to a friend like Finch, when he was working on a lucrative photographic assignment there.

Finch pressed him for more details of the tragic scene on the canal. "I need to fill this story out with whatever I can find," FJ continued. "I presume you took photographs? Would they be of any use?"

"They may give you a better idea of what went on, but they are not the sort of thing you can put in your newspaper."

Finch sucked in his breath as he examined the photographs. "A grim affair and no mistake. What a state the poor fellow was in. I wonder how Ramm could have worked out that foul play was involved?"

Blake shrugged and suggested there may have been witnesses, perhaps on the barge he had seen nearby. Hearing of the barge, Finch decided he should definitely visit the scene himself, not that he relished making his way through the snow. Before he departed, FJ glanced towards the stairs, lowered his voice and asked: "How has Cora taken all this, Nathaniel?"

"She was certainly distressed, FJ. It's a pity she was anywhere near the place. But her spirits seem to have picked up this week," Blake replied quietly, hoping his daughter could not overhear them.

"Are there developments between her and Oliver, do you think?" Finch continued. "Only he's been acting a little oddly these last few days. I'm sure he has something he wants to get off his chest and I presume it might involve Cora."

"Well, if something is afoot, I'm sure we shall find out soon enough. Perhaps there is some good news on the way for all of us!" Nathaniel said with a smile, clapping Finch on the shoulder as his friend left the studio.

It was another cold and uncomfortable journey to the County Asylum for Inspector Ramm that afternoon, the Inspector staring out disconsolately as the trap passed through Leekbrook, the chimneys of Wardle's dyeworks spewing steam and smoke into the frigid air.

"Well Inspector, are you any nearer to clearing up this matter? I am sure you are aware, the Lunacy Committee is anxious we should be free of controversy as soon as possible," Dr Gibson began as Ramm took his seat in the Medical Superintendent's office. It was clear that Gibson knew the Chief Constable had been contacted and was resuming his air of superiority. However, Ramm was in no mood to be browbeaten.

"Dr Gibson, how quickly we solve this case may depend on how co-operative you and your colleagues are," Ramm began. "Firstly, I am trying to find anyone who saw Dr Jervis on his final evening. Can I ask, where were you that night?"

"Seriously Inspector, are you really suggesting that I may know something about this death?" The colour rose to Gibson's usually pale cheeks.

"Dr Gibson, I intend to ask the same question of everyone I see fit."

"Well, I thought I had already made it perfectly clear that I saw little of Dr Jervis that Monday and I knew nothing of his *excursion* to the canal. Does that satisfy you?"

"Thank you," Ramm replied, privately satisfied that he had discomfited the asylum manager. He then continued undaunted. "I also want to ask about the weapon which we believe was used in the attack. We think it may have been a surgical scalpel of some sort."

"Do you mean Dr Jervis was stabbed?" Gibson spluttered.

"I am afraid so. Are such implements used in the asylum?"

"No, certainly not in the treatment of inmates."

"But there are scalpels here, are there not?"

"Well yes, but the only place they are likely to be found is the mortuary. And like every other item that could be harmful to inmates, they are kept under lock and key."

The Attendant in charge of the mortuary, a local man by the name of Braddock, was summoned. He led the Inspector to a detached structure at the rear of the main buildings. Compared to the warmth of the rest of the asylum, this was a chilly place, its walls lined with glazed bricks for hygiene. The first room they entered was a chapel of rest, furnished with an altar and pine benches. Next to it was a room fitted with slabs where, Braddock explained, the bodies of the deceased were kept prior to examination. Finally they entered the post mortem room. To Ramm it appeared well equipped and perhaps even superior to the facilities he relied upon at the Cottage Hospital. Braddock produced a bunch of keys and unlocked a cabinet. A variety of surgical instruments were neatly arranged in precisely shaped slots, including a number of scalpels.

Braddock pointed out that there were no spaces and so no scalpel was missing. He said that as no post mortems had been held, none of the instruments had been used for more than a month. There were only two keys to the cabinet, he added – the one he carried and another which was kept in a safe in the porter's office. He looked puzzled when Ramm asked about any recent purchase of scalpels from Leek.

"I don't know anything about that, Inspector. You could ask in the stores, but I can't see why they would want any," Braddock said. When asked what he was doing on the night it in question, he said he had been leading a choir rehearsal in the village Methodist Church, as the other singers could confirm.

"What did you think of Dr Jervis?" Ramm asked bluntly.

"I can't say I knew him. The last time I saw him was at the New Year's Eve dance," Braddock replied.

At that moment, the electric bulb hanging from the ceiling went dim and Ramm felt the floor vibrate.

"What is going on?" he asked.

"Oh, it's only the tram bringing folk up from the railway at Leekbrook. Wednesday is visiting day, two hours in a morning, two in the afternoon," Braddock explained with a smile that seemed incongruous in the post mortem room. "The tramline's just round the back of here, so it shakes this place a bit. And they still haven't got the electrics sorted out, so when the tram's running it sometimes drains the current from everything else."

Braddock then led the Inspector to one of the asylum's storerooms where he sought out the man in charge. Compared to the mortuary where he had just been, this was a cavernous space that made Ramm think of the great department stores he had seen on a visit to Manchester. Once again he was reminded of the sheer size of the community at the asylum and the huge operation needed to keep it supplied with goods.

Large tables were arranged across the linoleum floor. Around the walls were cupboards and shelving, all of which bore a great array of supplies, from dozens of thin rolled-up mattresses to sacks of sugar and chests marked 'Afternoon Tea'. At the upper floor level, a gallery ran along all four sides and through the wooden balustrades Ramm could see scores of neatly stacked boxes and wicker baskets. A lift had been installed to move goods to and from the upper level and numerous electric bulbs supplemented the weak winter light filtering through windows in the pitched roof high above them.

Wilkes, the storekeeper, occupied a cramped office, little more than a cupboard sandwiched between what appeared to be two tall bookcases but which, in fact, were filled with crockery, all of it bearing the asylum's name and crest. Wilkes was heavily built and looked like he could easily handle the largest boxes in his domain, however his size meant that he virtually filled the office as he squatted on a stool at his desk, his back to the store. Ramm cleared his throat to attract the man's attention and the storekeeper turned round and registered some surprise to see the uniformed officer.

Ramm questioned him on the purchase of scalpels in November. As with the mortuary attendant, Wilkes knew nothing of the matter.

"I can assure you that the asylum has purchased no surgical instruments from Wainwright's in the past six months," he said, somewhat exasperated.

"Could it have been bought without your knowledge?"

"No. Everything is recorded, Inspector," Wilkes pointed to a shelf of thick ledgers. "In a place this size we would be in a right pickle if people started ordering stock without obeying the proper system. We keep everything shipshape."

Ramm instinctively recognised a fellow ex-serviceman, as were many of the male staff at the asylum. Glimpsing an anchor tattoo on his forearm, he guessed the man had served in the Royal Navy in the late Queen's days and he was accustomed to a strict adherence to the rules. At last this was someone with whom he knew where he stood, the Inspector thought.

"But the asylum does have dealings with Wainwright?" Ramm asked.

"I seem to recall we had to buy extra medicaments from there when we had an influenza outbreak in November."

"And you handle such purchases?"

"To be honest, Inspector, we leave medicines and that sort of thing to our own pharmacist, Mr Standish. He has to fill in the proper paperwork, mind. That eventually comes across my desk, so the stores know exactly what's going on."

"Pharmacist? Perhaps he can help me. What sort of fellow is he? Approachable, would you say?" Ramm asked.

"Mr Standish is very efficient, I'm sure. But not very talkative. Keeps himself to himself, you might say."

Although he thought this had the makings of a wild goose chase, Ramm asked to be taken to the asylum dispensary. It was a considerably less flamboyant place than Wainwright's shop with no jars of colourful liquids and pills on view. The room was lined with cupboards and drawers of varnished wood, their small white labels bearing numbers not Latin names. It was clear that only one person would know where anything was to found and that was the pharmacist.

Standish, a balding man in his forties, gave no reaction when Ramm walked in and announced who he was. He proceeded to tell the Inspector that he knew nothing about the purchase of scalpels.

"Why do you ask?" he asked in the clipped tones of someone educated at a public school and an ancient university. Ramm told him of the investigation into James Jervis's death.

"Jervis, dead? I wasn't aware of that," Standish replied, showing no emotion.

"Did you know him well?"

"I know we shouldn't speak ill of the dead, but I am afraid I found the fellow rather irritating. A charmer with the ladies, was Jervis, and he knew it. And of course, once he had his violin out.." Standish almost snorted with derision.

"Dr Jervis played the violin?" Ramm remembered the small black case he had seen in Jervis's bedroom on Monday and now realised it must have contained his instrument.

"That's how he got the job, of course. Dr Menzies tends to favour musicians when he's appointing staff, either that or cricketers. He is always keen to find new recruits for his asylum orchestra. Music is good for the patients, he says."

It was plain to Ramm that Standish was not only sceptical about the orchestra, but had disliked the dead man. There were the same hints of jealousy over Jervis's success with women that he had sensed from Arthur Forbes.

"We're trying to trace Dr Jervis's movements in the early part of last week. Did you see him on Monday at all?" the Inspector asked.

"I can't say that I did. I don't think he came to the dispensary for any reason. But then we don't administer medicines regularly to the patients. They tend to be employed in particular circumstances, such as a sedative or to treat some physical complaint."

"What about in the evening? Did you happen to see him in the grounds or down by the canal, perhaps?"

"The canal? Why would I go there in the middle of the winter?" Standish frowned in confusion. "I spent the evening in my room reading, as I do most nights. Sometimes I am needed to dispense a sedative draught at short notice, so I tend not to venture too far."

After ending the conversation with the pharmacist, Ramm managed to find his way back to the Medical Superintendent's office where he asked if Dr Forbes could be summoned again. He had to wait for him to be fetched from the depths of the asylum.

When Forbes arrived, Ramm went with him to a meeting room across the corridor to speak in private. They sat either side a long polished table. Once again Ramm asked him about the last day he had seen Jervis. "Think carefully. Was there anything different about that day? Did Dr Jervis mention anything that might be troubling him or some reason for changing his plans to visit his parents?"

Forbes's pale face was marked with dark patches below his eyes. He appeared to have slept little since identifying the body and discovering that Jervis had been murdered. He was silent for a moment, his gaze fixed as if he was reliving the events at the start of the previous week.

Finally he spoke. "Something arrived in the post for him that morning. It was a postcard, a picture of Leek Market Place I think. I saw it on the hall table at Villa Road."

"Did you see who it was from?"

"Well, I picked it up…but only to check who it was addressed to." Forbes appeared embarrassed that he should have read a card intended for Dr Jervis. Ramm immediately thought of the sodden remains of a postcard which they had found in the dead man's pocket.

"What did it say?"

"To be honest, I could not tell. It was written in that silly fashion that people use sometimes. Capital letters with the spaces all in the wrong place." Forbes gave a small smile. "I guessed it was from one of his lady friends."

"I saw him pick it up when he came down from his room. He

read it, I think he might have frowned, and then he put it in his pocket," Forbes added.

Ramm found it odd that a busy doctor like Forbes would have taken the trouble to observe a colleague so closely and also to look at the postcards he received. He decided to press him on his relationship with Jervis.

"Dr Forbes, what did you really think of James Jervis's goings-on with women? Were you jealous, perhaps, of your friend's success with the ladies?"

"Aren't we all a little jealous of people who are more popular than ourselves, Inspector? But I didn't begrudge him his friendships… with anyone," Forbes replied, then added with a touch of bitterness: "As it happens, I suspect he paid for much of his time with those women."

"And what about his betting? I got the impression that was something else you were not so keen on."

Arthur Forbes stared down at the table. He blew out his cheeks in an exasperated sigh and dragged a hand through his thick blond hair. When he spoke again, Ramm was struck by the fervour in his voice.

"James had got himself into a pickle with this damned betting. He was in debt, deeply so I believe. His parents had bailed him out when he got into difficulties in the past, but now he was too embarrassed to ask them again. He told me he had borrowed to cover his losses and was convinced he would win it all back eventually."

He paused, then continued: "It was tragic really. He was probably as fixated as some of the people we see in here. In his case it was on betting and he couldn't treat himself. That's why he would indulge himself with women. He said that took his mind off his problems."

"Do you know whom he borrowed from?"

"Well, I loaned him some money and so did a couple of other

colleagues. He was desperate, so I felt I couldn't refuse and it was only a modest amount. But he had to keep it all very quiet. Dr Menzies is completely against the staff getting into debt, he feels it could tarnish the asylum's good name. In fact he has just fired the Chief Attendant for failing to pay his debts.

"It was a bad business. I was starting to think I might not see my money again, but it turns out it is poor old James I won't be seeing..." Forbes' voice tailed off as he seemed to struggle to contain his emotions.

"What about others he owed money to?" asked Ramm.

"I think that was where his real trouble began. Someone put him in touch with a moneylender. I think it was one of those damned bookmakers who did it, just so that James would have the means to carry on wasting money with them." Forbes shook his head in despair. "James told me all about it one evening after we had a glass or two of wine. Apparently he had started to fall behind with his repayments and this moneylender – some grim character from Manchester, I believe – was becoming rather impatient. They even sent a bully boy here to put pressure on him."

"When was this?"

"It was just around Christmastime. Apparently this thug twisted James's arm and he nearly didn't play his violin at the New Year's Eve dance. I think that's why he was going to visit his parents. He had finally decided to ask them for more money."

"It's a pity you did not tell me about this affair with the moneylender a little sooner, Dr Forbes. This is something we are going to have to investigate," said Ramm. "In the meantime, I think I need to look at Dr Jervis's room again."

Forbes led the Inspector back to the Medical Assistants' accommodation. As soon as they were out in the yard he produced a packet of cigarettes and, after looking to check no one was near, lit one. "You have to be careful. The Superintendent insists there should be no smoking in the asylum. Although I've heard he has a smoke in the tunnel each morning," he explained.

"What do you mean by the tunnel?" Ramm asked.

"There's a covered passageway and a tunnel that connects Dr Menzies' house to the main buildings."

When they reached the villa, Forbes produced a key and unlocked the door to Jervis's bedroom. It was just as Ramm had left it two days earlier.

He went straight to the desk and began to search the muddle of papers on the top in the hope there was something relating to the moneylender. Then he started to examine the contents of the drawers. Newspaper cuttings about horse races were mixed with tickets to classical concerts, there was a dried rosebud with its stem tied with a pink ribbon, and a bundle of what looked like medical notes. Finally, in the bottom drawer, he came across a brown envelope containing what he was looking for: an advertisement for the Reliance Credit Co. of Great Ancoats Street, Manchester, together with receipts for cash forwarded by them. There were counterfoils for postal orders which appeared to represent Jervis's repayments, as well as two terse telegrams demanding immediate settlement of outstanding loans.

"This looks like what we need," Ramm said as he returned the papers to the envelope and put it the pocket of his coat. He turned to Forbes, who was standing by the door. "It surprises me, Doctor Forbes, how much you seem to have discovered about James Jervis – his character, his habits, his money troubles – in such a short space of time. After all, you had only known him for, what was it, six months?"

Forbes sat down on the edge of the bed, took a long puff on his cigarette and looked earnestly at Ramm. "I think it's only fair for me to be completely honest with you, Inspector. I had known James for much longer than our time here at Cheddleton. We had been friends right from our days at university together, close friends, you might say."

Forbes cleared his throat, obviously uncomfortable at making his confession. "I... I admired James in many ways," he stammered. "When I found out he had applied for a post here, I did the same. I thought it would be a way for me to – how shall I put it? – for me to be near to him. We could share thoughts on our work and so on."

He added hastily: "Obviously Inspector, my motives were entirely honourable."

Ramm simply nodded. How many times had witnesses admitted something simply by denying it too keenly. In this case, he saw that Forbes was conflicted, trying his best to conceal his real feelings about James Jervis and how deeply he had been affected by his loss.

"Did Dr Jervis reciprocate your *admiration*?"

"James was a complicated fellow. He had so much going on in his life, and sometimes I don't think he really knew what he wanted... from any of us."

The short winter afternoon was over by the time Ramm boarded the trap to take him back to Leek. Jolting along the icy road in the dark, he thought about the gambling debts that Forbes – and Davis the bookies' runner – had told him about. He was intrigued by the story of the 'bully boy' who had apparently assaulted Jervis. Had this man returned to Cheddleton? Had there been an altercation on the canal path?

Arthur Forbes had also revealed much about himself and his relationship with Jervis. Whether his admiration strayed beyond the bounds of propriety and legality, Ramm might never know, but this was something else he could not afford to ignore. Once again he wondered if jealousy had driven him to violence.

Then there was the postcard Jervis had received on the morning before his death. Had it drawn the man to the canal? Could there be a woman involved? Tomorrow he would try to figure out what was written on it.

As the trap finally reached the town, the Inspector thought of the picture he was gradually building up of the man found in the canal. Alongside clergymen, a qualified doctor would normally be one the most respected members of society, but James Jervis appeared to be a complex and flawed character. A gambler, a philanderer, eventually the target for a violent attack, yet dedicated to his challenging work at the asylum. And the man even found time to play the violin.

Chapter Ten

Cora was on her way home from the studio that evening when she called at the *Lion* office to speak to Oliver. As she walked up the staircase she saw Alfred, the compositor who put together the newspaper's pages for the printing press. He was busy in the work room on the first floor, surrounded by trays of metal and wooden type. He nodded as Cora passed then went back to nimbly arranging tiny pieces of type with a pair of tweezers. When she reached the top floor, Oliver swivelled round from his typewriter. Cora was relieved to see he was on his own in the newsroom.

"Cora dear, I did not expect to see you," he smiled as he rose to embrace her.

"When you called at Father's studio yesterday I forgot to ask you about the Bioscope Entertainment tomorrow night. I would very much like to go. It sounds so interesting, some of the moving pictures will even show Leek, they say."

Cora saw Oliver hesitate. "Oh yes, that does look rather good. I've read that those moving pictures are quite something. But…"

"Don't tell me, you are going to be working," said Cora before he could complete his excuses.

"I'm sorry, Cora, but you know what it's like at this place," Oliver continued, hoping to placate her. "Thursday is always such a rush before we go to print on a Friday night. And this week I've got more on my plate than ever, what with Father dashing about to try to build up a big the story on this murder."

Cora had been prepared for this, in fact she had already talked about the bioscope with her friend Ellen Simms. "Well, that's a pity, but I think I shall be going anyway. Ellen says that she will go with me. There was someone from the bioscope company taking pictures outside the Great Mill a few weeks ago, so she is very keen to see what is shown."

"I do wish I could be there, but I simply know I will have work to finish. But don't worry, it will not be long before we are spending much more time together."

Mention of their future made Cora want to embrace Oliver again, but she resisted the temptation because she felt awkward that Alfred was working just below.

She refrained from asking if Oliver had told his father of their plans. She knew she had to be patient and, after all, it was only two days since she had said 'Yes'. Instead, she raised the other subject that was on her mind and asked if he had spoken to Gwendoline Cope yet.

"I think I have found out where she lives in Chorley Street. I plan to go there this evening and see if she will talk to me." From Cora's expression he saw that she was still doubtful about the story. "Please do not be concerned, Cora. I am confident this will be for the best."

"I do hope you are right," she replied. Secretly, she hoped he had been mistaken and Gwendoline Cope was not the person being haunted by a strange man. Miss Cope had been so calm and collected when she played the flute. That tranquillity being shattered by some sinister person was too awful to contemplate.

People were calling it 'smog' in London and that night it seemed a similar noxious cloud had descended on Leek. Freezing fog, mixed with the smoke of countless chimneys, choked the streets as Oliver Finch walked to find Gwendoline Cope's house. Since leaving the office, he had been rehearsing in his mind how he should approach the young woman. He knew she was fearful of an unknown man and worried about being identified in the *Lion*, but she had also appealed for help and that was exactly what he intended to offer.

He walked down St Edward Street as far as the town's impressive new Post and Telegraph Office which had opened a few weeks' earlier. The lights were still burning as it would be open until eight. He took a right turn where the narrow Strangman's Walks had been widened to make a proper street. On his right he saw the large stable block which had been built recently for Leek and Moorlands Co-operative Society's growing number of horses. From behind the high brick walls, Oliver could hear sounds of activity as the animals were being bedded down for the night. Early next morning they would be out again on the wintry roads, pulling carts of coal and heavy goods around the town.

Further along, the great bulk of Wellington Mill loomed on his left, the topmost of its four floors shrouded in the fog. Chorley Street was on the right, lined with terraced houses and the outline of another large mill, Brunswick Mill, just visible at the far end.

Pools of yellow light from the gas lamps had little effect on the gloom as Oliver picked his way down the street. Halfway along he stopped and knocked on a door. He held his breath, waiting for the young woman to appear on the threshold.

He would never admit it to anyone else – especially Cora – but the sight of Miss Cope outside the newspaper office two nights' earlier, only her dark eyes visible above her scarf, had added to his fascination for the story. An attractive, defenceless young woman pursued by a stranger, a man the *Lion* might be able to stop and even publicly disgrace.

Through the thin curtains at the front window he detected the dim light of a lamp, but no one came to the door. He knocked again. Long minutes passed and finally the door opened. Oliver stumbled over the words he had rehearsed because it was not the beguiling and vulnerable Miss Cope who stood before him. It was a short, white-haired woman probably into her seventies, stooped and holding onto the door as if to support herself.

"Yes? What is it young man?" she asked, her neck stretching from her woollen shawl as she peered up at him in the dim light.

"Good evening, Madam. My name is Finch, from the *Leek Lion*. Is Miss Cope at home?"

"I'm Miss Cope!" came the sharp response.

"Oh, I mean Miss Gwendoline Cope. I would very much like to speak to her, if it is of no trouble, Madam." Oliver realised this aged woman must be the aunt that Cora had mentioned and thought it best to be as polite as possible.

"Gwendoline? Why, what is it about? Her next concert? Only I don't think she will see you, she's a little out of sorts this evening. And it is rather late to be having visitors."

"I promise I will not to keep her long, only I think she may want to talk to me. Could you tell her I am here, perhaps?"

"I will ask. Wait there," the aunt instructed, pointing to the cleared patch of pavement beneath Oliver's boots. She left the door ajar and he could hear murmured voices from within. Moments later, he spotted the curtain move. No doubt Gwendoline was looking to find out who was at the door, perhaps fearful of whom the caller might be, he thought.

Miss Cope Senior returned and ushered Oliver into the front room, where he remained standing uneasily. He looked around the sparsely furnished room: two faded armchairs faced the unlit grate, in one corner a small table bore an oil lamp and in another stood a metal music stand. The room was cold and Oliver surmised the two women spent these chilly evenings sitting next to a range in the kitchen, though they would think that was no place to receive a visitor.

When Gwendoline Cop came into the room, she gave a slight nod in Oliver's direction and then looked down at the floor. He could tell immediately how nervous she was. He felt guilty that he also noticed how graceful her movements were.

"You should not have come, Mr Finch. I said in my letter that I wished to remain anonymous," she said quickly, apparently anxious to get the conversation over with as soon as possible.

"You asked for our help, Miss Cope, and the *Lion* is prepared to offer it. But we need to know the facts. The more accurate our story, the better it may assist you."

She hesitated as she considered this, then gestured for him to sit in one of the chairs. She took the other.

Finally her dark eyes focused on Oliver. "How did you find me?" she asked.

"After seeing you in the street on Monday…" Oliver paused as he tried to mask the excitement he had felt that night. "I made some enquiries. My father and I were shocked at your predicament and agreed that I should speak to you as soon as possible."

Gwendoline glanced towards the door. "Please speak softly, Mr Finch. My aunt knows nothing of my troubles. The shame she might suffer is one of the reasons I decided that no one must know who I am. I owe her so much, she gave me a home when my parents died and I have been very content here… until now. You must promise to guard my privacy."

She swept back her glossy dark hair with both hands, as if trying to wipe away the unhappy thoughts from her mind. She then began to recount how her fears had grown over the past six months. First it had been the footsteps that made her suspect she was being followed on her way home, particularly late in the evening after music rehearsals and performances. She had begun to peep through the curtains each night and convinced herself that there was a solitary figure in the shadows between the gas lamps or at the mouth of an alleyway just up the street.

"He is probably out there now, watching what is going on," she added, glancing towards the window. "I have worried that it might be a person in the audience when I play in a concert. Or perhaps it could be someone I have known for years. I have begun to suspect everyone. Sometimes when I am in a shop or at the market I have thought that someone was standing so close that I could feel their breath on my neck. When I turn around, there is no one there."

"Do you suspect anyone in particular? Could it be someone you work with?" Oliver asked.

"I'm at Miss Heath's millinery in the Market Place and we never see a man in there. But…"

"Yes?" Oliver, thinking that she may be holding something back, was anxious for her to continue. She tensed as she saw how much he was writing in the notebook on his knee.

"I have wondered whether it might be someone in the orchestra that I play in, the Moorland Philharmonia. There are several of the men who… look at me," she continued.

"Anyone in particular?"

"Well, perhaps I am being unfair, but Mr Alsop, the conductor, can be a very difficult person sometimes. I have wondered whether he might do something just to spite me. And then, of course, the awful note was pushed through the letterbox." Gwendoline's pale cheeks went pink as she recalled the incident. "I could not possibly repeat what it suggested," she continued breathlessly, "but I was simply relieved that I picked it up before Aunt Nancy saw it. Naturally, I burned it."

"And you think Mr Alsop might have written that?"

"I hardly dare imagine what sort of thing might be going on in his mind. But who am I to know what depraved desires an old man may have?"

As she recounted her growing suspicions and anxieties, Oliver could see how Gwendoline Cope's predicament was building into a compelling story for the *Lion*. He could even use her anonymity to add a greater air of mystery that would fascinate readers. But before writing any of it, he wanted to be sure the tale would not be appearing in this week's *Moorland Argus*.

"Have you told anyone else about all this?" he asked.

Gwendoline hesitated, apparently unsure how to answer. Oliver wondered if she was keeping something to herself, perhaps the fact that someone else was involved.

"I have told no one," she said, looking at the floor once more.

As Oliver left the house he resolved not only to write a story his father would be proud of, but to rescue gentle Gwendoline from her ordeal. He stopped to peer through the fog in both directions along the street, hoping to spot the miscreant lurking nearby, perhaps in one of the alleyways that led to the back yards. He saw no sign of the man.

Chapter Eleven

As soon as Inspector Ramm arrived at the station the next morning, his first act was to take from his desk the battered postcard which had been found in James Jervis's pocket. He had wrapped the card in a sheet of blotting paper and it had now dried out, no longer likely to disintegrate at the slightest touch.

Just as Arthur Forbes had said, the front bore a sepia photograph of Leek Market Place filled with stalls, a view which Ramm surmised Nathaniel Blake had taken from an upstairs window of The Black's Head Inn at the bottom of the square. There was nothing unusual about the picture, but it was the reverse side which the Inspector was interested in.

It was still no easier to make out the writing which the canal water had washed to ghostly traces of blue ink. However he could see that the message had been written in capital letters, and it looked to be signed with a single letter, most probably a "G".

He screwed up his eyes as he tried to bring the jumbled words into greater focus, but it was to no avail. According to Forbes, the card had arrived on the Monday Jervis was last seen and the postmark showed it had been posted in Leek the previous day. It was certainly the only item they had found in the victim's pockets. Did it have some connection with what had happened to Jervis? Even if he managed to decipher the message, Ramm wondered if they would ever identify the "G" who had written it.

An idea occurred to him. He had heard of people going to Nathaniel Blake with faded and creased pictures of loved ones from years ago. Blake used a combination of photographic skill and artistry to bring such pictures back to life, much to the families' delight. Perhaps Blake could do the same with the writing on this postcard? Ramm wondered.

He placed the postcard in an envelope and ordered Constable Phillips to take it to Blake's studio and ask him to produce, with all haste, a restored copy with the writing hopefully clear enough to be read.

Next, Ramm spread out the items he had taken from Jervis's desk the previous afternoon relating to the moneylender. Arthur Forbes' revelation about the unpaid loans and, more disturbingly, the "bully boy" who had been sent to extract a repayment, could point to a motive for the attack. However, he was not totally convinced of this. Somehow stabbing did not seem the sort of brute force a vexed lender might employ.

Although he had the name and address of the moneylender, he had no means of following up this line of enquiry himself. He would have to rely on the Manchester Constabulary and, without a proven link to the murder, they may not give it the priority he would like. He would make a telephone call to the city's police, explain the situation and impress on them the urgency of the situation. He also decided it would be prudent to speak to his Chief Constable again and forewarn him that enquiries at the County Asylum were likely to continue and even be expanded, whether the worthy members of the Lunacy Committee liked it or not.

The poor weather had once more kept clients away from the Blake studio that morning. Nathaniel was about to delve into his files again in search of a picture of the canal victim when Constable Phillips arrived.

"The Inspector wants you to do your best to improve the writing so that he can read it," the officer explained as he handed over the postcard. "And it's urgent, Mr Blake," he added.

A trace of a smile passed across Blake's face when he saw it was one of his own views of the Market Place. He remembered taking the picture on a busy Wednesday the previous summer. The card had obviously been damaged by water and he guessed it had probably belonged to the man found in the canal.

The constable left and Blake began work immediately, first taking a photograph of the reverse of the card and then making a selection of prints, developing each one differently to improve the contrast and make the writing more visible. There was a tap on the darkroom door and Cora came in to see what he was doing.

"Is this something to do with that poor man?" she asked. She had obviously overheard the constable's instructions and Blake knew better than to mislead her. "Yes, it looks like it was sent to the victim. Finch told me his name was Dr Jervis and he worked at the asylum. But it is difficult to see what the message says," he said.

In the red shaded glow of the darkroom lamp, Cora peered at the prints which were pegged up to dry. "What if I take one of these and try tracing over the top of the letters? Then I can see what words might fit," she said.

Nathaniel was loathe to involve his daughter in the tragic affair any more than she already had been, but he could see the sense in what she suggested. She was neat with a pen and pencil and had decorated – and sometimes improved – his picture postcards in the past.

When the prints were dry, Cora took two of them to her work table downstairs and set about tracing bolder letters on top of the original writing. Some of the writing was completely lost, so a little guesswork was needed. At first she thought she must have made a mistake because the words did not make any sense. Then she realised that the spaces had not been put in the correct places. This was the way some of her friends disguised messages they did not want the postman or other people to read, especially if they were writing to a young man.

She copied out the letters onto a fresh piece of paper and started to mark where she thought the words and spaces should be. After several attempts she was satisfied she had the message complete:

DEAREST J, I AM DESPERATE TO SEE YOU. MEET ME ON MONDAY EVENING, I BEG YOU. 8 O'CLOCK AT THE USUAL PLACE. G

Reading it through she felt a pang of sadness. Just think, the man might have had this in his pocket when he perished in the canal. A woman must have sent it, Cora thought, someone who was close to him. But now she had lost her 'Dearest J'. I wonder if they managed to meet for that last time? she thought.

Then Cora's romantic ideas were swept away by a more shocking notion. Perhaps their meeting 'at the usual place' had led to the tragedy. Suddenly she realised how important this postcard could be to the investigation. She gathered up her papers and dashed upstairs to her father. Blake was soon on his way to the police station to show Inspector Ramm what his daughter had discovered.

Reading the message, Ramm was convinced it had drawn Jervis to the canal on the fatal night. But had the person who wrote the message been responsible for the attack? Could a woman really be the murderer? Or was the card some sort of forgery, he thought.

Some years' previously he had investigated a crime where a man was lured to his death by what looked like an innocent letter from a local vicar. It transpired the letter was forged. Coincidentally, that gruesome affair was the first time Nathaniel and Cora Blake had assisted him.

One thing was obvious. If this message had led to the attack, the writer knew enough about Jervis to be sure the doctor would take the bait and go to 'the usual place'.

When Blake went to check his stock of photographic supplies a little later that day, he noticed that he had only half a bottle of developing solution left. He asked Cora if she would go to the chemist's to fetch some more.

"Where do you want me to buy it from? Cope's in Cawdry Buildings, as usual?" she asked.

"Wainwright's in Derby Street is nearer, it will be easier in this weather. And they stock the same developing fluids as Cope's. Get two bottles and have them put it on my account. But mind you don't slip on the ice, my dear," said Nathaniel.

A flurry of snowflakes accompanied Cora as she entered the chemist's shop some minutes later. Walter Wainwright was his usual efficient self and, nodding enthusiastically at her enquiry, immediately located two quart bottles of developing solution.

"It's Miss Blake, isn't it?" he asked, looking earnestly at Cora as he placed the bottles on his polished counter, then started to wrap them carefully in brown paper. "On your father's account, I take it?" he added.

Before Cora could reply, Wainwright went on talking, seemingly glad of the chance for conversation. "How is Mr Blake after that tragic business on the canal? According to the newspaper, he was there when that poor fellow was found, was he not?"

"Actually, we both were, Mr Wainwright. And yes, it was an awful affair," said Cora, trying to retain her composure despite being reminded of the horror of the body under the ice.

"I'm sorry to hear you were involved, Miss Blake. That was unfortunate indeed," the chemist continued, now warming to his topic. "Goodness knows how such a thing could happen. Then again, so many people risk themselves on the ice in this weather, do they not? I suppose the fellow must have stepped out on it and then… calamity struck!"

"I am sure I have no idea," Cora stammered, reaching for her parcel. However Wainwright was not to be deflected. "Still, I suppose the police will soon have the affair settled, a mishap such as that. Has your father been told who the chap was? I expect Mr Blake will be asked to give a statement, especially if it is needed for an inquest."

"Excuse me, Mr Wainwright, but I must get back to the studio, Father is waiting for this," said Cora, clutching the package and turning for the door, cutting short the awkward exchange. Wainwright remained at the counter, his mouth turned down in disappointment.

It was not until the end of the afternoon that Blake resumed his search for a photograph showing the canal victim. His interest had been piqued by the intriguing postcard.

He was leafing rapidly through prints from the previous October when he stopped and seized one in particular to take a closer look. A group of men and women were in formal dress. Blake remembered the occasion without looking at his pencil note on the back. Near the centre of the group, staring confidently at the camera, was the man he was looking for.

"I knew I had seen him before, poor fellow," he murmured to himself. It was a sobering thought that the next time he photographed this man, his body was being hauled from the frozen canal. Blake looked closely at the rest of the group and recognised several people he had seen in the town over the years.

Glancing out of the window, he saw it was getting dark and decided to wait until the next day to take the photograph to Inspector Ramm. He wanted to close the studio early so that he and Cora could have an early supper. They were both going to the Temperance Hall to watch the Bioscope Entertainment and that was a performance he definitely did not want to miss.

Chapter Twelve

An excited buzz of conversation spread around the Temperance Hall in Union Street that Thursday evening as the audience gathered to witness the display of "animated photographs" presented by the International Bioscope Company. This would be the first time moving pictures had been shown in the town, though one or two wealthier inhabitants had already seen displays of the fascinating new entertainment when visiting London or Manchester.

Although the entertainment was due to start at seven o'clock, Cora Blake and her friend Ellen Simms had arrived soon after six to make sure they had the pick of the cheapest sixpenny seats at the back of the hall. They knew there would be many people in front of them, some paying as much as two shillings for reserved seats in the best positions, but the two friends were ready to stand up all evening if necessary, to get a good view of the cloth screen which had been draped at the opposite end of the hall.

Cora saw that a space had been cleared in the middle of the floor for the projection machine and standing next to it was her father, in earnest conversation with a man she took to be the machine's operator. Both she and her father had finished work early that afternoon and Nathaniel, just as excited about the Bioscope Entertainment as she was, had wolfed down his evening meal so that he could be in the hall when the equipment was being set up. Nathaniel had read much about the rapid advance of moving pictures and wanted to talk to the operator and have a close look at the equipment before the show got under way.

He was now examining the workings of the projector, a

complicated device of black enamel and polished brass. Parts of it, such as the long lens and the carbide lamp with its chimney above, were similar to the projector he used to present his own lantern slide entertainments. Cora usually helped with these shows which Nathaniel put on in halls in the town and local villages. But this machine had additional features, including several large cogs that meshed together and two metal spools which carried the thin flexible film. On one side of the apparatus was a handle which the projectionist would endeavour to crank at a steady pace to create the magic of moving pictures on the screen some yards away.

The projectionist, a young man in his twenties with a southern accent and wearing a flannel three-piece suit, seemed happy to answer Blake's technical questions about the type of film and the projector, obviously pleased to impart his knowledge of the exciting new technology.

"I must say, I would love to dabble in these moving images myself. It seems an extraordinary thing. Although I don't know whether I could afford the equipment," said Blake, standing back to admire the projector once again. In truth he was a little jealous of an entertainment that seemed to make his own static images seem rather old fashioned.

"Take it from me, Sir, this is the future," the projectionist replied, straightening his spine with pride. "Once people see the International Bioscope Company's animated photography there is no going back to boring old photographs, if you will pardon the phrase. Mark my words, in a few years there will be bioscopes in every town – it's already happening in America."

Blake nodded thoughtfully. Perhaps he could not afford to ignore this new development. Already there was talk of a new theatre being built in High Street that would be equipped for moving picture performances if the owners saw a profit in it.

Their conversation was interrupted when a senior fellow with lank white hair and a serious expression came up to the projectionist and said he needed to discuss the musical accompaniment. Blake recognised him as Mr Alsop, conductor of the Moorland Philharmonia, who was in the photograph with Dr Jervis which he had found that very afternoon. Tonight, Alsop would be playing the Temperance Hall's jangling upright piano throughout the show, providing a suitable accompaniment to match the silent scenes on the screen.

From across the hall, Cora smiled as she watched her father talking to the bioscope operator. "I knew Father would be fascinated with this. He loves new inventions, especially anything to do with photography," she said.

"Never mind photography, have you thought any more about the protest that's planned for next month?" asked Ellen. She and Cora had become fervent supporters of the Votes for Women campaign, partly because of Ellen's experiences at Leek's Great Mill and partly from Cora's frustration at the way she thought women in general were treated. Their protests had landed them in trouble more than once, but they were undeterred and their experiences had brought them closer than ever.

Seeing Cora hesitate, Ellen continued: "I know neither of us have been to London before, and the train tickets will be expensive, but it looks like we may be able to get some money from the fighting fund in Manchester. It's going to be a big rally and the womenfolk of Leek should be represented."

"It's not the money, Ellen. I have just had so much to think about these last few days," Cora replied.

"Seeing that man in the canal must have been awful, Cora. There's always something, isn't there?" Ellen reached across to give Cora's hand a friendly squeeze. She knew all about Cora's past troubles because she had been involved in most of them herself.

"Yes, it was horrible. But my mind has been full of other things …about Oliver." Once she began to talk to Ellen, Cora knew where it was going to lead. She could not keep the news of Oliver's proposal to herself any longer. She had to tell someone and her closest friend was the one.

"What is it?" Ellen leaned in close and her voice fell almost to a whisper, but that didn't disguise the urgency of her question. "Has he done something?"

"He's asked me to marry him," Cora announced, glancing around her to make sure no one else could hear her. Ellen gasped and her face lit up in a smile, but before she could speak, Cora went on. "Say nothing to anyone, Ellen. Our parents don't even know about it yet. It's still a secret."

"Cora that's marvellous! No wonder you've had a lot to think about."

"Agreeing to marry was the easy part. It's what I've been dreaming of. He had something else to say, though," Cora went on.

"What do you mean?" Ellen asked.

"He wants to emigrate – both of us – to New Zealand."

Ellen's face registered the same shock as Cora had when she first heard of Oliver's his plans the previous weekend. "What? Leave Leek, your family, everything?"

"Oh I know, Ellen, it's bewildering, isn't it? But at the same time it is the most exciting thing I can imagine."

"But what about wanting to be a photographer? Surely it's going to be harder for you to find work over there, especially without your father to help you."

Cora paused. Ellen's comment brought her back to reality. Over the past couple of years, her ambition to take photographs had become as important as her dream of life with Oliver. Was that something else she would have to give that up to stay with him?

"I've said 'Yes' to him, Ellen. If that is where Oliver is going, then so am I. And we shall see what happens."

Ellen's heart sank as she realised the hole that would open up in her own life when her friend left. She could hardly imagine what Cora's life would be like in another country so far away, but she knew it would be very different from her own here in Leek, living in a terraced house, working at the mill. Then she saw that Cora was looking at her with tears in the corner of her eyes, waiting anxiously for her to say something. Ellen knew she had a duty to support her friend.

"You never stop surprising me," Ellen teased. "This is the maddest scheme, but I'm sure you and Oliver will be so happy together, wherever you finish up."

Before the friends could say any more, the sound of a spirited introduction from Jeremiah Alsop at the piano signalled that the show was about to start. At the same moment, the caretaker and his wife went round turning down the gas mantles that lined the walls. When the hall was dark enough, the projector lamp came to life and the packed audience fell silent as the International Bioscope Company's title flickered onto the screen, accompanied by stirring chords on the piano.

A murmur of anticipation spread through the hall as the title of the first animated photographs, 'A Cruiser in a Storm', appeared on the screen. Some gasped in amazement as the moving pictures began, a great steamship being pitched about in heavy seas. A suitably stormy piece from Mr Alsop on the piano enhanced the entertainment. After a minute or so, during which time the images of the imperilled ship appeared to be repeated twice, the screen went blank and the audience started to applaud spontaneously. A wonder of the modern age had come to the town.

The evening continued with a variety of moving pictures, from important events at home and abroad to short dramatic sketches often of a romantic flavour. Each lasted a couple of minutes at most and was accompanied by different piano music, Mr Alsop seeming to play with increasing vigour as the night wore on.

Towards the end of the first half of the show came the spectacle which the audience had most wanted to see. The title ‘Mill Workers of Leek’ was greeted by gasps of excitement, followed by whoops, shouts and whistles as the moving pictures began. Almost unbelievably, there on the screen were workers streaming out of the Great Mill at the end of their shift. Waistcoated and whiskered men of all ages in caps, trilbies and bowler hats were dashing down the steps, women in bonnets or straw boaters and wearing capes, shawls or tightly buttoned jackets and coats, were appearing from the great doorway and heading in different directions.

A certain unsteadiness of the operator’s hand on the projector’s crank made the movements on the screen rather jerky and a little faster than real life. The whole affair began to look like a headlong rush from work. For the audience, most of whom had never seen anything like this before that evening, the speed didn’t matter. There was laughter and claps of delight, some people calling out when they saw someone they recognised. When the precious minute of moving pictures came to an end, a chant of “Show it again! Show it again!” broke out and, after some fiddling with the spool of film, the projectionist did just that. Cheers erupted as the mill workers once again started to dash out of the Great Mill.

The screen went blank and the gas mantles were turned up, indicating it was time for the interval. Edgar Bostock, a local entertainer, mounted the stage and prepared to begin a selection of amusing stories while the projectionist busied himself adjusting his equipment, trimming the lamp wick and changing the spool of film. Alsop, the pianist, was striding for the door, pushing a plug of tobacco into his pipe.

“That was amazing!” Ellen said to Cora. “I couldn’t believe it when I saw all those folk coming out of the mill. It was like watching it happen in real life. My uncle was one of them!” The two friends stood up and continued to talk excitedly about the moving pictures as they went to join the queue for refreshments at the back of the hall.

Blake, who had watched the show from near the front, turned to see his friend John Gibb sitting at the end of his row. Scotsman Gibb was a former 'man of the road' who had become a local hero after his exploits with Nathaniel and Cora. He now helped to run a farm at Abbey Green on the edge of town. Nathaniel, who regarded Gibb almost as one of the family, edged his way across the row of seats to speak to him.

"Well, John, that was quite a spectacle, was it not?" Blake said. "I have read much about these moving pictures and, I must say, I was suitably impressed."

"Aye, Mr Blake, it was a fair treat an' all," Gibb replied. "I've never seen the like of it."

Whilst the audience was being enthralled by the bioscope performance, Inspector Ramm was witnessing something rather less entertaining – weighty discussions about the allocation of funds for the town's needy. The Moorlands Lodge of the Grand Order of Oddfellows had gathered in an upstairs room at The Red Lion Hotel in the Market Place, and such lengthy debates made Ramm wonder why he had joined the organisation in the first place.

When he had arrived, he had been slightly relieved to see that Walter Wainwright was not yet present. The chemist had obviously been excited to assist the police enquiries, and very curious to know what it was all about, but the last thing Ramm wanted tonight was to be drawn into a conversation about his investigation, especially as he had made little progress with that matter at the asylum.

When Wainwright finally arrived, Ramm thought he seemed a little flustered. The man in the next seat leaned over and said in a confidential tone: "Brother Walter's probably having trouble with his wife, poor chap. She's an invalid, you know. He tells me she can be quite demanding."

"Is she indeed? I was not aware," Ramm replied.

"Yes," his neighbour continued, lowering his voice even further, "brain fever, so I believe."

The news about Wainwright's wife made Ramm consider whether he should have been more sympathetic towards the inquisitive chemist. After all, the man had only been trying to help.

The meeting was halfway through when Wainwright had left again. "Excuse me gentlemen, I have some pressing matters to attend to," he apologised.

"The wife, no doubt," whispered the man next to Ramm, knowingly.

A couple of hundred yards away from the Temperance Hall, Oliver Finch was in the *Leek Lion* office, typing his report about Gwendoline Cope's predicament. Although he would have liked to have seen the moving pictures with Cora, he was determined to finish his report that night. He wanted to make the most of the story, not only because he felt he owed it to the frightened woman, but also to please his father. He was looking for any way to improve his father's mood before telling him of his plans to leave Leek and his job at the *Lion*. The fact that Miss Cope had such a beguiling personality had nothing to do with it, he told himself.

Another hard frost had descended over the town that evening and the newspaper office was as cold as ever. Oliver, in his overcoat and fingerless gloves, stopped typing and dragged the paraffin stove closer to his desk. He started to cough as fumes swirled up, one of the drawbacks of trying to keep warm with such a stove.

Small sheets of paper, each bearing a single typed paragraph, were piling up on his desk. He was nearing the end of the story. Then Oliver leaned forward and gripped the sides of his typewriter, wracked by coughing a fit more violent than before. He began to feel disorientated. He was finding it difficult to breathe …and to see. He rubbed his knuckles into his streaming eyes and then reached for his mouth as he started to cough again.

As Edgar Bostock was finishing his last recitation, Jeremiah Alsop came bustling back into the Temperance Hall, looking around expectantly in case he was late, then resumed his seat at the piano and flexed his fingers. A murmur of excited anticipation spread amongst the audience as they settled down for the second half of the Bioscope Entertainment. However, conversation petered out when the sound of a bell was heard from somewhere outside. It was not the clock of the St Edward's Church tolling the hour, this was a constant and urgent clanging.

A man sprang to his feet and ran from the hall, followed by two more. Blake recognised them as members of the town Fire Brigade. He realised someone must be pulling the bell rope that hung from the tower of Leek Fire Station, only a short distance away near the top of Stockwell Street, and these men were responding to it.

The sound of concerned voices spread around the gathering and seconds later a man rushed into the hall and shouted: "Fire! There's a fire broke out. It's in Market Street!"

Others were now leaving their seats and making for the door, including Blake and John Gibb. Cora gave a cry and stood up. "Oliver is in Market Street! He's working tonight. We must see what is happening," she said. Ellen grasped Cora's arm and the two friends hurried from their seats, joining the mêlée in the hallway as more and more people decided to see what was going on outside. The projectionist looked around the hall, baffled by this turn of events just as he was about to start his machine, and decided to suspend the show until everyone had calmed down.

Blake and Gibb walked briskly the few paces up Stockwell Street, dodging curious drinkers coming out of The Union Inn. When they reached the gateway to the Nicholson Institute, they crossed into Market Street. They could see a crowd was forming, people pointing at smoke pouring from somewhere just beyond the Town Hall. All the while, the fire station bell was ringing persistently in the background, summoning the firemen to action.

"My God! It looks like Finch's place!" said a shocked Blake. He was horrified at the thought of a fire in a building he knew to be stacked with paper and tins of ink on the ground floor, and yet more paper and books in the office on the second floor. He and Gibb ran towards the scene, the Scotsman pushing his way through the crowd to get a better look. Behind them came a scream and Blake knew at once it was his daughter's voice. He swivelled round to see Cora clinging onto Ellen and staring up at the *Leek Lion* building, her face frozen in fear.

"Oliver might be in there!" Cora cried, then she started to shout Oliver's name, craning her neck to see if there was any sign of movement in the top floor windows.

John Gibb looked back at Cora then peered along the street through smoke which was spewing from the shattered panes of the ground floor windows. "Where on earth is the fire brigade? They've only got to come from around the corner," he growled. Moments later, the Queen of the Moorlands fire engine appeared in Market Street, the town's firemen struggling to push it through the snow.

"Stand back, stand back," shouted the Fire Brigade Captain, Arthur Machin, a white-bearded fellow in his sixties who had been first to run out of the Temperance Hall. The rest of the firemen, some with their tunics half undone, hauled the engine close to the building and began to unroll a hose. "Quick men, look lively, get the pump going," Machin ordered with brisk authority.

"There might be somebody inside," Gibb shouted desperately to Machin, pointing at the door. Its green paint was blistering in the heat.

"We need to get some water on the fire before we can do anything else, now move aside," Machin replied. The hose was out, but lay limply useless as the firemen were struggling to get the pump's steam boiler going in the freezing cold.

Gibb shook his head in exasperation and then, with not a moment's hesitation, rushed at the door, raising his heavy boot to kick it open. As an acrid cloud of smoke and ash billowed into his face, Gibb wrapped his tartan scarf around his nose and mouth and charged in.

"John, don't!" Blake called, but it was too late for Gibb to hear him. Cora, standing beside her father, tried to run to the door too, but Blake caught her by the shoulders and held her back. "No, my dear. There's nothing you can do."

"But Father, Oliver must be in there!" she pleaded, then looked around wildly, searching the faces in the crowd just in case her young man had escaped from the building.

Years earlier, John Gibb had distinguished himself for bravery in the army. Though now well past middle age, he was still powerfully built and, more importantly, he was powerfully single-minded. At times like this, he knew that he who hesitates is lost. The Finch family, like the Blakes, had been generous to him and, if Oliver really was in the building, he had to do something about it.

As he rushed inside, he expected to be confronted by a wall of flame or searing heat, but instead he came upon what seemed like a solid mass of choking smoke in the darkness. There was a reek of something smouldering akin to tar. Although he could make out virtually nothing of the interior, he knew that there was a staircase on his right which led to the upper floors and that was where Oliver might be found.

Gibb groped blindly, then caught the toe of his boot on the bottom step and stumbled forward onto his knees. Despite the stab of pain, he was relieved to find that the wooden staircase had not been burnt through. He might just be able to find his way upstairs, he thought. Unable to see the steps beneath his feet, he decided it make his way up on his hands and knees. He cried out as he put first one hand and then the other onto either hot timbers, pieces of burning paper and shards of glass, but he carried on doggedly.

On reaching the first floor, he scrabbled around in the dark until he found the next flight of steps which led up to the office where, in the past, he had seen FJ Finch and his son at their desks.

Below him he could hear shouts and barked commands. He guessed that the firemen had finally come through the front door and were trying to extinguish whatever was burning down there. He paused to catch his breath and to tighten the scarf across his face with his blistered fingers. How he wished he had thought to soak the cloth with a handful of snow before he had entered the building. He knew that in incidents like this, smoke could be the real killer. Fighting in the Sudan all those years ago, he had seen comrades perish in blazing buildings of wood and thatch, and usually it was the smoke that claimed them, not the flames.

At that moment the gloom around him was lit up by an orange glow. To his horror, he realised the stairs he had just climbed must have caught fire. He was cut off from escape.

Down in the street, Nathaniel had his arms wrapped around Cora as they gazed at the smoke pouring from the building, flames flickering in the background. With no sign of John Gibb or Oliver Finch, father and daughter were growing more desperate by the minute.

Nathaniel shook his head. "Whatever was John thinking, charging into a burning building like that?" he said despairingly.

"That's what he is like. He's so brave," said Cora, wiping the tears from her cheeks with her mitten. "He wants to save Oliver, just as he saved me before." She knew that she had Gibb to thank for her life when she had twice landed herself in dangerous situations in the past.

"But it's such a risk…" Nathaniel began. He stopped as he was pushed aside by someone trying to force their way through the growing crowd. It was FJ Finch, who had come running after hearing the commotion when he was on his way home to Bath Street.

"Let me through!" Finch shouted. "I must go inside! Let me through, I say!" There was a panic in his voice that Nathaniel had never heard before. He took hold of Finch's arm.

"Steady on, FJ. You cannot go in there, it's too dangerous, old fellow," said Nathaniel, hoping to calm his friend. "Leave it to the fire brigade, they are dealing with it now."

The editor glared at him with desperation in his eyes. "But the office is on fire, can't you see? Oliver will be in there. I have to find him... before it's too late!"

As a parent himself, Blake understood the gut-wrenching anguish that engulfed FJ at this moment. But he could not let his friend do something so foolish it would make the night even more tragic. He took a firmer grip of Finch's arm and spoke directly into his face. "Listen FJ, the brigade are putting the fire out. If Oliver is in there, they will reach him soon enough. And John Gibb has gone in after him, too."

"What? Gibb? Then I must go in! He's my son!" Finch tried to struggle free from Blake. He was staring at the open door of the *Lion* building, trying to make out what was going on inside, desperate to see his son appear safe from the building.

Blake heard the shrill sound of a police whistle, followed by a familiar voice bellowing across the crowd. "Move back from the building! It's too dangerous. Constables, move these people away."

Inspector Ramm had arrived on the scene and was immediately trying to get the situation under control. The two officers on night patrol who accompanied him began to force the onlookers back to the pavement on the opposite side of Market Street. They then took up position in the street, barking a warning at anyone who dared to move any closer.

Ramm surveyed the burning building and the fire brigade's frantic efforts, their hose snaking through the door. From inside came the crack of splintering wood, the roar of burning paper and muffled detonations as tins of printing ink exploded. In the street, the snow was coated with ash and dotted with shards of glass from shattered windows.

A man came running from nearby York Street carrying a bucket. He bent down and scooped snow into it before barging past a constable and flinging the contents through the doorway. "Fetch more buckets!" someone shouted and within minutes a chain of men were desperately casting showers of snow towards the building. Whether it helped or not, it seemed better than standing and watching.

The Inspector went across to where Blake and Finch were standing. "This is a grim to-do. Did you raise the alarm, Mr Finch?" he asked.

Finch shook his head sadly. "I only wish I had been here, then it might not have got hold. It's a nightmare, Inspector."

"FJ fears Oliver may be in there. He was working this evening," Blake interjected.

"Good Lord, that makes it even worse!" Ramm replied. He strode across to the Fire Brigade Captain and asked if his constables could assist. At that point, two more firemen appeared at the far end of Market Street, straining to push a hand cart which carried a long wooden ladder they had brought from the fire station. In front of the *Lion* offices, they hauled the ladder off its cart and extended it until it reached the second floor windows.

Inside the building, John Gibb had realised that, with no way down, he had no alternative but to carry on upwards. On all fours once again, he started to feel his way up the next staircase. His makeshift mask was proving useless and he began to cough almost ceaselessly.

When he reached the top floor, he was relieved to find no more flames. However it was too dark and filled with smoke to see where Oliver might be. If he was to help the young reporter, Gibb knew he had to clear some of the smoke and turned towards where light showed dimly through the windows in the front wall. He needed to open them to let the smoke out, despite the risk that a rush of air would feed the fire and make his situation worse.

His scarf fell from his face and Gibb held his breath as he staggered towards one of the windows. He kicked over some metal contraption and there was a sudden burst of flame from the floor. John realised he had upended a stove and a pool of paraffin was alight, threatening to set the room on fire. Instinctively he stamped on the flames.

When he reached the window, he began to frantically run his fingers over its many panes to find the latch. His lungs felt like they were bursting when he finally found the catch, twisted it and wrenched the window inwards. He gulped the frigid night air before he moved across to the other window and pulled it open, too. Smoke started to stream past him as it escaped from the room.

Gibb rubbed his streaming eyes and looked around the office. In the faint glow from a street lamp near the window he perceived the outline of two desks. Across one of them was another shape – a body slumped face down. He seized Oliver's lifeless form under the armpits and dragged him backwards towards the window.

"Hold ye on, my boy. We'll get ye outta here," he croaked, fighting for breath. From Oliver there was no reaction. Gibb could not tell whether he was dead or alive.

When he reached the open window, he laid Oliver on the floorboards and leaned out into the night, bellowing to the crowd below: "Get a ladder!"

Gibb did not know it, but the brigade's ladder was already in position just below the window. Moments later a shining helmet rose above the sill as a fireman reached the window. The Scotsman helped to haul Oliver's body across the fireman's shoulders. The man then began to slowly descend, holding Oliver in place with one arm.

Seeing a body brought out of the window, people in the crowd gasped in horror. FJ rushed forward, waving his hand and shouting his son's name. Cora, who had been crying in Ellen's arms, broke free, dodged one of the constables and was at the bottom of the ladder just as the fireman gained the pavement. Groaning in despair, she tried to reach up to touch Oliver, but was restrained by Nathaniel who had moved quickly behind her.

"Oh my Lord, Oliver! Is he alive?" came FJ's anguished cry. Then he turned around and shouted: "Quickly someone! We need to get him to the hospital!"

A constable, helped by a man who had emerged from the crowd, took Oliver from the fireman's shoulders. Carrying the young man between them, they hurried off towards the Cottage Hospital which was a few hundred yards away at the bottom of Stockwell Street. Cora struggled free of her father's grasp again and ran after them. FJ followed, as did Nathaniel and finally Ellen Simms.

Inspector Ramm watched them go, then looked up at the open second floor window where smoke was still drifting into the night sky. "Where's Gibb?" he frowned. Through the main door he could see flames licking up the wooden staircase, but then he saw a fireman going back up the ladder.

In the newspaper office above them, John Gibb lay senseless. Exhausted by his efforts to rescue Oliver Finch, the Scotsman had fallen backwards after passing him to safety. He had been stunned when his head hit the floorboards.

The crowd watched in admiration as the fireman climbed in through the office window, from where the smoke was clearing. Moments later he appeared again and shouted: "He's up here! Give me a hand to get him down." Another fireman scaled the ladder and soon John Gibb, now groggily conscious, was being manhandled through the window and guided with slow steps down to the ground.

When Gibb reached the pavement, his face blackened by smoke and his hands blistered, some of the onlookers started to applaud and one came forward to give him a steadying hand.

Ramm approached. "That was very brave, Mr Gibb, but you put yourself in peril," he said and, nodding at the Scotsman's hands, added: "You need treatment for those." Gibb was helped away in the same direction that Oliver had been carried.

Eventually the crowd in the street began to drift away, the excitement dampened after the drama of Oliver Finch being carried unconscious from the scene and John Gibb's rescue. Some would go straight home, others would make their way to the nearest hostelries – The Red Lion, The Cock, The Roebuck and The Union – to discuss what had gone on until closing time.

Inspector Ramm remained at the scene until the firemen – their faces, helmets and uniforms covered in grime and blackened by smoke – had extinguished the last embers. There would be no *Leek Lion* for a while, he thought. This was a catastrophe for the newspaper and the Finches, but he knew the incident could have been much worse if the fire had spread to the Town Hall next door, a conflagration far beyond anything the town brigade could handle.

His thoughts drifted to the huge fire that had broken out when the County Asylum was being built. Someone had cycled to Leek to raise the alarm in the small hours of the morning, but by the time the brigade arrived, the main hall was beyond rescue. The whole project had been set back by months. Following that incident, the asylum had recruited its own fire team and the Leek brigade had been supplied with the new steam powered engine that they had used tonight.

Looking at his pocket watch, Ramm saw that it was approaching midnight. He was anxious to find out what had become of poor Oliver Finch, but before he left for the Cottage Hospital he sought out Captain Machin again. Ramm knew the man had been fighting fires in the district for decades and asked if he had any idea what could have caused this one. Machin looked both filthy and dog tired and took some moments before responding. He needed to take a better look inside the building, he said, and would do so once it became light. The men agreed to meet at the scene at eight o'clock the next morning.

When he went through the main entrance of the Memorial Hospital, Inspector Ramm came across John Gibb slumped in a chair outside the Matron's office. The Scotsman pointed a bandaged hand to a door further along the corridor. "The lad's in there," he said, despondently.

A pitiful scene greeted Ramm in the small treatment room, lit by a bare electric bulb. Oliver Finch lay stretched out on one of the two beds, eyes closed, unmoving. Around him were grouped the solemn figures of FJ Finch and his wife Martha, Nathaniel Blake and his daughter Cora. All eyes were fixed on Oliver, all looked dazed by what had happened. Cora, seated on a metal framed chair, whimpered into a handkerchief she held tightly to her mouth.

Ramm's heart fell as he feared the worst. Then a strangled choking sound came from the bed and he realised Oliver was still alive, but only just. The Inspector was about to speak when Dr Handbridge came into the room. He was the hospital's most senior member of staff, and, as well as performing post mortems for the police, was called upon at all hours for urgent cases such as this.

"I'm afraid we need to clear the room so that he can rest," the doctor announced, then added with a little more sympathy: "I know you wish to be near him, but this is for the best. Matron will inform you when you can come back."

Ramm indicated to Handbridge that he wanted a word with him and the two went out into the corridor, leaving the others beside the bed.

"I know what you are going to ask, Inspector, and it's too early to say whether he will recover," the doctor began, keeping his voice low. "I have never seen anyone survive smoke inhalation as severe as this. It could well have damaged his windpipe and his lungs. We might try a steam treatment to ease his breathing, but that is the best we can do at the moment."

The doctor paused. "Something about his colour, his skin and his lips are very red, makes me think he might be suffering from the effects of poisonous fumes of some sort."

Their discussion ended as Oliver's parents and the Blakes came out of the room. Cora seemed to be walking in trance, supported by her father. Handbridge took a small white envelope from his pocket and handed it to Nathaniel. "Your daughter needs to rest, Mr Blake. Get her to take this sleeping draught when you reach home," he said.

Cora began to protest, her voice raw from crying, but Nathaniel drew her in close and said quietly: "We all need some sleep, my dear. In the morning, we will come back again to see how Oliver is faring."

FJ looked at Ramm blankly with hollow eyes, the shock seeming to have robbed him of the power of speech.

"Mr and Mrs Finch, please accept my sympathy for tonight's terrible events. We all know that Oliver is in good hands here," said Ramm.

“It was the damned stove, wasn’t it?” said FJ with a sudden anguished vehemence. Ramm looked puzzled.

“That started the fire. That did this to Oliver,” Finch went on, jabbing his finger towards the room where his son lay. He fell silent again, lost in thought, before turning to put an arm around his wife’s shoulders. The couple walked off down the corridor with leaden steps.

Blake watched them depart. “A tragic night indeed,” he murmured to Ramm.

Chapter Thirteen

It was the middle of the night and Cora woke with a start. She thought she had been having a nightmare, but quickly remembered that the horror was all too real.

She could recall that she had felt exhausted when they had returned home long after midnight, but she had refused to take the sleeping draught the doctor had handed to her father. She had just about managed to climb the staircase to her attic room and had fallen into bed, her mother pulling the eiderdown over her.

Lying on her back, staring upwards into the dark, Cora kept reliving the events of the last week, the most momentous of her life. All the turmoil of going to take photographs at the asylum and the shock of seeing the body in the canal. Then her joy and astonishment at Oliver's proposal and his plan for them to start life in New Zealand. But now… the happiness and hope had been swept away, all the excitement had been replaced by distress.

But tired as she was, Cora could not get back to sleep. Somehow she felt it was her duty to stay awake as long as possible while Oliver lay helpless in the hospital bed. And her mind was filled with the scenes from the night of the fire, most of all the sight of

Oliver being carried unconscious down the ladder. Her relief at his rescue from the burning building had lasted only a moment, replaced by sickening dread that he might be injured and severely so.

She thought again about Oliver's plan for a journey into the unknown and wondered whether the whole idea was now impossible. She had no inkling if he would recover or whether he would ever be fit to face the weeks at sea.

To make things worse, neither her father or mother knew the full truth of her heartache. Ellen was the only person she had told about Oliver's proposal and that was barely an hour before the fire. Now it would be a secret she would have to keep for a while longer – perhaps forever. Even if Oliver recovered from his injuries quickly, their plan to leave Leek might be turned on its head. After what had just happened, he would find it even more difficult to leave his father and the *Leek Lion* behind.

Cora finally drifted off to sleep again, but it could have been for only a short while and she certainly did not feel any better for it when she woke as morning approached.

It was still dark outside, the glow from a street lamp showing dimly through the frost covered panes of her bedroom window. There were sounds of movement in the street – footsteps in the snow and the occasional cart – so she guessed folk must be on their way to the mills to start their shifts at half-past six.

Cora got up and went downstairs to find her mother and father already in the kitchen. The stove was lit and they were drinking a cup of tea at the table, engaged in a quiet conversation that ceased when she entered. They both turned to look at her with sunken eyes that betrayed their own sleepless night.

"Cora, you should not be up yet. Please go back to bed," said Edith Blake gently.

"It is no use, Mother. I shall not sleep. Not until I know Oliver is better."

Edith glanced at her husband and he shrugged. “I’m sure he will be back to his old self soon,” he said, hoping to reassure his daughter. From Cora’s expression, he knew he had failed.

The smell of smoke was still in the air when Inspector Ramm met the Fire Brigade’s Captain Machin at the *Leek Lion* office, or what remained of it. By the time Ramm arrived, Machin had already removed a sheet of corrugated iron which the firemen had used to block off the doorway when they left the scene in the early hours.

“Watch your step, Inspector. The fire is extinguished, but there is broken glass and debris all over the floor,” said Machin, as he led the way inside.

Ramm looked around the sorry remains of the ground floor workshop where the newspaper was printed each week. He saw that the once gleaming printing press was covered in ash and surrounded by stacks of singed paper and buckled tins of ink. The white-painted walls had been blackened by smoke and the wooden staircase was burnt away in places.

He shook his head as he thought of the scene in there the previous night and of the courage of John Gibb who had charged into the fire and gone up those stairs to rescue Oliver Finch. The man was rash, but brave, he thought. Courage like that had won Gibb the thanks of the King two years before.

“I realise you are anxious to find out the cause, Inspector, so I have already been looking around for half an hour or so,” said Captain Machin.

“Mr Finch thinks it might have been a paraffin stove. Apparently they had one on the top floor and it would have been lit when his son was working last night.”

“A stove on the top floor, you say?” Beneath his white beard and bushy eyebrows, Machin’s face creased in a quizzical expression. “Please, wait here while I go to look up there.”

With infinite care the fireman scaled the damaged staircase, gripping the bannister and testing the strength of each tread as he went, striding over one or two that looked particularly unsteady. After some minutes he came back down, just as slowly.

"I have found the stove and that has confirmed my opinion," he said.

"What, that the stove was responsible?"

"No Inspector, it's my belief the fire started down here, on the ground floor. Just inside the front door, if I'm not mistaken. See this patch of burnt material," Machin pointed to a blackened area on the floor behind the scorched and blistered remains of the door.

"What could have caused it there, do you think? Was someone careless with a lamp, or a cigarette or something, next to all this paper and ink?" Ramm asked.

"Looking at the way the fire grew from this entrance area, I think some flammable substance was used. It burnt most of the door and started to spread through this workshop and then upwards. There is evidence of fire at several points on the stairs," Machin continued.

"This is very disturbing, Captain Machin. Are you sure of this?"

"Most certainly, Inspector, the fire did not start in the office. The paraffin stove was knocked over, perhaps when Mr Finch was being rescued, but that did not cause the fire down here."

"Is there any indication what could have been used to start it? Motor spirit, perhaps?" Ramm asked.

"It may have been petroleum spirit, yes, or perhaps a flammable chemical of some sort. I think the culprit must have brought the means with them. It was not some jape, such as ruffians stuffing a burning rag through the letterbox."

Captain Machin's explanation shocked Ramm. Suddenly there was a case of arson to investigate, a grave crime by any measure and, in this instance, made even more serious by the injury suffered by Oliver Finch.

They were about to leave when something caught Ramm's eye. He bent down and picked up one of the pieces of glass littering the floor. It was the remains of a container of some sort.

"There's more of that glass on the stairs. I thought they might be jars of some kind," said Machin.

Ramm looked at the rounded glass. To his mind it could be the remains of a chemical flask. Was this what the arsonist had used?

After ensuring the doorway was blocked again, Ramm headed for the hospital with heavy steps. He expected to find FJ Finch at his son's bedside and knew it now fell to him to break the news that the fire was no accident. The editor was distressed enough, but this was going to make matters worse.

When he went into the small ward, Ramm could see no change in Oliver. The young man was still unconscious, his breathing little more than a gurgle in his throat, his skin a curious pink. Finch Senior was seated next to the bed, as was his wife who was stroking her son's hand. Ramm thought of tragic happenstance of Oliver being in the wrong place at the wrong time. Unless, of course, the arsonist knew the young Finch was in the office…

"Mr Finch, could I have a word… in private, perhaps?" Ramm asked, beckoning FJ into the corridor and then leading him out through the main entrance. They stood outside the ivy clad building where they were less likely to be overheard.

"I see that your son has yet to recover," Ramm began, sparking a rapid response from Finch.

"Recover? We have seen nothing, not a blink, not a movement, barely a breath. He's dead to the world, Inspector."

"That is dreadful news, Mr Finch. I am sorry to add to your woes, but I have just had a meeting with the Fire Brigade Captain at your offices."

"What now? Has something else happened?" Finch asked

urgently, obviously impatient to return to the ward.

Ramm took a deep breath. This was almost like breaking news of a death, he thought. "Well, it appears that the paraffin stove was not responsible for the fire. According to Captain Machin, it was a deliberate act. Apparently, the fire may have been started by some flammable substance poured in the doorway."

Finch's expression registered disbelief. "You're saying that someone tried to burn down my building? While Oliver was in it? Who would do such a dastardly thing? Why?"

Finch went quiet as he stared blankly at a cart making its slow way along the street, then he burst out angrily: "Someone is trying to put me out of business! Surely it's not that damned *Argus*? Are they really that desperate?"

Ramm put a hand on FJ's arm to calm him. "At the moment, none of us have any idea who it could be, or why. But you can be assured, we shall begin an investigation without delay. This person must be found."

"Well, start with the *Moorland Argus* people," said Finch bitterly, before turning and going back to his son.

On his way to the police station, the Inspector made a detour to Blake's studio. He wanted him to photograph the damaged area at the entrance to the *Leek Lion* office before any cleaning was done. It was more than likely that this would develop into a crime investigation and a picture of the evidence might prove to be useful. He found the photographer and his daughter sitting together, each holding a cup of tea. They both looked drained from their experiences of the previous night, but Nathaniel's expression showed added concern when Ramm entered the shop.

"Inspector? What is it? Not more bad news I hope," he said, at the same time casting a worried look at Cora. "We were both at the hospital an hour ago and saw no change in poor Oliver then."

"No, no, Mr Blake. I myself have just come from there and it seems his condition is no different. However, there is something I wish to speak about." Ramm glanced from Blake to Cora as he considered how to proceed with the young woman present. Sensing the officer's hesitation, Nathaniel spoke while reaching for Cora's hand. "Do not worry about speaking in front of my daughter, Inspector. She is made of stern stuff, especially after last night."

"Well, it is indeed about the fire. We shall need to investigate the cause and, to assist us, I want you to photograph damage done to the premises, especially near to the entrance."

Cora seemed to wake from her daze. "The front door? So it wasn't Oliver's fault?"

"It seems the fire may well have started downstairs. Apparently the stove in the office where young Mr Finch was working could have had nothing to do with it," Ramm replied.

Blake realised that if there was to be a police investigation and Ramm wanted photographs taken, then he must suspect the fire was started deliberately. An appalling prospect, given the damage done to Finch's business and to Oliver. However, Blake decided not to question Ramm more closely as he thought it might be best to let Cora believe the fire was an accident, at least for the time being.

Nathaniel had misjudged his daughter. She too had guessed the implication of what Inspector Ramm had said and, after the officer left soon afterwards, she made plain her anxiety about the fire and who could have started it. "When I woke up this morning, I thought the situation could not get any worse, but now it has," she said. Her beloved Oliver had not suffered an unfortunate accident, she thought. He was the victim of a crime.

After a few minutes, Cora decided she could sit there no longer. "I just have to do something …anything," she announced. Snatching up her coat, she opened the shop door and said: "I'm going to see how Oliver is."

Blake heaved a great sigh as he watched her hurry down the steps onto the icy pavement, the door banging shut behind her. The sight of Oliver lying unconscious had been harrowing and, from the doctor's comments he had overheard, he knew the young man might be permanently affected by the smoke and fumes. He was fearful how this tragic event might turn out and what it might ultimately do to his daughter.

When Blake arrived in Market Street, camera case in one hand and a tripod in the other, he saw half a dozen older folk standing on the pavement staring at the *Lion* building. These were people who might have heard the commotion last night, or had been told about it in a shop that morning, and were curious to see what had been going on. Heads were being shaken solemnly, puzzled comments muttered.

After removing the corrugated iron sheet which barred the door, for a moment he stood appalled at the state of the press room. Then he set about taking his photographs. The blackened room was so dark that he had to use his chemical flash lamp to create an explosion of light to illuminate the mess of paper, wood, tins and dusty machinery. Pools of water on the floor were evidence of the fire brigade's efforts with their hose. He knew it was near the doorway which most concerned Inspector Ramm and he was able to partially drag the remains of the door into the daylight to take pictures of where it had been burned. He also photographed a blackened area on the flagstoned floor.

He was putting his equipment away when the light filtering from outside was dimmed by a figure standing in the doorway. It was FJ Finch, not moving, his expression fixed, simply staring into the destruction. Blake could see that his friend seemed to have aged ten years over one sleepless night. An unruly mess of greying red hair poked out from beneath his trilby, his waistcoat was unbuttoned, his tie was askew, the spark of curiosity had gone from his eyes, the restless energy gone from his body.

"Has Ramm told you?" Finch said in a monotone. "The fire was deliberate. Somebody did this to us."

"It is shocking, FJ. But I'm sure the Inspector will find who was responsible," Blake replied. "Probably some miscreant or other who dislikes the *Lion* and what you stand for."

"I told Ramm it must be the *Argus*. But who would stoop so low to put us out of business?" He shook his head and when he spoke again his voice was breaking with emotion as he looked around the room. "To be honest, Nathaniel, I cannot think clearly after what has happened here and to Oliver. But we have to make a start on this mess. I must speak to my men, and contact the advertisers, and…"

"FJ, you need to compose yourself," Blake interrupted. "You must tell me what I can do to help. Why not come round to the studio and we can sit with a cup of tea?"

"I have something important to do first," Finch replied. "I'm sorry to say that last night I was so preoccupied with Oliver's condition that I barely spoke to John Gibb. It need to put that right."

Cora had spent the last hour at Oliver's bedside, her heart aching to see her beloved so transformed. The energetic young man, full of exciting ideas, full of love for her, was reduced to this prone figure, an occasional uneven breath his only sign of life.

Mrs Finch went out of the room briefly and Cora clasped Oliver's hand. She whispered to him about things they had done and planned, willing him to wake up. But there was no response.

Her mood became bleaker and she started to think of what might happen if he stayed that way, all the things that might never happen. Not just the marriage, not just the adventure of a new life overseas, but an intimacy with him that she would never know.

Mrs Finch returned and Cora sat back in her seat, embarrassed to be seen so close to Oliver. As the minutes passed she thought once again about what had happened last night and what Inspector Ramm had said this morning. She began to convince herself that if the fire was started deliberately, then whoever did it must have known Oliver was in the office. They didn't care what happened to him, she thought.

Once again she felt the urge to do something. Visiting Oliver was not enough, especially when he did not know if she was there or not. She wanted to find out why this awful thing had happened, who was to blame. She had done it before when Ellen Simms had been in trouble, and two years later when her friend Sarah had been killed. Except no one was going to die this time, were they? Definitely not, she thought, looking back at Oliver, hoping his eyes would open.

As she left the hospital, Cora puzzled over why someone would want to destroy the *Lion* office. Was it because of something they were going to print? If the fire was to hurt Oliver, was it because of some story he was working on? She started to wonder what had been so important that he could not go to the Bioscope Entertainment.

On her way to the studio, she found herself drawn to Market Street once again, back to scene of last night's fire. Looking up at the smoke blackened panes on the top floor, she relived the shock of seeing Oliver manhandled from the window by John Gibb and carried down the ladder by the fireman. Then she had an idea. If Inspector Ramm was correct and the upstairs had not been on fire, then perhaps Oliver's notes and the story he was writing last night, were still there.

She looked around and saw that two people who had been standing looking at the damaged building had now walked off. For a moment at least, she was on her own in the street. Cora seized her chance and darted across to the *Lion*'s door. She was slender enough to edge past the sheet of iron, although her long coat snagged on one of its rusty edges.

She put her hand to her mouth to stifle a cough as she was enveloped in the smell of charred wood and the newspaper ash still swirling in the air. She heard voices outside and stood perfectly still, praying no one had seen her going inside.

In the gloom she could make out that the staircase was still in place, though some parts had been almost burnt through. If she was going to find Oliver's papers, she needed to find a way up those stairs. After all, John Gibb managed it last night, in the smoke and the flames and the dark, she thought.

Trying to keep her steps as light as possible, she picked her way up the staircase, clinging to the bannister when a tread creaked ominously. The higher she climbed, the less serious the damage seemed to be. The first floor workroom, normally a hive of activity, was eerily quiet. On a workbench, trays of metal type were coated in white ash as if they had been left untouched for years.

Her heart fluttered when she reached the top floor. Two days ago she had been in that room, talking to Oliver. Last night he had working in here as usual, when… "There's no time to go over it all again," she told herself. "I need to find Oliver's notes and leave before anyone comes."

Cora knew the office Oliver and his father shared was not the most tidy place at the best of times, filled with a profusion of books, directories, files of old newspapers and stacks of documents. Today, it looked worse than ever, with dust on every surface. Papers were scattered around, some stirred by a cold wind coming through the open windows. Oliver's chair was tipped over and so was the small stove which had leaked paraffin across the floorboards. Cora guessed that much of this had been caused when John Gibb rescued Oliver and, as she had heard afterwards, when Gibb himself was pulled out of there by the firemen.

On Oliver's desk, next to his sturdy typewriter, lay a small hardback notebook, black with a red spine. Cora had so often seen him pull a book like this from his pocket and start to make notes. She picked up the book and held it to her chest briefly, almost overcome with misery again, then opened it. It was full of writing in pencil, some of it a rapid scrawl, other parts she recognised as the shorthand which she knew Oliver had studied.

Still held in the typewriter was a piece of paper, half filled with typed lines. Carefully she unwound it from the roller and held it with the notebook. Then she spotted more of the sheets – she had heard Oliver and his father call it copy paper – on the other side of the desk and on the floor next to it. She gathered them all up. These might give me a clue, she thought.

When Finch arrived at Dieulacresse Cottage Farm, he found John Gibb sitting in the low ceilinged kitchen with his bandaged hands on the scrubbed table. The Scotsman looked at a loss, for he liked to be active whenever he could, helping widow Rosa Carter on her smallholding at Abbey Green. He was a lodger and slept in the barn, although it would be no surprise to Finch if John and Rosa married at some point in the future.

But Finch discovered Gibb's gloom was not only because his injured hands stopped him working. His mind was still full of what had gone at the scene of the fire.

"I cannay believe what happened to your son, Mr Finch. Thank God I managed to get him out. Aye, I thought I was trapped in there m'self for a moment," he said.

"Martha and I will never be able to thank you enough for what you did last night, John," said Finch, his voice wavering with emotion. "Your bravery put the rest of us to shame."

"It's only what anyone would have done…" Gibb began modestly, but Finch did not let him finish.

"No John, you were the only one who went to see if Oliver was in there, certainly before the firemen did. I dread to think how things might have turned out if you had not acted so quickly." He reached forward to shake the Scotsman's hand, but seeing the bandages thought better of it.

"So, how is the young man doing?" From Gibb's tone it was obvious that, from what he had seen of Oliver's condition, he was not expecting particularly good news.

Finch shook his head sadly and poked a finger to wipe one of his watering eyes. "No better, I'm afraid." Nodding at Gibb's hands, he added. "And what of yourself?"

"Oh, they'll heal, Mr Finch. I had worse in the Sudan. The doctor says to take it easy for a couple o' days."

They both went quiet, lost in thought. In the background a cow could be heard bellowing in a barn. Finally Finch spoke. "It was no accident, you know."

"I thought as much. That fire was coming from below, not that stove upstairs." Gibb paused. "Somebody mustn't like you, Mr Finch. Or they've got something against the *Lion*."

Or something against Oliver, Finch thought.

Assuming the Fire Brigade Captain was correct, Inspector Ramm and his men had a second grave crime to investigate alongside the murder of Dr Jervis. At the very least, it was a case of arson and the culprit would face years in prison. At worst, it could be attempted murder or, should Oliver Finch not recover, something even worse…

Having returned to the police station, the Inspector called a meeting in the canteen to tell his team of the latest developments and to share out the tasks which now faced them. The constables on night patrol in the town were now off duty, however they had reported seeing nothing suspicious near the scene. Ramm dispatched two of his officers to visit houses and shops close to the newspaper offices and ask if anyone had seen anyone loitering in the street before the fire. Both the Town Hall next door and Brunswick Methodist Church, which was directly opposite, were empty and in darkness as the drama unfolded, however Ramm ordered that the Town Hall caretaker and his wife, who lived on the premises, should be questioned.

Ramm wondered how seriously he should take Finch's claim that the *Moorland Argus* could be to blame. It seemed outlandish to think the fire was the result of a business rivalry, especially between educated and respected individuals such as newspaper owners. But it was something he could not afford to ignore, especially as, at that moment, it was the only lead he had. He decided to visit the *Argus* office as soon as possible.

Turning to the murder of James Jervis, he instructed another constable to go to Cheddleton and find any other members of staff who may have seen the doctor during his final hours at the County Asylum. Sergeant Reynolds announced that nothing had been heard from the Manchester Constabulary, however the Coroner's secretary had called to ask what progress was being made and to inform them that an inquest was to be opened on Monday. Finally, Knowles said that James Jervis's parents were due to arrive by train from Carlisle that evening.

Ramm gave a great sigh. He was feeling almost overwhelmed by the complexities of the case. The unusual weapon, the betting, the moneylender, the women, the suspicious colleagues, the postcard with its mystery message – his enquiries were pointing in many directions, none leading to an arrest. But he consoled himself with the thought that it had been only a week since they had discovered that the "accident" was in fact a murder.

As Cora returned to the studio, her father was anxious to leave.

First he needed to take his photographs of the damaged premises to the police station. Next, on FJ's behalf, he was going to find the newspaper's workers – Alfred the compositor, Tom who operated the printing press and Jacob his apprentice. Finch wanted them to begin cleaning up the mess as soon as it was safe.

Cora had managed to hide Oliver's papers under her coat and, once her father had hurried out, she started to examine them. Even if they did not help her investigation, the notebook and the type-written sheets gave her some solace. She had saved the last things he was writing before the fire broke out.

The black notebook was a little disappointing because she could not decipher much of what seemed to be a combination of words and squiggles. She bit her lower lip and gripped the notebook tighter as she remembered Oliver trying to teach her some Pitman shorthand symbols one rainy afternoon. Turning towards the back, she saw a heading, 'Miss Cope', and below it an address in Chorley Street. Further down she spotted mention of Miss Heath's Millinery in the Market Place.

She then spread out the typed sheets on her work table. Reading each one quickly, she realised that several stories were mixed up – something about the livestock market, another one about delays on the railway. Finally she saw a sheet referring to 'the mystery of the frightened woman'.

She gathered together other sheets from the same story. Thankfully they were numbered, so she could put them in the right order, the last sheet being the one she had pulled from the typewriter. Oliver had indeed been writing about Miss Cope when the fire started, she thought.

The story revealed Gwendoline Cope's unhappy experiences as the victim of an unknown prowler. Reading it through rapidly, Cora saw that Oliver had been true to his word and there was nothing to identify Miss Cope. But there was much to stir the reader's sympathy. And Cora was a little surprised at some of the descriptions of ‘the attractive and innocent young lady’ who had ‘revealed her innermost feelings to our reporter’.

She was about to read the story again when the shop door was opened. Thinking it was her father returning, Cora started to hastily gather up the papers, but she looked up to see that it was her friend Ellen.

“Is Oliver any better?” Ellen asked immediately. “You must be so worried, Cora.”

“He is no different to last night,” Cora replied sadly. “The hospital has tried some sort of steam treatment for his breathing, but he seems no better.” Cora swallowed hard to stop herself crying, “And he’s still unconscious.”

Ellen drew nearer and gripped Cora’s hand. “He *will* get better, Cora. He only choked on some smoke.”

Cora nodded, her lips pressed tight.

“I just had to find out what was happening,” Ellen went on. “I only got a pass-out because I told the foreman my sister’s at home with whooping cough and I had to make her dinner. He believed me, thank goodness, but I only have half an hour and then I need to be back at the mill.”

She looked at the typed sheets spread over the table. “What’s all this about?”

“Oh… it’s what Oliver was working on last night when… when the fire started,” Cora explained, then added sheepishly: “I found them in his office this morning.”

Ellen couldn’t contain her surprise. “What? You went into the *Leek Lion* office? It was on fire last night! You might have been hurt!”

“But I have to do something, Ellen. You see, they think someone started the fire on purpose. I want to try to find out who it might have been. And concentrating on this stops me thinking about the rest of it, about what has happened to Oliver.”

Ellen had seen Cora’s determination before. This urge to act, to throw herself into something, was the way she coped with distressing situations, just like when Sarah Hulme died two years' before. But Ellen had also seen her friend's headstrong behaviour land her in real danger.

"Cora, should you really be doing this? If there's something suspicious, why not leave it to the police? What if things go wrong?"

Ellen's comments seemed to make Cora more determined than ever. "Someone has harmed Oliver. I owe it to him to find out about it. After all, I… I am his intended." Her voice trailed off as she thought once again about how their romantic plans had been turned upside down in an instant.

Ellen was quiet for a moment, wondering whether Cora's father was in his studio upstairs. "Does anyone else know about you two, yet? I mean, what you told me about last night?"

Cora gave a great sigh. "Oh, if only he had asked Father's permission and told his own parents about it! Who knows when that will happen, now? Until Oliver's well enough, I will have to keep the whole thing bottled up!"

Ellen saw how much her friend had changed since they had sat together at the Bioscope Entertainment. Then, Cora's eyes had shone with excitement at what she and Oliver were planning. Now they were dull and red-rimmed from her sleepless night and her hours of distress.

"But I'm so glad that I told you about it, Ellen," she went on. "It makes it seem more real, something I can hang on to."

"And that's why you must stay safe, Cora, and be ready for when Oliver has recovered. Then you can start your lives together."

After his trap had brought him back to the hospital, FJ Finch saw Oliver's condition was no better. He soon found himself restless – just as Cora had done earlier. He felt he simply could not spend the rest of the day confined to the small room, waiting, hoping and just staring at his son. He had tried to persuade his wife to take a respite herself from this agony of uncertainty, but she had refused to leave Oliver's side.

Inevitably, Finch returned to the scene of the fire. He was standing outside the damaged building, ruminating on how his business would survive, when an office boy approached. "Mr Finch, is it? Mr Eaton sends his regards, Sir, and asks that you attend his office as soon as you are able," he said.

Finch was taken aback. William Eaton was the printer behind the *Moorland Argus*. Although FJ had done business with him in the past, they had not spoken since the rival newspaper was launched. And Finch had told Inspector Ramm that the *Argus* could be to blame for the fire. Now the man wanted to see him. Perhaps he wants to offer some paltry sum for the *Lion* because he thinks I'm desperate, he thought.

The boy was waiting patiently for a response. "Tell Mr Eaton I shall be there directly," Finch said shortly. Even though he was suspicious what this might be about, he could not contain his curiosity. On top of that, he was in a mood to tell the printer exactly what he thought of him.

Minutes later, ready for the confrontation, Finch strode into the premises of WH Eaton Printers, Booksellers and Stationers in Derby Street. '*Home of the Moorlands Press*' proclaimed a gold-painted sign above the door. The two windows were crammed with books and magazines, including a prominent display of religious texts. Inside, the shop's shelves were stacked with printed items of every kind. The smell of printer's ink wafted from the works at the rear, accompanied by the rhythmical clank of a printing press. The sound and smell rekindled Finch's sense of loss at the destruct-ion of his own press room.

A woman assistant showed him upstairs to Eaton's office, where a young man whom Finch recognised as the journalist editing the

Argus was just leaving. He looked at Finch with an embarrassed expression and seemed about to speak, but FJ brushed past him without a word.

Eaton, a portly man in his sixties, was seated behind a desk covered with printing proofs. "Mr Finch, thank you for coming so soon," he began in an emollient tone. "I wanted you to know how very sorry I am – how sorry we all are – about the accident at your works last night. A most distressing affair, indeed. How is your son?"

"My son? Are you really so concerned, Mr Eaton? When you are trying to put me out of business? By any means possible, I might say," Finch replied, ignoring the printer's attempt at conciliation.

"Now, now, Mr Finch. I am sympathetic…"

"The fire was no accident, Mr Eaton," Finch interrupted. "But perhaps you knew that before anyone else."

"Mr Finch, whatever are you suggesting?" Eaton's cheeks went red and he seemed to struggle for breath. He unfurled a large handkerchief and put it to his face. "I can assure you that I had nothing to do with the fire. I am shocked you should even think so. It is the very last thing I would wish on a fellow businessman. Bring up the holy book from downstairs and I will swear to the Lord, if you like."

Finch was silent as he tried to judge whether the man was being honest. He knew that Eaton was a prominent churchgoer and doubted he would tell a lie on the Bible.

"What about your man, your *editor*? What was he up to last night?" FJ asked.

"Mr Finch, I am sure his time can be accounted for. But let me get to the other reason I wanted to see you so urgently – apart from expressing my sympathy, of course. I wanted to offer you my assistance."

Finch was immediately on his guard, preparing himself for some pathetic business offer. "And what is it that are you offering?" he asked warily.

"To print the *Leek Lion* for you, or at least what part of it you can rescue from your premises. As soon as you wish. It will allow you to keep the *Lion* alive, as it were, until you are back on your feet."

"But you are my competitor. You have your own newspaper now, so why would you wish to help me?"

"Call it Christian charity. Call it self-interest. It might not be helpful if the town saw that I was trying to benefit from your predicament, particularly with your son lying injured." Seeing Finch hesitate, Eaton went on, opening the palm of his hand as if to show he had nothing to hide. "Come Mr Finch, we have done business in the past, before all this… all this unpleasantness with the *Argus*. Let me offer you a hand of friendship now."

Suddenly Finch felt emotional. Here was someone he had begun to think was his enemy, even his attacker, offering to help him. He realised that, although at least one person had sought to do him and his family harm, there could be many more in Leek who might rally to support him. Perhaps there was a glimmer of hope for the future, after all.

"Mr Eaton, I barely know what to say," FJ stammered with a reticence rarely seen before.

"Say no more than 'Yes' to my offer, Mr Finch. I presume a good part of this week's edition is already set into type. If this has survived, we could put some semblance of the *Lion* onto our press. We can do it tonight."

Their discussion was interrupted when the shop assistant came into the office looking somewhat flustered. She announced that Inspector Ramm was downstairs and wished to speak to Mr Eaton immediately. The printer looked across to Finch who said apologetically: "I know what this is about. It is perhaps better that I stay."

Ramm was surprised to find the two men seated together, but before he could say anything, Finch spoke in tone which conveyed some embarrassment.

"Inspector, I hope I have not wasted any of your time, but I may have been a little hasty in what I said about the fire earlier today. To be frank, I was giving vent to my anger." He shifted uncomfortably in his chair. "Mr Eaton has assured me he knew nothing of the incident. In fact, he has made the very generous offer to print some part of the *Lion* until I my own facilities are restored."

"Exactly so, this will be an emergency edition to keep Mr Finch's title in business," said Eaton, nodding vigorously. "It is very worrying to hear the fire may have been deliberate. We must stand together against such an attempt to silence the local press."

Ramm saw that William Eaton – who was a fellow parishioner at St Edward's Church – had successfully placed himself above any suspicion, certainly in Finch's eyes. However, he still needed to get to the bottom of the affair.

"Well, I am happy that you two have made some sort of peace, but I would still like to speak to your editor, Mr Eaton. Even if he knows nothing of the fire, he may have heard of some animosity towards Mr Finch," said Ramm.

Eaton tried to conceal his discomfort that the Inspector still considered the *Moorland Argus* of some relevance to the affair, but agreed that his editor should co-operate "for the good of the community".

Finch left to see how much of the *Lion*'s work could be salvaged from the damaged building. As he hurried along Derby Street, scuffing the snow with his boots, he was already thinking which advertisements and stories could be crammed into the two pages Eaton had agreed to print. Now he had some work to focus on, Finch's mood improved a little. If he could put a reduced edition on the streets, the prospects for his newspaper were better than he had feared.

But then he was struck by a pang of guilt. The real cost of the fire was not the damage to his business, it was the harm done to his son. "I pray to God that Oliver recovers soon. We need you back at the *Lion*, my boy," he said to himself.

Chapter Fourteen

Later that Friday afternoon Cora went upstairs to tell her father she had finished her work and he decided to ask her about Ellen's visit earlier. He had been curious when the young women stopped talking as soon as he had entered the shop.

"It was good of Ellen to call round at lunchtime, wasn't it? I suppose she wanted to know how things were. She certainly looked concerned," Blake said.

"Yes, she's as worried about Oliver as I am, Father. She was there last night and saw it all."

"What were those papers?" He had seen Cora hastily put away some documents which he was sure she did not want him to see.

"It was just some notes I've been making."

"Oh, what about?" he persisted.

Cora sighed. She was finding it difficult to contain her anger about what happened to Oliver. "The fire, Father! The more I think about it, the more I am sure someone was trying to hurt Oliver!"

Nathaniel tried to placate her. "Cora dear, please try to calm yourself. I know you are upset, we all are, but it's too soon to know why the fire was started or who did it. I am sure Inspector Ramm will find out. We just have to be patient."

"But it might be because of something Oliver was writing," Cora replied. She was determined to have the last word.

Just then she spotted one of the photographs on her father's desk. It showed a group of musicians, most likely the local orchestra, she guessed. In the middle stood the white haired old fellow who had played the piano at last night's Bioscope Entertainment, but she gasped in surprise when she recognised a tall young woman standing on the right, holding a flute: Gwendoline Cope.

Looking at the elegant Miss Cope, she felt a twinge of uncertainty – or was it jealousy? Oliver had been so keen to speak to this woman and, judging by what she had read of his article, he felt deeply about her predicament. If it wasn't for Miss Cope's story, he might not have been in the office when the fire started, she thought bitterly.

She flipped over the photograph and, sure enough, it was marked in pencil as the Moorland Philharmonia. Surely Oliver's father had not been planning to print Miss Cope's picture in the newspaper?

"Has someone asked for a reprint of this one, Father?" she asked. After the heat of their previous exchange, Cora tried to adopt a more casual tone.

"Oh, that? It's one I took some months ago. Dr Jervis, the poor fellow who was found in the canal, he's one of the musicians," he said. "I wanted to show it to Inspector Ramm, but with all the other things going on, I simply haven't had chance." Nathaniel pointed out which one was James Jervis.

Cora gazed at the photograph again, a glimpse into the life of the man found under the ice. Like the rest of the gentlemen in the picture, the tall and handsome Dr Jervis was dressed in evening attire. He was standing close to the conductor, a violin in his hand, looking confidently at the camera.

How poignant, she thought, little did he know what the future held for him. Her eyes roved over the rest of the group and she realised that, as well as Miss Cope, some of the other performers were familiar. Several of them were shopkeepers in town, although they looked very different than when they were in their white work coats and aprons.

She was struck by the coincidence that Miss Cope was in the same photograph as the man who had been murdered. Two people who had been so much in her thoughts. Her mind went back to the postcard with the unusual message which she had deciphered for Inspector Ramm. She was struck by an idea. It might be fanciful, but it was one she knew she had to pursue. And that would mean going to see Gwendoline Cope sooner rather than later.

Blake observed his daughter studying the picture so intently. What was going through her mind now? he wondered. As he turned to go into his darkroom, Cora asked if she could leave for the day as she intended to call at the hospital. When she hurried downstairs, he didn't notice that she still had the orchestra photograph in her hand.

Inspector Ramm sat at his desk, seeking inspiration for the murder investigation. He reached into a drawer and took out the items he had collected – a watch, two postcards, a notebook and a bundle of receipts from the Manchester moneylender.

First he took up his magnifying glass and examined the two postcards to see if the handwriting was the same. The few words on the embroidered card were in a curled script, whilst the faint message on the mysterious card found in Jervis's pocket was in capitals. Ramm could not make a decision one way or the other.

Next he leafed through the notebook which had revealed Jervis's betting habits. He came upon a page bearing a list of initials with a sum of money noted against each.

When he had first examined the book, Ramm originally thought this was a list of yet more wagers, but now he realised it was likely to be something else – a record of people to whom Jervis owed money. He spotted '*R.C.C. £105*' which he guessed must represent the Reliance Credit Company, the moneylender from whom he was seeking answers. On another line he saw '*A.F. £25*'. Arthur Forbes had said that he was amongst a good number of people Jervis had borrowed from and here was the proof. There were more than a dozen sets of initials and Ramm quickly calculated that the total sum the doctor owed came to several hundred pounds. If the murder was connected with the doctor's debts, the killer might be on this list, he thought.

With an exasperated sigh, he pushed the items aside and contemplated the inky stains on his blotting pad as his mind turned to his other most pressing case. He feared the implications if the fire at the *Leek Lion* was not an isolated attack. There would be more damage, more injury if the arsonist was not apprehended quickly.

Although Finch had relented in his allegations against the rival newspaper, Ramm had still spoken to the *Argus* editor. The journalist had a sound alibi for the previous night. He could name a host of witnesses who would have seen him at a meeting of the Leek Liberals and their MP Robert Pearce.

Ramm had also drawn a blank with people living near to the scene. On a freezing night when most folk had chosen to stay indoors, no one had seen anything suspicious. Nor had his officers been able to discover who had raised the alarm. Apparently, a unknown man had been seen pulling the bell rope at the fire station and shouting about something going on in Market Street, but he left when the firemen arrived.

The Inspector resolved to speak to Finch again to ascertain if there was any dispute that could have prompted the attack. Now the editor had calmed down a little, he might give a more considered view as to who may have a grudge against him, his son or his newspaper.

The substance used to start the fire was a further puzzle. Motor spirit was a possibility, although there were only a handful of motor cars in the town, owned chiefly by prominent people. Surely none of those could be involved, thought Ramm, but what about their chauffeurs and mechanics? Several motor engineers and cycle shops had begun to sell petroleum and he decided a constable should do the rounds to ask about recent sales or thefts. The same officer could also visit the hardware shops that sold paraffin.

Or the arsonist may have ignited some sort of chemical. Ramm thought again about the glass containers found amongst the debris. He might need help in identifying what chemicals they should be looking for.

Cora had looked in the window of Miss Heath's shop in the Market Place many times before, but had never been inside – most of its fashionable large-brimmed creations were beyond what she or her parents were prepared to pay. This time, as she grasped the brass doorknob, she had even less interest in the hats balanced on their wooden pedestals. Gwendoline Cope was why she was there and she was relieved to see that the assistant, standing tall behind the polished mahogany counter, was the only person in the shop.

Gwendoline's features registered a vague recognition of Cora and she immediately adopted her professional mode. "Miss Blake is it not? Can I be of any help? Were you looking for something in particular?"

Cora hesitated. She had rushed from her father's studio without considering how she was going to approach Miss Cope on delicate subjects. But she was determined to find some answers. She caught sight of herself in a large ornate mirror at her side. She thought she seemed small and out of place amongst this finery.

"Miss Cope," she began, dipping her head with uncertainty before looking up at this woman who was so annoyingly attractive, so poised and tall. "I have come to speak to you about the *Leek Lion* and my… my acquaintance, Mr Finch Junior. I believe he came to see you on Wednesday evening."

A momentary tremor of concern passed through Gwendoline's dark eyes before she regained her calm demeanour.

"I am afraid I do not know what you are talking about, Miss

Blake. I do not think I know the gentleman," she said.

Cora took a deep breath. She felt guilty at having helped Oliver find Miss Cope. Otherwise he might never have been in the office when the fire was started. But if she was to get some answers from this woman, Cora knew that she too had to be truthful.

"It was me who told him who you were," Cora blurted out, "after you sent your letters to the *Lion*."

Gwendoline gasped and her whole body tensed. She glanced from side to side as if wondering what to say or how to remove Cora from the shop. The sound of movement came from above and Gwendoline looked at the ceiling nervously. She lowered her voice. "We cannot talk here. Miss Heath is in her workroom upstairs. Come into the storeroom," she said, turning and opening a door behind the counter.

The small storeroom was lined from floor to ceiling with shelves which were piled with hats, mostly black or the darkest purple and wrapped in tissue paper. Gwendoline moved a box of umbrellas out of the way, but there was still barely room for the two of them. Cora was conscious how unnervingly close they were standing, compared with when they faced each other across the counter. It was oddly intimate and the air of confrontation between them began to thaw.

Gwendoline gave a great sigh, then began in a voice that had lost some of its confidence. "You are correct, Miss Blake. It was me who wrote to the newspaper – but no one else must know that, you must promise. I was at my wits' end, I did not know who to turn to. Mr Finch promised to help." She paused. "But why should you want to know about such things?"

"Because Oliver… Mr Finch Junior, I mean… was writing an article about you last night when the fire was started at the *Lion* offices. If he had not been there working, today he would be safe and well. Instead he is…" Cora choked as she tried to continue. "He is in hospital and… and he may never recover!"

"Good heavens! In hospital!" Gwendoline reacted, then went on: "But you said the fire was started. Do you mean it was not an accident, that someone did it deliberately?"

Cora nodded, tears now running down her cheeks.

Gwendoline appeared to understand the situation and instinctively gave Cora a sympathetic squeeze of the shoulder. The two women stood silently in the claustrophobic space for some moments, the only sound their breathing and the hiss of the gas mantle on the wall. Then Gwendoline whispered: "I am so sorry to hear your awful news. Mr Finch is special to you, isn't he?" Cora nodded mutely, pulling a handkerchief from her coat pocket.

"I know it is not your fault, Miss Cope, but I think the story Oliver was writing might be connected with what happened last night. You have no idea who is watching you?"

Gwendoline looked away, lost in thought, then shook her head. "Who knows the evil that men can do?" she said at last. "I told Mr Finch to take care, in case he was seen by the fiend who is haunting me. I do so hope that what has befallen him had nothing to do with my own sorry affair."

Cora took a deep breath to calm herself. She reached into the cloth bag she carried over her shoulder and pulled out the photograph of the orchestra which she had taken from her father's desk.

"There is something else I wanted to ask, Miss Cope. What do you know about this man?" Cora held the photograph towards Gwendoline and pointed at the figure of James Jervis.

Gwendoline gasped and then seemed so flustered that she did not know how to reply. Finally she said: "Why do you ask? It is plain to see that Dr Jervis was playing in the same orchestra as myself. I know nothing else."

Cora sensed that Miss Cope was no happier with the turn in the conversation, but to her dismay, she also realised that perhaps the flute player was not aware Dr Jervis was dead. Was Cora herself to be the bearer of the shocking news? However, first she wanted to pursue her fanciful idea that Gwendoline was the mysterious 'G' who had sent the postcard seeking a secret rendezvous. "Were you not friends, close friends with him?" she asked.

At first Gwendoline's features were set in defiance and she started to shake her head vigorously, but then she stopped abruptly and instead dissolved into tears. Her defence had crumbled.

"Excuse me, Miss Blake," she said, pressing a tiny embroidered handkerchief to her nose. "Dr Jervis was, in truth, a very good and caring friend. I cannot deny it. It pains me to say it, but I have not spoken to him since long before Christmas which is why this other matter, this devil who is pursuing me, has become so fearful. I have felt so alone!"

"Did you not write to Dr Jervis last week?" Cora persisted.

"Write to him? Why would you ask that?" Gwendoline seemed startled by the new question. "No, I have had no contact with him for weeks."

"Did you meet sometimes, other than at the orchestra?"

Gwendoline looked down to hide her embarrassment at having met the man secretly. "Yes. When the weather was better, we would see each other somewhere quiet. That seems so long ago."

Cora felt a jolt of grief as the tragic image of the man under the ice flashed before her. "You do not know what has happened, do you?" was all she managed to say.

"Happened?"

Cora stammered on. "Dr Jervis has died. I was there when… when he was found …in the canal last week."

Gwendoline's dark eyes were suddenly wide with shock. "Dead? How can this be? He…" her words tailed off as she started to topple forward as if in a faint, almost on top of Cora in the confined space.

"Miss Cope, Miss Cope," said Cora as she struggled to keep Gwendoline upright, shaking her gently by the shoulders to bring her back to her senses.

"He cannot be gone from me, for ever," Gwendoline moaned.

After the pain of the previous night, when Oliver had almost perished, Cora could understand what Gwendoline must be feeling. Fate had dealt harshly with them both. Unfortunately she had something to say which was going to make matters even worse.

"Miss Cope, I must tell you that the police think it was not an accident."

Gwendoline greeted this with a fresh gasp of distress, her eyebrows were knit in a look of complete confusion and horror.

"It seems he was attacked on the towing path," Cora went on, passing on the details she had heard her father and FJ Finch talking about. "My father and I were working at the County Asylum when the doctor was brought out of the water. That is how we came to be involved."

The whispered exchange was interrupted by Gwendoline's name being called from the room above.

"That is Miss Heath. I must go to her." Miss Cope suddenly switched back to her normal demeanour, straightening her dress and apron. "Please wait here," she added before hurrying out of the storeroom and shutting the door behind her.

Cora heard rapid footsteps on the stairs, followed by indistinct conversation from above. She looked around at the piles of hats without really seeing them. Her mind was filled with the predicament she had put herself in and what she should do next. In her haste to see Miss Cope, she had not thought what she might achieve or that she might have to convey such tragic news. It was clear Gwendoline had been deeply attached to Dr Jervis, but she said she had not been in contact with him for weeks. So the mysterious postcard could not have been from her.

Just when Cora started to think this strange secretive meeting should never have taken place and perhaps she should leave as soon as possible, she heard someone descending the staircase. She gave a start when the storeroom door was flung open, but it was

Gwendoline returning to their hiding place.

"Miss Heath wanted to tell me about some orders that need to be delivered, but I wasn't really listening," Gwendoline began breathlessly. "After what you told me about poor dear James, I cannot concentrate on anything else, and certainly not Miss Heath's worries about her silly hats. To be honest, I simply want to wake up from this nightmare. I do not think I can cope with much more of it." She reached for her embroidered handkerchief again.

Cora began to feel guilty about being jealous of Miss Cope's good looks and the way Oliver had been so keen to meet her. She was about to express her sympathy when Gwendoline started to speak again, this time with a desperate resolve in her voice.

"I want to go to the place where James died," she said. Seeing Cora's shocked reaction, she went on quickly: "I know you must think me strange, Miss Blake, but I need to be there. I feel it would be a way for me to perhaps make a connection with him, with his spirit. Who knows, he may have thought of me in those last moments..." A distant look came into her eyes.

Cora was too surprised to respond immediately.

"You said it was it was on the canal?" Gwendoline continued. Her distress had turned into the sort of determination that Cora herself showed in trying circumstances. "Somewhere near the asylum where James worked, was it?"

Cora realised she could not refuse to give Gwendoline the details, no matter what the outcome. She had gone too far to back out now.

"Yes, there is a path which leads from the asylum across the fields to the canal. Father ran down to see what was going on and I followed afterwards. No one could do anything to save him."

There was another small gasp from Gwendoline and she started to dab her eyes.

"I know the place," she whispered, barely loud enough for Cora to hear only inches away. "That is where we used to meet sometimes on a summer's evening." A faint smile crossed her lips as she remembered happier days. "James would send me a message and slip out from the asylum – although he wasn't supposed to. I would be waiting for him. I am sure that is where I could still be near to him."

Gwendoline went quiet, once again lost in thought. Then she came out of her reverie. "Do you think me forward, Miss Blake? A single woman meeting a man in secret? You might be too young to know the influence a man can have, a man like James." She paused. "But perhaps not, perhaps young Mr Finch has the same effect on yourself. If that is the case, I pray you do not lose him."

Cora thought of the secrets of her own love for Oliver, the marriage proposal, their plan to leave Leek. Yes, she knew what it was to come under a man's spell. "Oliver is still alive and I still have hope," she said.

Gwendoline fixed Cora with a direct look and reached for her hand. "So, Miss Blake, will you go with me to that place by the canal? I feel I cannot go alone, that would be too… too painful… and you are the only person in the world I have told of my meetings with James there, our special place."

As much as she felt there was a growing bond between her and Miss Cope, Cora feared returning to that lonely spot on the icy canal. It was a place she had hoped to forget. If she went back so soon, she might never rid herself of the memory.

"I, I cannot say, Miss Cope," she stammered. "I must think about what all this means… to both of us."

"But I must know," Gwendoline pleaded, gripping Cora's hand tighter. "Come tomorrow and tell me your decision. Miss Heath will be out after luncheon and, in this weather, we are seeing hardly any customers."

Cora knew she would have to give an answer, one way or the other. "I will return tomorrow then, after I have had time to decide," she said.

A minute later, she was out of the cloying atmosphere of the cramped storeroom, thick with the smells of fabric and burning gas and Gwendoline's perfume, and into the frigid air of the Market Place, its chill prickling her cheeks. After all the emotion of her exchanges with Gwendoline, Cora wanted one thing: to visit Oliver.

Chapter Fifteen

The light was fading and the temperature falling by the time Inspector Ramm left the station and headed for the *Leek Lion* office, hoping to find FJ Finch. He was passing Wainwright's shop in Derby Street just as the chemist himself was coming out of the door carrying a leather briefcase.

"Busy as usual, Brother Albert?" asked Wainwright, not noticing Ramm wince at the word 'brother'. "You must have had a disturbed night with that conflagration in Market Street. What an awful affair to befall the *Leek Lion*. Some carelessness, I presume?" Wainwright's intense gaze betrayed his desire to find out more, a curiosity which he probably shared with half the town after the incident at the newspaper office.

Ramm was about to press on along the street when he remembered Captain Machin's suggestion that a chemical could have been used to start the fire. Could he risk asking Wainwright about it without sparking the man's curiosity even further? He knew he might need advice on combustible substances and, in any case, the chemist had tried to be helpful about scalpels.

"Actually Walter, we are looking into the cause of the fire. Some type of chemical may have caught alight," the Inspector said. He realised it was only a matter of time before it became public knowledge that the fire was arson.

"Indeed! A chemical?" Wainwright looked positively excited at the news. He dragged a few strands of hair across his balding head with a slight shake in his hand. Ramm noticed that this was something the man seemed to do every few minutes, obviously self-conscious of his thinning hair.

"Yes, and I may need your advice on chemicals which burn easily. Simply so we can ascertain how the fire developed, you understand."

"I should be only too pleased to help, Albert. If you wish, I could prepare a list of substances, their combustible properties, means of storage, availability and so on."

"Many thanks, Walter. I shall send an officer round for the details," said Ramm, turning to continue along Derby Street.

"By the way, have you made any more progress with your other investigations? I heard that awful death in the canal was someone connected with the asylum, was it not? And there was the business with the scalpel which I helped you with. I do hope you have cleared matters up." The chemist leaned closer to Ramm, apparently hoping to glean any new titbit of information.

Ramm resisted a groan at the man's inquisitiveness. He reminded himself that assisting a police inquiry had probably been the high point of Wainwright's week, particularly if he had to cope with a wife who was indisposed.

"Investigations are still going on, Walter, and there is little I can say on the matter. However, your assistance is much appreciated."

With that, the Inspector managed to extricate himself and walked around the corner into Market Street where he found oil lamps had been lit in the blackened interior of the *Lion* building. Stepping through the doorway he saw that the man who usually ran the printing press was groping about in the gloom, stacking up piles of singed paper and buckled tins of ink. His clothes, hands and face were covered in dirt and ash. A young lad was sweeping up debris with a large brush, raising clouds of dust in the process.

Planks of wood had been nailed in place as a temporary repair to the staircase and from upstairs he could hear the sound of voices, including that of FJ Finch. After a closer look at the rickety nature of the repair, Ramm decided against scaling the stairs himself and instead shouted up: "Mr Finch, can I have a word?"

With a fearsome creaking of wood and a new fall of dust, Finch descended, followed slowly by a man in overalls who was carrying a shallow metal tray with great care. Ramm saw that it contained metal type arranged in columns. Finally Nathaniel Blake came down to join them.

"Inspector, we have been busy making rough repairs and then rescuing some of our stories and advertisements which Mr Eaton has kindly agreed to print tonight. Nathaniel came round to help. The upstairs was not really damaged, so we have been able to piece together enough for a couple of pages, haven't we Alfred?" Finch clapped the compositor on his dusty back in congratulations.

Ramm was struck by the change in Finch's demeanour since earlier in the day. The prospect of salvaging something of his newspaper and being able to throw himself into some work, seemed to have given him respite from his distress over his son.

Alfred marched off with the tray of type, bound for Eaton's printing works, and Ramm asked Finch about likely reasons for the attack.

"I have been puzzling over that all afternoon, Inspector," Finch replied. "There are one or two ne'er do wells who regularly appear in our pages, but I cannot believe they would risk something as serious as last night's fire. And there have been the usual disagreements in our correspondence columns, mainly about council matters, but nothing to warrant attacking my offices."

"What about business disputes?"

"Nothing springs to mind. Obviously my first thought was the *Argus*, but…" Finch's explanation trailed off in embarrassment.

"Their editor is definitely in the clear, Mr Finch, and I think Mr Eaton has shown himself to be distinctly honourable."

"Of course, of course. I was overcome about Oliver when I made those rash comments," Finch responded hastily.

"Is your son showing any sign of recovery?" Ramm asked. Though the light from the oil lamps was poor, he saw Finch's expression darkened instantly.

"He is no different, I'm afraid," said Finch, his voice little more than a whisper.

"That is unfortunate. I don't want to trouble you any further, but there is something else I must ask. Did you and Oliver always lock the front door when you were upstairs in the office at night?"

Finch's shoulders sank. "I must admit there have been times when neither of us bothered to check the door."

The three men fell silent as they considered the implication. How simple it would have been for someone to enter the building and cause mayhem.

Ramm was about to leave when Blake spoke up. "There was something I wanted to tell you, Inspector."

"Why, did you see something suspicious last night?" Ramm asked earnestly, ready to seize on the merest crumb of a clue.

"No, it was about that other matter, the death on the canal. I was sure I had seen the fellow before and I have found a photograph I took in the autumn. Dr Jervis was a member of the Moorland Philharmonia."

"Was he indeed," said Ramm, thinking of the coincidence that Edna had watched the orchestra the previous weekend. "I knew he played the violin, but I thought that was just at the asylum – they have their own orchestra, can you believe? I did not realise he had been coming into Leek to perform."

"I have a copy of the photograph, but I was not expecting to see you here. I can drop it off at the station, if you wish. If you want to know more about the orchestra, Mr Alsop, the conductor, is probably the best one to speak to," Blake added.

"Yes, I've come across Mr Alsop. It may be worth me making some enquiries, but to be frank, this affair is leading in many different directions and other avenues may prove more rewarding. It appears that Dr Jervis led quite a colourful life."

The Inspector was about to leave when Blake spoke again. "Actually, there was something about the fire that I ought to mention."

Ramm fixed Blake with an alert gaze. The photographer had been a source of useful information – and sometimes wild theories – in the past and he knew he should take notice.

"It is probably nothing, but Cora seems to have convinced herself that the fire was started by someone who wanted to harm Oliver. She thinks it could be connected with something he was writing."

"Miss Blake is a very resourceful young lady," said Ramm. He still remembered their first encounter five years earlier when Cora, a bloodstain on her dress, had appeared at the station to report a murder. "Perhaps it is something I should bear in mind. Mr Finch, I presume you know what your son was working on?"

"I shall be able to give you details in the morning, Inspector, after I have looked on his desk. I have just been up to the office and at the moment it is in complete disarray," Finch replied. He knew about the article that Oliver was writing and wondered just how much he should reveal.

Despite her winter boots, Cora tried her best to tiptoe along the corridor at the Cottage Hospital. Unsure about how many visitors Oliver was allowed, she was wary of being discovered by the Matron and being ordered out. She came to the door of the small ward where Oliver lay and opened it cautiously, fearful of what she might find. But her heart leapt when she saw that his eyes were open and he seemed to be breathing more steadily.

Mrs Finch, still in the chair beside the bed where she had been all day, turned to look who had come into the room. Cora was surprised to see her mood appeared little changed, her expression as downcast as before. Why isn't she pleased that he's getting better? Cora wondered. Then Oliver spoke and she understood.

An unintelligible ramble came from Oliver's mouth, a confusion of unrelated words, exclamations, even foul oaths she had never heard him utter before.

"He has been like this since he started to come round an hour ago," Mrs Finch told Cora quietly. "It is as if he cannot talk or think straight. He doesn't know where he is or even who I am," she added, wringing her hands.

At the sound of a voice, Oliver's head turned and he looked towards Cora with apparently unseeing eyes. "Who is that?" he asked in a cracked voice that sounded like his throat was parched.

"Oliver it's me. Cora."

He showed no sign of recognition. He turned to face the wall again and began to mumble to himself.

Cora gasped and held her hand to her mouth, stifling a cry of despair. The situation was worse than ever. Oliver was conscious, but was no longer the same person. It was as if his brain was addled. She gazed at him, too despondent to think of anything to say to Mrs Finch.

Their silent vigil, disturbed only by the patient's bizarre utterances, continued for some time until the door opened again. It was Dr Handbridge. He stepped up to the bed and took out a stethoscope to listen to Oliver's breathing. Then he took the young man's chin, moved his head from side to side and peered into his eyes. Finally the doctor sighed and gave a shake of the head.

"What do you think, Doctor?" asked Mrs Finch.

"Perhaps I could have a word with you, Mrs Finch," he replied, indicating they should move away from the bed. He glanced towards Cora and was about to say something else when Mrs Finch divined his intention. "It's all right, Doctor. Miss Blake is almost part of the family."

Hearing that gave Cora the nearest thing to happiness she had felt all day. Although she knew Oliver had not told his parents he intended to marry, perhaps his mother guessed it was inevitable.

"Well, Oliver's breathing is a little easier, which is encouraging. The damage to his airways may not be as serious as we feared," Dr Handbridge began in a confidential tone. "But it looks like his senses have been affected, probably by the smoke and fumes."

"But he doesn't know us! And the things he's saying!" said Mrs Finch urgently.

"Try not to distress yourself, I'm sure he has no idea what he is saying. He's in a confused state."

"How soon will he get back to his old self, Doctor?" There was desperation in Mrs Finch's voice now.

"Only time will tell, Mrs Finch. This appears to be some sort of gas poisoning which I have not come across before."

After what she had talked about with Gwendoline Cope, Cora had wanted to speak privately to her friend Ellen that evening. In her own home it would have raised her parents' suspicions if she had taken Ellen up to her bedroom, and the Simms' cottage in Cruso's Yard had barely enough space for the family with its numerous children, let alone visitors.

They chose to meet in the porch of the Old Church, just up the street from where Ellen lived. The outer door was open and it was freezing cold in there, but at least there was a bench where they could sit. With no service or choir practice that evening, they thought they would not be disturbed.

On the other side of narrow Church Street there was much activity, however. Carter's pawnbrokers was doing a brisk trade as people used coins from their new wage packets to reclaim treasured items. Next door, folk were seeking a bed for the night at Ma Duggan's lodging house. Nearby, Friday night drinkers were heading for The Golden Lion Inn and the Conservative Club.

In the church porch, talk of Miss Cope had to wait because the first thing Ellen asked about was Oliver's condition.

"It is so upsetting, Ellen," said Cora. "His breathing seems a little better and his eyes are open much more. But when he's awake he seems to be agitated because he doesn't know anyone or where he is. And his words are all jumbled up. It's almost a relief when he drifts off again, because at least he's at peace."

"He didn't recognise you?" said Ellen in horror.

"No! Nor his mother," Cora replied. Then she told Ellen what Dr Handbridge had said about how fumes from the fire could have caused Oliver's confusion and the memory loss.

"So will he ever remember?" Ellen asked bluntly. She was too shocked at what it could mean for her friend, the marriage proposal and their plans to leave, to think of a gentler way of putting it.

Cora shook her head, doing her best to hold in her tears. "The doctor doesn't seem to know. We just have to wait."

"What else has happened?" Ellen asked with some trepidation. She had been concerned at how Cora was behaving when she saw her poring over Oliver's papers earlier in the day. She hoped her friend had calmed down a little now.

"I have been to see Gwendoline Cope," Cora announced.

"Who?"

Cora took a deep breath and began to explain. "She's the person who has been writing to the *Lion* about being followed by a man, the one that Oliver was writing about when the office was set on fire. No one is supposed to know her name, Ellen, so this is in the strictest confidence."

"Of course, Cora! I won't mention it to anyone. But why did you go to see her?"

"It's complicated, but I thought it was important. The thing is, as well as this horrible business at the *Lion*, Miss Cope knew the man who was found in the canal last week." Cora gave an embarrassed smile. "In fact I think she was totally smitten with him. They played music together and they used to meet in secret. But she didn't know that he had been murdered or even that he was dead – I had to tell her."

Ellen couldn't hide her dismay. "Murdered? Don't tell me you are getting mixed up with a murder as well as the fire. Leave it to the police. Please, Cora!"

"I'm already 'mixed up' with it. Father and I were there when he was found, weren't we? And I've seen a postcard that was in the man's pocket. His name was Jervis. He was a doctor at the asylum and he played in the orchestra with Miss Cope. I thought perhaps she had sent the postcard, but now it looks like it was someone else."

Cora was talking faster and faster as she unburdened herself of the complicated affair and all her theories. Ellen was becoming more concerned. It seemed her friend was behaving more recklessly than ever. It was as if what had happened to Oliver had made her care less what became of herself. But before Ellen could calm her, Cora ploughed on to the most surprising part.

"She wants me to go with her to see the place where Dr Jervis died, out on the canal. She says it's where they used to meet." Cora fell silent and looked at her friend, waiting for her reaction. She guessed what Ellen would say – even Gwendoline had admitted the idea might sound peculiar – but Cora did not know how to say 'No' to Miss Cope.

"Don't do it, Cora, please," begged Ellen. "This Gwendoline, whoever she is, must be upset – who wouldn't be? But going to the canal is really strange. What does she want to do? Take some flowers? She might even try to throw herself in!"

"She says she wants to contact his spirit. I think she might be a spiritualist," Cora replied. A few months earlier she had read an article about spiritualism in one of the ladies' magazines her father bought to keep his portrait clients occupied. A growing number of people, including some famous characters, believed they could commune with the spirits of loved ones.

"I've heard of those people, they do some very odd things," said Ellen warily. "You need to steer clear of this. Let her go on her own."

That was the sort of level-headed response she had given to some of Cora's wilder schemes in the past. Ellen's life was rooted in the daily grind of work in a silk mill and years earlier she had suffered at the hands of its malevolent owner. She was not given to flights of fancy, she knew how things could go wrong. Above all, she was concerned for her friend's safety.

In her icy bedroom that night, Cora lay thinking how her life had skewed in new and disturbing directions over the last 24 hours. Seeing Oliver so confused and hearing that his memory could be damaged had been a crushing blow. It brought home her worst fears. Their golden plans for married life seemed a long way off. He might not even remember he has proposed to me, she thought bleakly.

She started to wonder whether it would have been better if she had never accepted his hand and his exciting scheme for their life in New Zealand. Perhaps her sense of loss would have not been so great.

She shook her head to cast away the thought. There was no going back. She had said 'Yes' to Oliver and that meant 'In sickness and in health', no matter where they finished up.

Her thoughts turned to Gwendoline Cope. In truth she knew she should tell Inspector Ramm what she had discovered, although it would mean revealing things Miss Cope was desperate to keep private.

It would be difficult to face going back to that fateful spot, but the more Cora thought about Gwendoline, the more she had sympathy for her plight – robbed of someone she cared for, pursued by someone else she did not know. Trying to commune with Dr Jervis's spirit had sounded decidedly odd, but visiting the place might bring the woman some comfort.

Cora decided not to heed Ellen's warnings. Tomorrow she would visit the hat shop and tell Miss Cope she would go with her to the canal. And no one else would know.

Chapter Sixteen

The Leek Lion

SATURDAY, JANUARY 18TH 1907

Special Edition

Following the destructive fire at our premises on Thursday last, we present this Special Edition courtesy of Mr. W.H. Eaton of the Moorland Press. Circumstances dictate that only a selection of our normal content is available today, but we feel duty bound to maintain the service to readers and advertisers of which we are justly proud.

We will strive to publish a more extensive edition in the near future and resume the level of reportage which readers have enjoyed for the past twenty years. Although the incident has caused considerable physical damage to our premises, disruption to our business and significant family distress, our spirit is undaunted. But no matter what, the *Lion* will continue to roar!

On a personal note, the Editor would like to convey thanks to Captain Machin of Leek Fire Brigade and the town's firemen for their tireless efforts on Thursday evening, to members of the public who gave assistance, and chiefly to Mr. John Gibb for his selfless act of bravery.

It had just passed eight o'clock on Saturday morning. In any other week FJ Finch and his son would have been in the office, looking back with satisfaction, grimacing at the occasional typesetting error, looking forward with enthusiasm.

This morning was far different. Finch was at his kitchen table, the *Leek Lion* was reduced to a single sheet, Oliver was in a hospital bed and FJ had little desire to think about the future.

The fervour which had buoyed him up the previous afternoon

had drained away and the reality of the dire circumstances which faced his newspaper and his family had set in. It might take weeks to get the printing press back in action, for a new stock of paper and ink to be delivered, the staircase safely repaired, the upstairs rooms cleaned, windows and doors replaced. And he would have to try to put the newspaper together on his own. Oliver, his right hand man, his beloved son, was not there to help.

Looking again at the two sides of the broadsheet page, FJ was satisfied to have rescued at least part of that week's offering. The front was filled with advertisements: keeping advertisers happy and retaining a slice of his revenue was vital if the business was to survive the fire. The reverse side was a ragbag of small news items.

But Finch felt a twinge of regret that two important stories were not to be seen. He had delayed writing his report on the murder of the County Asylum doctor until the very last minute and had never had chance to complete it. As for Oliver's investigation of the mystery woman being pursued by a stranger, FJ suspected his son was typing it on the fateful evening when the fire started. He had no idea whether it would ever be found.

However, the loss of a story was a small matter compared to what the Finches had really risked – the loss of their only son. FJ and his wife had discussed Oliver's condition long into the night. They were both struggling to come to terms with what the future might hold for him, whether his sharp brain would be permanently blunted. They were equally at a loss as to who would have wanted to inflict the calamity upon them.

It was barely coming light when Martha Finch had set off along Bath Street to the hospital and FJ intended to go there himself shortly. He would dispense with his usual Saturday stroll around the town, chatting to acquaintances. He would spend the time with Oliver instead, hoping to see an improvement.

At the Blake house, Nathaniel gave a sigh as he perused the *Leek Lion* over breakfast. "I must say, Finch did well to have this printed so quickly, but there are still some difficult times ahead," he said, casting a concerned look across the table at his daughter.

Both he and Edith had been concerned about Cora when she came home from seeing Ellen Simms the previous evening. They had seen how downcast she had seemed after visiting Oliver, but later her mood seemed to swing between anxiety and agitation. Nathaniel was worried that she may be embarking on one of her headstrong campaigns to find the truth, this time about the dreadful fire.

Cora avoided meeting his eye and said nothing, apparently concentrating on her slice of bread and jam.

"Perhaps you should not come to the studio this morning. You need to rest," Nathaniel suggested.

"No, I want to keep myself busy, Father. It stops me thinking about other things," she replied.

Half an hour later, when they were walking to the studio together, Nathaniel remembered the photograph she had been so curious about the previous day.

"You recall that picture of the orchestra you were looking at? Where did you put it? When I came to take it to Inspector Ramm I couldn't find it," he said.

Cora gave the impression of thinking the matter over, although she knew it was safely in the bag on her shoulder. "I think I put it in one of the drawers, Father. It must have got covered up. When we get to work I shall find it for you."

She hoped she could return the picture to her father's desk without him noticing. Her other task would be to find a copy of the postcard which had been sent to Dr Jervis. She was curious to hear what Gwendoline Cope would say about it.

Inspector Ramm arrived at the police station that morning to be told that Manchester Constabulary had already been in touch by telephone. However any spark of hope that a breakthrough was imminent was dashed when Sergeant Reynolds conveyed what had been said.

"They have been to see that moneylender character. Yes, he admits he sent a *colleague* to chivvy up Jervis with his payments a couple of weeks ago. Apparently his man had told him things got a bit physical when Jervis started to argue the odds. But since then he says he has had no contact with the doctor."

"Well, he would deny anything else, wouldn't he?" said Ramm, sceptically.

"It looks like the Manchester lads are going to wait for further instructions, Sir."

"Let me think about it," Ramm replied as he turned to leave the front desk.

"Oh, and Mr and Mrs Jervis have sent a message. They spent the night at The George and say they will be here in half an hour," Reynolds added.

James Jervis's parents had had several days and a long journey from Cumberland to digest the news of their son's death. However the white-haired couple still appeared confounded by the situation when they faced Inspector Ramm across his desk.

They immediately began to pose questions, or rather, it was Mrs Jervis who did most of the talking. Her husband, a tall gaunt figure, sat as if in a daze, struggling to come to terms with what had happened.

After telling the couple how James Jervis had been found in the canal, the victim of an attack, Ramm produced the gold pocket watch to confirm it was their son's. That was the point when Mr Jervis Senior came alive, reaching forward to grasp the watch. He ran his thin fingers over an object that was obviously dear to him, then he opened it to check the engraving inside.

“Oh yes, this belonged to James,” he said, wiping a tear away. “We gave it to the dear boy when he qualified.” He spoke with an educated accent which betrayed both his north country origins and a life in the professions. The man was probably a doctor himself, Ramm thought.

“What we want to know, Inspector, is exactly what happened to James and why,” said Mrs Jervis, a frustrated firmness in her voice.

“If we knew that, Mrs Jervis, we might be a lot closer to finding his attacker. But I am afraid we have no definite idea at the moment,” Ramm replied. “I gather your son was intending to visit you last week.”

“Yes, we were expecting him on the late train into Carlisle on the Monday, the sixth I think it was,” Mrs Jervis explained. “When he did not turn up we were not alarmed. We thought it might be something to do with all this snow, or that he had to stay at Cheddleton for an extra day. We knew he had his work cut out looking after his patients.” She paused and a blank look came into her eyes as if she was picturing her son’s busy life at the County Asylum.

“We started to become worried as the week passed and we had still heard nothing from him. When the telegram arrived from the asylum on Sunday night, asking if he was with us, we knew something was amiss.”

There was a lull in the conversation as the parents took in the mystery of it all. A constable came in with tea, Ramm stood to poke the office fire and then returned to his seat. He felt the time was right to broach the rather delicate subject of James Jervis’s character.

“I believe your son had a keen interest in horse racing,” he began.

“James was an enthusiast for all kinds of sport. He was an athlete, you know,” Mrs Jervis began quickly.

“What I actually meant was betting on horse races,” said Ramm.

The doctor's mother looked unhappily at her husband and it was he who spoke next, clearing his throat loudly as if to show his difficulty in finding the words. "When it came to horses, to betting, James was weak." He almost spat out the last word. "The boy never seemed to learn from his mistakes. We helped him where we could, but there was no end to it. We had to tell him 'No more, we've done enough'."

Mrs Jervis reached across and patted her husband's hand. "But he was so clever. He did so well at university and with his music," she said, anxious to give the other side of her son's character. "And he was so dedicated to his work at the asylum, and that's something not everyone could face."

"Yes, Dr Forbes has told me how accomplished he was," said Ramm, taking the opportunity to introduce Jervis's friend into the conversation.

"Forbes? Arthur Forbes? What does he know about it?" asked Mrs Jervis sharply.

"Well, Dr Forbes has told me he had been your son's friend for years. And now he is on the staff at the County Asylum. He joined last year, at the same time as your son. Did you not know?"

"James had mentioned it. We have heard plenty about him in the past. He was always pestering James," she replied dismissively. "Not really our type," she added.

Ramm considered whether it would be indelicate to press her on what she meant by that, but in view of Forbes' importance to the investigation – both as a witness and possible suspect – he felt he had no alternative. "Type?" he asked simply.

"The man's effeminate," Jervis Senior blurted out, gruffly. "Not to be trusted, in my opinion."

"Was there something in particular about his trustworthiness?" Ramm asked, looking from one to the other.

"I always thought he was a bad influence on James, some of the things they used to get up to at university. And he's a secretive sort.

But then he would have to be, wouldn't he?" Mrs Jervis replied with a knowing look.

The Inspector saw they were prejudiced against Arthur Forbes and blamed him for influencing on their son. However, from what he had already gleaned about James Jervis, the fellow had needed little encouragement to get into trouble.

Towards the end of the morning, Blake left Cora to lock up the shop and set off for home. On the way, he went via Market Street to see if Finch happened to be at the *Lion* office. Seeing the doorway was not blocked, he went cautiously inside and shouted his friend's name.

"I'm up here, Nathaniel!" came the reply from the upper floor. Blake made his way carefully up the roughly repaired steps and found Finch in the office on the second floor. The room was smeared with dust and stains from the fire and still smelled strongly of smoke despite a sharp wind coming through the broken window. Finch appeared to be trying to return the office to some sort of order, darting from one place to another, picking up documents which were scattered on the floor, then glancing at each one before adding it to one of the piles on the two desks. There was nervous energy to his erratic movements.

"I came to see how Oliver is," said Blake.

"The same, I'm afraid. I spent an hour with him this morning. Martha is frightfully distressed. He still doesn't seem to know where he is or be able to say anything sensible. I thought I may as well come here and try to do something practical, but this is going to take an age," he said despondently.

"Oh, I'm sorry to hear that. You and Martha must take care not to exhaust yourselves, FJ," said Blake. Looking around at the confusion in the office, he added: "I never thought I would see a *Leek Lion* out today after what happened here on Thursday night."

Finch seemed to brighten slightly at the mention of the special edition. "It's not perfect, Nathaniel, but better than nothing. In fact, one or two people have already called round to wish us well. Of course, there were plenty of stories missing, including my piece on the canal murder. Ramm might have collared his man by the time I can print that. And there is a good one that Oliver was working on."

"Oh, which was that?" Blake immediately thought about Cora's idea that one of Oliver's stories had been the reason why someone had started the fire.

"He had spoken to that woman who says she is being harassed by some stranger. She's the one who wrote to us anonymously. It was only thanks to Cora that he was able to find her."

"Cora? How was she involved?" Blake asked with growing anxiety.

"Apparently she knows this woman through some musical events, or something."

Perhaps that was why she was so interested in the photograph of the orchestra, Blake thought. By strange coincidence, the same picture that included Dr Jervis.

"Did Oliver tell you her name?"

"It is supposed to be confidential, Nathaniel, but I think he said it was Gwendoline."

Blake felt increasingly ill at ease, he was sure that Cora was keeping something from them.

"I've been thinking about what Cora says about the fire, how it might be connected to Oliver's work," FJ went on. "The strange thing is, I cannot find that story anywhere. I'm sure he told me he was going to be working on it on Thursday night, so I expected to see at least some of it here."

He waved a hand towards Oliver's untidy desk. "Of course, there's paper everywhere, but I've searched on his desk, on his typewriter, on the floor and there is no sign of it. I can't even find his notebook and he was never without that."

FJ paused and became agitated. "Perhaps Cora is right! Perhaps some rotter was in here going through Oliver's things. Who would do that, after all that's happened?"

Blake was too flabbergasted to respond. He suspected he knew precisely who that person was.

Inspector Ramm considered his conversation with Mr and Mrs Jervis and concluded that he had not really learned anything to assist his investigation. What he needed was something new, some fresh information that would be a clue to the attacker or their motive. The only aspect of James Jervis's colourful life which he had not yet explored was his music. Perhaps he should act on Blake's suggestion and speak to Jeremiah Alsop, he thought.

He had been surprised to discover that the doctor had found the time to come into Leek and play in an orchestra. Thinking of Jervis's dalliances with the fairer sex, he wondered if there was another attraction in the town as well as the music.

Sergeant Reynolds checked a directory and informed him that Alsop lived only a short distance away in Southbank Street and so Ramm decided to visit him in person, rather than summon the conductor to the station. It might soften the attitude of a man who was known for being rather stand-offish.

True to his reputation, Jeremiah Alsop was somewhat grudging when he showed the Inspector into the tiled hallway of his substantial terraced house. He led the way into the front parlour which was hung with heavy velvet curtains. The grate was fitted with a cast iron gas fire, but it was unlit and the room was decidedly chilly.

In the crowded parlour there was no feminine touch. This man is married to his music, Ramm thought. The sloping lid of an office desk was open, revealing a profusion of papers and crumpled concert programmes. The dining table was covered with sheet music and by one wall was a dusty piano, its ornate candle holders dripping with old wax. In a corner, Ramm spotted the polished brass horn of a phonograph gleaming in the gloom. On a shelf below, he could make out more than a dozen phonograph cylinders in cardboard tubes marked 'Edison Bell Records', and next to them was an open tin of steel needles. How Edna would like one of those contraptions, he thought.

Alsop noticed what he was looking at. "Not as good as listening to the real thing, of course," he said with a wave of the hand, as if dismissing the costly machine as a mere trifle. "I have one of the new ones on order from London, they use flat records instead of cylinders, you know," he added with false modesty.

"So Inspector, is there something you require from me?" he continued, gazing quizzically at the officer.

"I wanted to speak to you about the Moorland Philharmonia and in particular one of your players, Dr Jervis."

"Oh yes? Violin One? He's on some sort of holiday at the moment, I believe, so I cannot help you if you are looking for him."

"I'm afraid that Dr Jervis is not on holiday. He is deceased," Ramm replied. The fire at the *Leek Lion* and the failings of its rival newspaper meant that the identity of the body in the canal was not yet common knowledge in the town.

"That's a pity. I need players of his quality. Now I shall have to find a new leader for the violins," said Alsop, shaking his head and pursing his lips in disappointment.

Ramm realised this man saw life through the lens of his orchestra. Alsop did not seem affected by the news and had not asked how Jervis had died. Matters of life and death were perhaps secondary to his music.

"It would help to know how Dr Jervis got on with the other players in the orchestra. Was there any discord, as you might call it?"

Alsop suddenly appeared suspicious. "Why? What would the orchestra have to do with this?" he asked, sweeping his long white hair back with a dramatic gesture.

Ramm knew that if he mentioned the word 'murder' the conductor would be even less co-operative, and so decided not to go into details. "Probably nothing, Mr Alsop. I am just gathering information on his activities. So, were you aware of any dispute with the other musicians?"

"As far as I could tell, he had got on well with everyone since he joined us last summer. Although my focus is always on the music, of course. I did notice that he was particularly popular with our ladies – we have three in the orchestra. Womenfolk can be easily impressed, can they not?"

"Perhaps you could give me their details?"

"I don't know whether that would be quite in order, Inspector."

"Mr Alsop, if you are not prepared to help the police, I can make a note accordingly."

With much huffing, Alsop shuffled through the papers in his desk to find the addresses of the members of the orchestra.

"By the way, did you happen to lend Dr Jervis any money?"

"Why on earth would I do that? The man was a doctor!" Alsop tried to appear shocked, but there was something in his hasty response that led Ramm to think he knew more than he was admitting.

"But perhaps some of the other musicians may have done so?"

"Occasionally I saw banknotes being exchanged, but I preferred not to ask what was going on. It was really none of my business."

After closing her father's shop at lunchtime, Cora walked the short distance into the Market Place to the hat shop. She saw that Gwendoline Cope was arranging long and elaborate hat pins in a glass display case. Perhaps it was her dark mood, but to Cora these sharp things looked as much like weapons as decorations.

Gwendoline looked up nervously as Cora went in. "Oh, Miss Blake. I am so glad to see you, I was worried that you might not come. Miss Heath has gone out as I expected, so we are alone," she said breathlessly. She hurried to the door, twisting the key and flipping a sign in the window to say 'Closed'.

She turned and fixed Cora with an anxious look. "Well? What have you decided?"

"Miss Cope, I will go with you to the canal where I saw… the incident. It would not be my own choice, but if this gives you some peace of mind then I feel should help to you."

"Oh, thank you! This means so much to me," Gwendoline replied, reaching forward to touch Cora's arm. "I have been thinking so much about dear James and what might have happened to him. I feel I must reach out to him, one last time."

Cora nodded uncertainly, trying not to reveal her misgivings about Gwendoline's spiritualist quest.

"I think we should go tomorrow, if that is convenient with you," Gwendoline continued. "In the morning I shall be at a prayer meeting, of course, so perhaps in the afternoon? I think it will be most convenient to catch the train to Wall Grange and then we can walk along the canal from there. I have checked the timetable and a train departs at half-past one. We could return by a later train, there are several in the timetable. And of course, I shall buy the tickets – it will only be sixpence each."

Cora realised that Gwendoline had it all planned out and there was little room for discussion. She agreed to meet Miss Cope at the railway station in time for the train.

Then she reached into her bag and pulled out a copy her father had made of the postcard which had been found in Dr Jervis's pocket. "Do you recognise this?" Cora asked.

Gwendoline glanced at the picture, then studied the faint writing on the back as if trying to make out what it said.

"How very strange!" she said, frowning as she continued to look at the message. "I did sometimes send messages to Dr Jervis, but not this one. I have never seen it before." Then she faced Cora and asked urgently: "Where did you get it from? It must be someone pretending to be me!"

Gwendoline gasped when Cora told her where the postcard had been found. "It must have been sent by someone who knew about us," Gwendoline murmured.

"Miss Cope, I know this matter is very private, but shouldn't you speak to the police? It might help them find out what actually happened to your friend."

"No, no, it would be too embarrassing. Please don't tell anyone!" Gwendoline begged.

Cora reluctantly agreed and left without delay. She did not wish to be late for luncheon in case her mother asked where she had been.

There were few people in the Market Place and she did not notice a man in a long dark coat, sheltering in a doorway on the opposite side of the square. His head and neck were swathed against the cold. He had been there for some time, observing the milliner's shop and the young woman with whom Gwendoline Cope had been talking.

When Ramm returned to the police station he decided to check on Oliver Finch's condition. If the young man recovered sufficiently to be interviewed he might be able to shed some light on what happened on the night of the fire. At the moment no other witnesses had been found.

He picked up the telephone on the reception counter and asked the operator to put him through to the Memorial Hospital. The call took some time to connect because the Matron had to go in search of Dr Handbridge to bring him to the receiver.

"Ah Inspector, I'm glad you called. Oliver Finch's condition is proving to be quite a conundrum. It's far worse than other cases I have seen where victims were overcome by smoke. He lapses into unconsciousness and when he comes round he appears very confused. It might be temporary, it might not."

"And this is as a result of the smoke?"

"Rather more noxious than that, I think. I have been looking through some Medical Journal reports on carbon monoxide poisoning and the effects of chemical gases. Some of the symptoms recorded look very similar to what Oliver has now. I'm supposing it must have been fumes from some substance in the fire. Perhaps it was something they used in the printing works?"

Doubt about Oliver's recovery was not what Ramm had hoped to hear. He thought once more about whether a chemical had been used to start the fire. Was that the substance which had also robbed Oliver of his senses?

Cora spent the afternoon in her room, reading through letters and notes that Oliver had sent her occasionally and which she kept in the cabinet next to her bed.

Although it was colder up in the attic than down in the kitchen, she wanted to be alone. Her spirits were low. Her father had passed on the news that Oliver was no better and she wondered when she could face going to the hospital again. Reading his letters might remind her of what he was really like.

Was it only a week since Oliver had proposed to her in the tea room at Rudyard? So much had happened since then! It was frightening to think what another week might bring.

She began to worry that she had been too hasty in going to see Miss Cope and in agreeing to the adventure with her the next day. She was no wiser as to who might have started the fire. However she believed that Miss Cope's friendship with Dr Jervis was really something Inspector Ramm should be told about, as well as the fact that the postcard had probably been forged.

Cora came to a decision. She would steel herself for the excursion to the canal and once it was over and done with, she would tell the Inspector what she knew.

When the family gathered for their evening meal, the improvement in young William's cough seemed to lift the mood. Although it was good news that he might return to St Luke's School on Monday, Cora sensed that her parents were making an effort to be positive for her sake.

"Do you have anything planned for tomorrow Cora?" her mother asked as she cleared away the dishes to the scullery.

"Well, after church I thought I would pop to the hospital to ask after Oliver," Cora replied.

"Who knows? By tomorrow there might be some improvement," said Nathaniel.

"And then after lunch I am meeting Ellen. We have a lot to talk about, what with the things planned for the women's campaign." Ellen had covered for her in the past and Cora thought that mentioning her friend would reassure her parents. "After that we might go to see someone else," she added casually.

"Oh? Who is that, Cora?" asked her mother.

"Er..." Cora hesitated, "just someone who used to play the flute at the dance school concerts sometimes. Gwendoline Cope, you may not remember her."

"I don't recall you mentioning her before," said Edith with a puzzled expression.

Nathaniel sat suddenly rigid when he heard the name Gwendoline. This must be the woman that Finch had referred to that morning, the one Oliver had been writing about. Neither he nor Edith had heard of this friend of Cora's before.

He was becoming convinced that their daughter was concealing something. In the past Cora had pursued wild theories and gone on secretive jaunts, and not all of them had turned out well. He already suspected she had taken Oliver's papers from the *Lion* office. Now she might be planning something else, just as foolhardy.

"After everything that has happened this last week, Cora, I think you would be better staying in tomorrow and resting," he said.

"Oh Father, please do not concern yourself. Spending time with a friend might be good for me," Cora replied.

Nathaniel said no more, but was still not satisfied. He knew his daughter was up to something.

That evening Albert and Edna Ramm were enjoying a peaceful hour by the fire. Ramm was staring into the glowing coals and musing on the day's events, the rather awkward conversations with Jervis's parents and Jeremiah Alsop. He mentioned the phonograph he had seen at the conductor's house and Edna was immediately envious.

"If the fellow is buying one of those new-fangled ones that play flat records, he might want to sell the one he already has. I might drop him a note to ask what he's planning to do with it," he said, much to his wife's delight.

A comfortable silence followed. Edna was leafing through her new copy of *Enquire Within*, a weekly women's magazine which offered fashions, recipes and 'homely reading'. Albert was thinking back over the week and the many things he had learned, from the workings of an asylum to the wiles of a bookmaker's runner.

He hoped to recall a neutral topic, not connected with violent death or crime, to talk to Edna about.

"By the way, I didn't know that Walter Wainwright's wife was an invalid," he said.

Edna looked up from her magazine. "The chemist's wife? It's her mind, apparently. They say she's in Cheddleton, poor woman."

"Do you mean she's in the asylum?" responded Ramm, musing on the number of times his enquiries seemed to cross the threads of townsfolk's lives in a place like Leek. And the times that Edna came up with interesting titbits of gossip that had passed him by. Then he realised she was still talking. "What was that you said?" he asked.

"I was just saying," Edna continued, a little exasperated at her husband's inattention, "that no matter what is going on with his wife, the chap looked happy enough when I saw him at the Town Hall last Saturday night."

"At the concert? Was Wainwright in the audience?"

"No! He plays in the orchestra, Albert! Didn't you know? He was there on the front row with his violin. And he seemed to be well pleased with the attention he was getting."

Ramm was dumbfounded. If the chemist played in the Moorland Philharmonia, then he must have known James Jervis. It was strange this had not come up when they had spoken over the last week, he thought. On the other hand, perhaps Wainwright, like Jeremiah Alsop, was unaware that it was Jervis who had been found in the canal. Ramm himself had never mentioned the doctor's name to the inquisitive chemist.

Yet another of those coincidences that cropped up in this small town, and one that could perhaps be of use, he thought. The helpful chemist might give some new insight into the tragic doctor's life.

Chapter Seventeen

For patients of the County Asylum, Sunday began like any other day. A seven o'clock breakfast of two slices of bread and butter was accompanied by a steaming mug of tea – the hundreds of loaves having come fresh from the asylum's own bakery that same morning.

The size of the congregation in the asylum church an hour later would have delighted any clergyman. The impressive Gothic styled church had space for 500 and, as was usual on a Sunday, every pew was full. Admittedly, there were one or two differences from a normal church gathering: men and women went in through separate doors and sat on either side of the aisle, and two smaller rooms were set aside for members of the congregation who might need a little extra attention during the service.

Going to church was seen as an important part of the treatment for patients at the asylum, just like the opportunity to attend a concert by the staff orchestra or watch a dramatic entertainment in the main hall. Dr Menzies, the Medical Superintendent, believed it was reminder of what life was like in the outside world and encouraged orderly behaviour.

The Chaplain, the Reverend AH Boucher who was also Vicar of St Edward's Church at Cheddleton, arrived in some haste just before the appointed time. He was somewhat flustered, his duties at the asylum alongside those at the village church were always a challenge on Sunday mornings. When he reached the doorway he was surprised to see Dr Gibson, the Senior Medical Assistant, waiting for him.

"Good morning to you, Reverend Boucher. I just wanted a word about your sermon, in case you were considering making reference to the loss of Dr Jervis," said Gibson.

"Yes, I thought it was appropriate to pay some tribute to his dedicated work. A tragedy indeed, the poor man was drowned, I believe. Is there something in particular you wish me to say?"

"On the contrary, Chaplain," Gibson replied, his expression revealing a certain embarrassment. "I would prefer you not to mention it at all." Seeing the clergyman's puzzled look, he continued: "It is just that the matter is still being, how shall I say, looked into. It would be unfortunate if you said something which compromised the issue. The least said about Dr Jervis at the moment, the better for all of us."

Reverend Boucher gave an abrupt nod and strode off down the aisle, his robes flapping as he went. He liked to think he knew best when it came to his sermons, as had his father who had been Vicar of Cheddleton for many years before him. Dr Gibson followed behind to join his wife in the private pew usually reserved for the Medical Superintendent.

The hundreds in the congregation fell dutifully silent and then got to their feet with precision when the organ piped up for the first hymn. Their singing would be swelled by the choir made up of nurses and attendants.

Most of the patients enjoyed the shared experience of the service and joined in the hymns and prayers with gusto. Many in the congregation also had their minds on the day ahead. As it was

Sunday, they would not be expected carry out their tasks around the asylum buildings or in the workshops, except for those who helped in the kitchen. Some of the women would spend their time knitting or sewing sitting by the coal fires in the wards, the men might play cards or dominoes, and every ward was provided with books, newspapers and 'cheap publications of a cheerful nature'.

Others were looking forward to a walking party which was being organised for the afternoon. Accompanied by an attendant, groups of patients – especially those due for release – were allowed to go rambling in the countryside beyond the grounds. Some local folk were wary of the asylum residents wandering down the lanes, however it was only occasionally that a patient would go missing.

There was also talk of a football match. A pitch had been cleared of snow the previous day, so a good number of patients were hoping to go out later to cheer on the asylum team. The footballers were drawn from the ranks of the male attendants. The men were given extra pay for playing and the team was amongst the best in the district.

In Leek, a little later that morning, Albert and Edna Ramm were taking up their usual places in St Edward's Church. Ramm had slept badly, unable to rid himself of thoughts about murder and arson which were swirling in his mind. Even in church there was no escape from the cases. He glanced round to be confronted by Mr and Mrs Jervis sliding into a pew behind them. Then Mr Eaton, the printer who was also a sidesman at the Old Church, walked past. There was no sign of the unpleasantness caused by Finch's original suspicions about the *Moorland Argus*, in fact the Inspector sensed satisfaction in the look that Eaton gave him.

When Albert and Edna left the church after the service, he saw James Jervis's parents standing near the lychgate onto Church Street. Mrs Jervis approached. "This is the first chance we have had to attend a service since finding out about James. We wanted to remember him in our prayers," she said. "We do so hope you can find whoever did that to our son." Mr Jervis again left most of the talking to his wife, but Ramm noticed he appeared even more haggard than the previous day. That man has had a bad night too, he thought.

In view of the wintry weather, cups of tea were going to be served in the Maude Church Institute on Clerk Bank, the hall named after the previous vicar of St Edward's. However this morning Inspector Ramm could not face the chit chat. The encounter with Mr and Mrs Jervis had brought home the need to press on with his investigations. Sunday was to be no day of rest.

"You go along to the Maude, Edna. I am going to the station. There's something I need to look at," he said.

"What, on a Sunday morning? Surely, you can have a rest from it today?" came her response.

"There will be plenty of people you can talk to, I'm sure. And anyway, there is something I have to look at, otherwise I won't rest all day," he said.

As Ramm plodded towards the police station, his mind returned to what had bothered him in the middle of the night. Simply too many coincidences were coming to light.

On reaching the station, he gave a curt greeting to the surprised constable who was on duty at the front desk, ordered a mug of tea and headed for his office. There he pulled Jervis's betting notebook from his drawer and turned immediately to the page which listed the doctor's debts. "I should check this list every time I interview someone," he said to himself.

He ran a finger down the column of initials and stopped when he came to a pair that he now recognised. He took a sharp breath as the implications hit him like a blow to the stomach.

At the Blake house, Nathaniel was in the kitchen, brooding. Edith and Cora were at St Luke's Church and William had been well enough for Sunday School. Left on his own, Blake could think of nothing apart from what Cora might be getting involved in.

Two days ago, it had seemed she was on one of her crusades, convinced that someone had been trying to hurt Oliver in the fire. But now she had gone quiet and that was what worried him. It was not like her. He was sure she was planning something in secret, perhaps with Ellen, perhaps with this Gwendoline Cope.

He was still curious about Cora's interest in the photograph of the orchestra. Was Miss Cope in the picture as well as Dr Jervis? Did Cora have some wild theory about the murder, too?

He decided he must go to the studio. When he arrived he immediately brought out the orchestra photograph. Once more his eyes roved over the smartly dressed group: Dr Jervis in happier times, Mr Alsop looking as stern as ever. There were three women, two looked too old to be friends of Cora, but the other one was younger and was holding a flute. She was tall, wearing a lace trimmed evening dress and had dark hair which was pinned up. Was that Gwendoline Cope?

He tried to imagine why Cora had not mentioned her before. Then a memory of something else stirred. He quickly found a copy of the postcard Cora had deciphered for Inspector Ramm. He could see it was signed with a 'G'. A horrible thought struck him. What if Miss Cope really was mixed up in Dr Jervis's death as well as the story in the *Lion*?

He went downstairs to the table where Cora worked when she was not standing behind the counter. He opened the drawer where she kept some of her own papers and soon found what he was looking for. These were the pages which Oliver must have been typing on the night of the fire, the ones FJ Finch had not been able to find. He quickly read them through and realised that this would indeed have been an important story for the *Lion*. But he was equally sure it was something that his daughter should not become involved in.

Inspector Ramm knew that Edna would not be best pleased if he was late for Sunday dinner, especially when he was supposed to be having a day of rest. However his suspicions about people he now knew were involved with James Jervis were driving him on. Accordingly, on his way home, he went via King Street. There was someone there whom he needed to speak to.

The house was part of the tall three storey terrace which had been built in the time of King George, nearly a century before. The top floors had the wide windows of the workrooms, known in the town as 'shades', where some silk workers still went about their trades.

He raised the brass knocker and rapped on the door. As he waited for a response he looked across the street and saw a nun come out of the Loreto Covent and hurry towards St Mary's Catholic Church which was built in the garden behind. His mind went back a couple of years to a mysterious attack which had occurred virtually on the convent doorstep. What a case that turned out to be!

He turned back to the door and used the knocker again, this time forcefully enough for the sound to carry down the street. He was about to walk away when the front door of the next house opened and an aged woman looked out.

"He's out, Inspector. As usual," she said. Even though Ramm was not wearing his uniform, his features were well known in town. "I hear that door opening and shutting all hours of the day and night. The man never rests. No wonder his wife… well, it's not for me to say, is it?"

Ramm thanked the woman and turned for home, disappointed to have made no progress on his latest quandary.

As he was walking through Sparrow Park, Ramm caught sight of Nathaniel Blake at the bottom of Derby Street, carrying a brown envelope. He waited to speak to the photographer.

"On the way from your studio, Mr Blake?"

"I'm glad to have seen you, Inspector. Here is the photograph of the Moorlands Philharmonia I promised, the one with Dr Jervis in," Blake replied, handing the envelope to the policeman.

Ramm held the photograph in one hand and smoothed his moustache with his other, deep in thought. "Actually Mr Blake, if you have a few minutes I would welcome the chance to chew over the facts in this Jervis affair. It might help me to put my theories in some sort of order."

Minutes later the two were sitting in the parlour of the Ramm house, the smell of a Sunday roast floating from the kitchen. The Inspector had been looking intently at the picture of the orchestra. Finally he gave a sigh.

"This Jervis case is a complicated one, Mr Blake. Every day it seems there is a new suspect to consider, and sometimes more than one."

Nathaniel sat forward to show that the Inspector had his full attention.

"Dr Jervis led a very full life and, as the man's dead, I don't think he will mind me sharing a few of his secrets," Ramm began.

"He was keen on horse racing, which in his case meant betting – and losing – large sums. He was in debt to a string of people, from a Manchester moneylender to some of his colleagues and acquaintances. I suspect one of these debts could be the reason he was attacked, because I'm convinced it was no random incident. He was lured down to the canal."

Ramm tapped the photograph. "I'm sure some of these people will have loaned him money, and one of them may have even been driven to do something desperate. I've spoken to Mr Alsop as you suggested, but I believe he is in the clear. There is at least one other musician I would very much like to speak to, however."

"Oh? Who is that?"

"I shouldn't really say, but you might have noticed yourself that Walter Wainwright is in the photograph. He must have known James Jervis and I believe he also loaned him money."

"The chemist? He has always appeared an inoffensive sort to me. Perhaps a little talkative," said Blake.

"That's what puzzles me, Mr Blake. I've spoken to him three or four times in the last week and he has never given any hint that he knew Jervis. Then again, he perhaps didn't know the doctor had been found in the canal."

Blake fell silent as he mulled over just how many people might have had contact with Dr Jervis.

"Then there are the women," Ramm continued, prompting Blake to raise his eyebrows. "It appears that he used to meet various ladies on the towing path, virtually at the very place where he was eventually killed. Unfortunately, I haven't been able to identify any of those yet.

"Another of my theories was that there may have been some professional conflict. At least one person at the asylum, another chemist in fact, has made no bones about disliking Jervis. Something I didn't tell you – and this is definitely not to become public knowledge – is that Jervis was knifed. The weapon could well have been a surgical instrument and, according to Dr Handbridge, the attacker knew exactly what they were doing."

Blake blew out his cheeks at this latest revelation. "Are you suggesting it could be another doctor?"

"Or someone with some medical knowledge at least. There's a doctor at the asylum that I've considered, but he says he was a devoted friend since university days. If he's the killer, then it could be a case of jealousy, but I am not convinced."

Ramm paused. "Added to all that, I have the Coroner and the Chief Constable breathing down my neck to get this sorted out as soon as possible. You can see why I am feeling a little overwhelmed."

"And of course there's the fire at the *Leek Lion*," said Blake with some sympathy.

"Exactly, but I have only just begun on that one. Once again, the motive is the key because I'm sure it was planned in advance."

While Ramm had been speaking Blake realised he should reveal what he had discovered about Gwendoline Cope, even though Finch had given him her name in confidence. The police were investigating murder and arson and Blake felt it his duty to help.

"Well, Inspector, I am sorry to add to your burden, but there is something more you should know," he began. He went on to explain what he knew of Miss Cope, and how Oliver was writing an article about her on the night of the fire. Finally he told him that Cora had taken documents from the *Lion* office. "I know it was foolish, Inspector, but I think she had the best intentions. You know what she is like. She's convinced one of Oliver's stories was the reason the fire was started."

"So Miss Blake searched the office? After the fire? Dear me, this is disappointing. It could have disrupted my own investigations," Ramm frowned. "I saw that letter in the *Lion*, but if Finch knew more about the matter he should have told me rather than chase the story for his newspaper."

"There is something else, though," Blake continued, taking a deep breath. "I think Miss Cope played in the orchestra alongside Dr Jervis." He took the photograph from Ramm and pointed to the tall young woman he surmised was Gwendoline. "I even wondered if that postcard, the one signed by 'G', may have been from her."

Ramm sat back and considered the revelation. At last he might have discovered one of the women whom Jervis was involved with. And if Miss Blake's theories were correct, the woman could also be linked to the motive for the fire. "Where do I find this Miss Cope?" he asked.

"She lives in Chorley Street, I believe," Blake answered. "I should also tell you that Cora is friendly with her, apparently."

"I hope Miss Blake is not becoming too deeply involved in these affairs. At least until we know the truth about what went on."

"My thoughts entirely," said Blake with a sigh.

By the time Nathaniel reached home, the rest of the family had returned from church. While Edith was preparing lunch and William went to his room to look at his *Boys' Own* magazine, Nathaniel decided to have a serious word with his daughter in the parlour.

"There's something I want to ask you, Cora. I need to know exactly what is going on between you and Miss Cope!"

Cora hesitated and Nathaniel ploughed on. "I'm afraid I know it was you who took Oliver's papers, Cora. That was a foolish thing to do, but involving yourself with Miss Cope might be even worse. As well as this business with the *Lion*, I presume you found out that she knew Dr Jervis, too?"

Cora realised it was useless denying it all, but was still stung that her father had been doing his own investigations. "Have you been looking at my things, Father?" she said hotly.

"They are not exactly your things, are they Cora? You know that Inspector Ramm should have been told about all this," he replied. Seeing they were on the verge of an argument, he decided not to tell her that he had already spoken to the policeman.

"I intended to tell him. In the meantime, Miss Cope is very upset. I wanted to give her some comfort." Cora guessed what her father's reaction would be if she told him precisely what was planned.

"Well, that is very noble, my dear," Nathaniel conceded. "But what if there is something dangerous going on? She says someone is spying on her, doesn't she?"

"Father, I will be safe enough and I shall be back before it goes dark."

They left it at that. Nathaniel realised he would not be able to keep her in the house. She was a grown woman, not a schoolgirl.

Edith had been listening and after Cora had left the room she tried to calm him down. "Don't let your imagination run away with you, Nathaniel. Spending time with a friend might be just what Cora needs," she said.

"Yes, Edith. But do we know what sort of friend Miss Cope is?"

Chapter Eighteen

Cora excused herself from the Sunday lunch as quickly as possible and was on her way to the railway station by one o'clock. As she walked down Broad Street she passed the Leek Brewery, enveloped as usual with the aroma of malt and yeast. On the opposite side of the street were the Grace family's builders yard and a large furniture shop. Further on, the advertising hoardings fixed to a high stone wall towered above her: *Robin Starch does not stick to the iron; Triumph Bicycles, easy payments one shilling and sixpence a week; Nestle's Swiss Milk, the best cream.*

But it was a newspaper poster outside the newsagents' shop across the street that caught her eye: *LEEK FIRE. INJURED MAN IN HOSPITAL.* She swallowed hard and walked on. She had called at the Cottage Hospital after church and been told that Oliver was not well enough for her to see him. Visitors might disturb him too much, the Matron had said.

When she reached the bottom of the hill, she saw traps and carriages were lined up in the cobbled courtyard outside the railway station. The horses stood patiently in the snow, their heads down, waiting to take new arrivals into the town.

Once on the platform, she had no trouble spotting Gwendoline Cope. The tall Miss Cope was wearing an elegant black coat which reached down to her patent leather boots. A vivid red scarf gave a splash of colour and her outfit was topped off by a large, expensive looking hat which Cora guessed had come from Miss Heath's shop. An elaborate jewelled hatpin glinted amongst its black velvet folds.

Glancing down at her own grey woollen coat, thick stockings and scuffed leather boots, Cora felt a little drab. Miss Cope was obviously making a special effort, she thought. Perhaps that showed how much this afternoon meant to her.

On seeing Cora, Gwendoline took a step forward and held out a gloved hand. "Miss Blake, thank you once more for coming with me. I don't think I could have done this on my own," she said.

The train bound for Stoke and the five small stations in between arrived in a cloud of smoke and steam. Its brakes screeched as it came to a halt by the platform. Miss Cope had already bought the sixpenny return tickets and they climbed into a second class carriage.

The journey to Wall Grange took less than ten minutes so there was little chance for conversation, which was a relief for Cora. Her mind was too filled with doubts about what she had become involved in, especially after Gwendoline made an unexpected comment. "Oh, I do wish we had a medium with us, to help me communicate with Dr Jervis," she said. "There is a very good one, Miss Cook is her name. She has been helping me to contact my parents."

Cora was too preoccupied to notice anyone else stepping onto the single platform at Wall Grange Station. In a siding stood a row of trucks, loaded with bricks packed in straw. Cora guessed these had come from the brickworks a short way up Park Lane behind the station.

As they crossed the road bridge over the line, Cora saw the County Asylum stretching along the hilltop in the distance. It was easy to pick out the water tower standing high above the many slate roofs, as well as the tall clock tower.

Along the road they passed the entrance to the Staffordshire Potteries Water Company's huge pumping station and then came to the bridge over the Leek Arm of the canal. Just as Inspector Ramm had done a week earlier, they took the stone steps down to the towing path and set off back towards Leek and the place where the attack had taken place.

Miss Cope began to make polite conversation as if they were on a normal Sunday afternoon stroll.

"Dr Jervis was so… so inspiring," she said at one point. "I'm thinking of becoming a nurse myself, more rewarding than hats. He loaned me some books to study. That was before… before we stopped seeing each other."

As they came closer to the tragic spot, Cora sensed Gwendoline becoming more agitated. She looked about her anxiously, her head jerking to the side when a bird moved in the bushes or snow was dislodged from a branch.

They rounded a bend and the view opened up, the asylum looking surprisingly close across the valley to their right. Cora could make out where the pathway had been worn down the slope from the group of great buildings and up to the canal embankment. It was the path where she and her father had run that fateful day, the path that had led to the man's body.

Gwendoline halted, a faraway look in her eyes as if she was recalling the last time she had been there with James Jervis. "This is the place," she said breathlessly. "This is where we used to meet. I can feel his presence."

She stroked her hand against one of the bushes, sending a shower of frost to the ground, then turned to face the frozen canal. Suddenly she sank to her knees, her long coat pooling around her, and stretched out her arms towards the surface.

Cora darted forward and reached for Gwendoline. She thought

the distressed woman was going to throw herself onto the ice, just as Ellen had suggested she might. But Miss Cope shrugged her away. "No, no, I am all right, Miss Blake. I am trying to reach out to my dear James. I am sure his spirit is here." She closed her eyes as if she was going into a trance.

Cora backed away, uncertain what she should do or say, or what her companion might do next. Miss Cope had been right about the spot on the canal, this was exactly where Cora remembered the men trying to pull the body out. She looked at the ice and tried to rid herself of images of what it must have been like under there.

She glanced around to see if anyone else was on the path, worried what they would think of the strange spectacle of Gwendoline on her knees in the snow. There was a figure some distance away in the direction they had come. Whoever it was, they seemed to have stopped and were looking the other way.

Back in Leek, Nathaniel was pacing about in the parlour. It was more than an hour since Cora had left the house and he knew he would not be able to rest until she was home safe. Finally, to Edith's surprise, he said he was going out. "I want to call at Ellen Simms' house," he said.

"Cora might not be too pleased that you're checking up on her," Edith warned.

"It's for her sake that I'm going," he called from the hallway.

Ellen's mother answered the door of the cottage in Cruso's Yard and shouted her daughter. When Ellen saw Blake she looked worried.

"Have you seen Cora this afternoon?" he asked. "Only she said you two were calling on Gwendoline Cope."

Ellen hesitated and then closed the door behind her so that her family would not hear. "I'm sorry, Mr Blake, but she hasn't been here today," she said.

"Listen Ellen, I know you and Cora have been through a lot together. I wouldn't ask you to betray her trust, but I am worried what she might be getting involved in."

"So am I, Mr Blake," Ellen sighed.

"Do you know Miss Cope?"

"All I know about her is what Cora told me and, honestly, some of that sounded a little peculiar," Ellen replied. "I think she lives in Chorley Street, but they've probably gone somewhere else this afternoon."

"Where?" Nathaniel urged, his mind racing with possibilities. He never imagined what Ellen was going to say next.

"The canal. Miss Cope wants Cora to take her to where that man was found, the one you and Cora saw in the ice. Apparently the two of them were… er… friends, " she said, then added a little defensively: "I told her not to do it."

Blake was baffled. Going back to where Jervis died? Why would she want to do that? Ellen seemed to read his thoughts. "Cora said she thinks Miss Cope wants to contact the dead," she said.

Didn't Cora realise the risks she might be taking? Blake thought. Leading someone she hardly knew, a woman who was writing strange letters to the newspaper, to a spot where a murder had taken place. But if they had already set off, what could he do about it?

He thanked Ellen and hurried home. He decided he would go along the canal himself and to save time he would take his bicycle. With any luck he might meet them somewhere on the way and then he would know that Cora was safe.

"Miss Cope, do you think we should move away now? You must be frightfully cold down there."

Cora felt she had to speak. There was sure to be someone coming along the canal soon. It was ten minutes since Gwendoline had sunk to her knees, though it seemed much longer. Her eyes had been closed the whole time, her eyelids flickering occasionally. Sometimes she would mumble, to Cora it sounded like she was saying she was sorry.

Cora's words roused her companion from her trance, although when she turned her head her eyes still seemed unfocused. Cora went to help her to her feet and she rose unsteadily, grasping Cora's arm briefly then apparently regaining her composure.

"I am sure he is there somewhere. I have so many memories of this place, happy ones and sad," she said, then announced: "I still need to get closer to him."

"I thought that is why we came here. Isn't it time we went back to the station?" Cora asked. The low winter sun had started to dip behind the hill on the other side of the canal, turning the sky purple. She was worried the light would soon start to fail and she definitely did not want to walk back along the canal in the dark.

"There is a train back to Leek at half-past three and I am sure we shall be in time to catch that," Gwendoline replied. "But first I feel I must visit James's room. That is the place where I shall be closest to his spirit."

"His room? You mean at the asylum?" Cora was shocked by this new idea. She was worried how unpredictable Miss Cope was becoming, or was this what she had planned from the start?

"It will only take us half an hour," Gwendoline reassured her, then she pointed across the valley to the asylum. "He had a room in one of those villas near the church."

"How do you know about his room?"

Gwendoline looked down in embarrassment. "James took me there once," she replied, then added hastily: "It was only briefly, when he knew there was no one else about. Nothing untoward happened, I can assure you, Miss Blake. I just want to look in his room for one last time."

Cora didn't like the idea of venturing onto the asylum grounds without permission. Apart from all the memories it brought back, she was worried what someone would say if the two of them were seen there. But she was touched by Gwendoline's pleading. She opened her coat and looked at the pendant watch that had been a gift from her late grandmother. If they hurried then perhaps, as Gwendoline suggested, they could be back at the railway station in time for the train.

"James showed me a path that runs from the asylum towards the station at Wall Grange – I think some of the workers use it. It will save us time and we need not come back along the canal," Gwendoline added. Then she opened her handbag and produced a posy of artificial flowers, the sort with fabric petals which decorated expensive hats. As she bent down and laid it at the water's edge, Cora saw there were tears in her eyes.

They turned and Cora put out her hand to help Gwendoline down the steep embankment from the towing path. Then they started across the snowy field towards the great buildings on the hill. Cora shivered, as much from trepidation as from the cold. She was beginning to regret ever having agreed to come with the unpredictable Miss Cope.

Chapter Nineteen

The ice was cracking beneath his tyres as Blake rode his bicycle along the towing path, hoping desperately not to lose balance and plunge into the frozen canal. His handlebars were jolting painfully in his gloved hands as his front wheel skewed over frozen snow and hoofprints that had filled with ice.

He had joined the canal just off Newcastle Road at the wharf where barges were loaded and unloaded. The Leek Arm first ran straight for half a mile to the point where it crossed the River Churnet and was joined by the feeder from Rudyard Lake. It then followed a winding course.

Riding a bicycle along the path was officially forbidden by the Railway Company which owned the canal, but Blake had done it plenty of times before and that afternoon he had more important matters to concern him.

Soon he had to dismount to pass under a low arched bridge which carried a farm track over the canal and shortly afterwards he pushed his bicycle over the hill where the Leek Tunnel had been excavated a century earlier. This was the path that draft horses took while bargees legged their boats through the narrow tunnel, although nowadays more craft were driven by steam engines.

After rounding another bend, Blake came to the spot where Dr Jervis's body had been pulled out of the ice. He stopped and looked around, but there was no sign of the two young women. He spotted a splash of colour on the snow and bent down to see a posy of fabric flowers. Had Miss Cope laid this? he wondered.

A man came lumbering towards him, but turned abruptly to go down the canal embankment. Like most folk, he was wrapped up against the cold. His dark coat was long enough to skim the snow and his wide brimmed hat was pulled down over a voluminous balaclava helmet.

"Excuse me, have you seen two young women recently?" Blake called after him. "One of them is my daughter," he added, hoping to justify why he was asking.

The man stopped. When he spoke his voice was muffled by the knitted helmet, as was his face. He had indeed seen two women some minutes earlier. They were walking towards Wall Grange, he said.

Blake thanked him, mounted his bicycle and continued in that direction, however he saw nothing of Cora and Miss Cope. When he reached the bridge over the canal at Wall Grange he climbed the steps onto the road. A locomotive was pulling out of the nearby station, black smoke pumping from its chimney as it set off towards Leek. Perhaps they had caught the train, he thought. If that was the case, Cora would be home before him.

Blake decided to turn back. The daylight was fading and the icy path was too risky for him to rely on his carbide cycle lamp. Although he had not found Cora, he was relieved to have seen no sign of any incident on the canal.

On the ride back he thought about the fellow in the woollen helmet. He wondered whether the man was connected with the asylum, as he had seemed to be heading across the field in that direction. Blake had not been able to see his face clearly, but now he thought he recognised the voice.

When they reached the gap in the asylum fence, Cora had been surprised how well Miss Cope seemed to know her way around the grounds and wondered if the woman had been there with Dr Jervis more than the once she had admitted to.

Gwendoline led the way to the row of semi-detached villas. She hesitated at the door of one of the houses, then twisted its round brass handle. It was unlocked. She opened the door, took a cautious step inside and listened for a moment before setting off up the stairs.

Cora remained on the doorstep until Gwendoline appeared again. "This is really annoying! I cannot open the bedroom door, it seems to be locked," she said.

"Shall we go then? We don't want to miss the train," Cora replied, anxious to be away from the asylum as soon as possible.

Gwendoline gave a sigh. "Oh, if we must. I was so hoping to see James's room for one last time."

Cora looked around, wondering where the path was that Gwendoline said led towards Wall Grange station. The rear walls of the asylum's main buildings stretched before them in both directions. Close by was the asylum church, with its arched windows and great sloping roof. From somewhere in the grounds, on the far side of the buildings, she could hear the sound of shouts and cheers and presumed some sport was being played in the grounds.

"I think it's this way," said Gwendoline, pointing away from the church. They had begun to follow a path around the outside of the asylum when a figure approached. Cora was immediately on her guard because she could not see the man's muffled face. She wondered if he might be a patient. However, as he drew nearer he took off his hat and woollen helmet. They both knew who it was.

"Mr Wainwright!" said Gwendoline in surprise.

The chemist looked first at Gwendoline and then at Cora, raising his bushy eyebrows. "Why, Miss Cope, Miss Blake! What a coincidence to see you both," he said with a smile. "What brings you here?"

"Oh…" Gwendoline began, her eyes darting around as if searching for an answer, "we were out walking and thought there was a shortcut back to the station." Although Cora did not think the excuse was very convincing, Mr Wainwright seemed to accept it with a nod and another smile.

"And what of yourself, Mr Wainwright? Why are you here?" Gwendoline asked.

"Visiting someone, a patient in fact," he said, sliding a hand over his ruffled strands of hair. Something made Cora ill at ease. It was not only Wainwright's over friendly manner, but his claim to be visiting a patient. Her father had told her there were strict rules that visitors were only allowed on Wednesdays.

Gwendoline turned to Cora and explained: "I know Mr Wainwright slightly. He plays the violin in the orchestra."

A pained expression passed across Wainwright's face. "Slightly? Surely we are better friends than that, Gwendoline."

Cora felt shocked by the man's change in attitude. He was clearly offended by what Miss Cope had said, but his over familiar use of her first name was equally unsettling.

Gwendoline was taken aback. "Mr Wainwright, I… I am not sure what you mean," she stuttered.

Wainwright cleared his throat and paused as if gathering his strength before speaking again. "How can you not know what I feel for you, Gwendoline?"

Miss Cope appeared even more startled. She was at a loss for words.

"I have the deepest respect for you, Gwendoline. I always have, I always will," Wainwright continued, looking longingly at Miss Cope. "No one could be as devoted, not even a doctor." He reached forward and tried to grasp Gwendoline's hand, but she flinched away before he could touch her.

Her eyes widened in a shock of realisation. "Have you followed us here?" she asked, her tone cold and hard. "Are you the one who has been watching me?"

Cora was becoming afraid at what might happen. "Come Miss Cope, we really must leave! We do not have a moment to spare," she urged. Minutes earlier she had hoped they would not be noticed by anyone at the asylum, now her dearest wish was for someone to appear and help them escape this strange man.

"Gwendoline, Gwendoline, I have always wanted the best for you," Wainwright began to plead. "I have watched over you, cherished you, tried to protect you from rogues like that fellow Jervis. I love you!"

Cora stared at Wainwright. She could hardly believe what she was hearing. The man seemed unhinged. She glanced across at Gwendoline and saw that she was breathing rapidly, struggling to contain herself. There was hatred in her eyes, not love.

"You! You are the one who has been making my life a misery!" she scowled.

"Miss Cope, please come away," cried Cora, looking around desperately for help. At the same moment Wainwright lurched forward to seize Gwendoline in his arms. There was no telling whether he was driven by passion or violence.

With a cry of fear and anger, Gwendoline managed to struggle free from his grip. She reached upwards and pulled out the long pin that secured her hat and sank it into the back of Wainwright's hand. He yelped in pain and staggered back, blood dripping scarlet onto the snow.

"You creature!" Gwendoline shouted, glaring at the man. She raised the hatpin again, but Cora grabbed her hand and pulled her away. "We must get away from him!" she shouted.

When Blake arrived back in Portland Street, he put his bicycle away in the outhouse and went in through the back door. From the expression on Edith's face he knew Cora had not returned home.

Earlier in the day, it had seemed that she thought he was making too much of his fears for Cora. Now she too was worried. "It will be getting dark soon Nathaniel and she's not back yet. Have you not seen anything of her? If I had known about this canal business, I would never have allowed her to go."

"I have been as far as Wall Grange, but saw no sign of them. Someone did tell me they had seen two young women on the towing path," Blake replied. "With any luck she will probably be home at any moment."

Edith was not convinced and she could tell that her husband felt the same. "Please Nathaniel, if she is not back in half an hour, you need to do something. What about Inspector Ramm, can he help?"

With each passing minute, it became clearer that he would have to speak to the officer again.

Cora and Gwendoline ran towards the asylum buildings and followed railway lines which curved into a yard. There was an open shed where it looked like the tram was parked. Straight ahead was a door into another building and Gwendoline pushed it open. Inside was a cavernous storeroom stacked with boxes and crates. They looked around wildly hoping to see someone who would help, but the place was deserted at this time on a Sunday afternoon.

Gwendoline leaned against a work table. "I cannot believe this is happening," she panted. "I have barely spoken to him before and now this." She stopped abruptly when they heard Wainwright calling her name outside.

"This way," said Cora, pointing to another door. They ran out of the storehouse and into a courtyard which was enclosed by buildings on all sides. At its centre loomed the huge water tower, almost blocking out the sky.

Standing this close to the great tower, Cora found it truly intimidating. It was the tallest building she had ever seen, higher than Leek's biggest mill. She craned her head back and saw that the eight-sided column rose eight floors high, topped by a wider crown of brick and stone and slate.

Gwendoline ran across the courtyard to a door which looked like it was a way into the main asylum block. It was locked. Cora remembered that when she had been at the asylum with her father, most of the doors had to be unlocked by an attendant. "We're trapped!" cried Gwendoline wildly.

Cora darted across to the tower. Through a window on the ground floor she caught a glimpse of sides of meat hanging from hooks. It must be a meat store for the kitchens, she thought. On another side of the tower was a door. She tried the handle and it opened, not into the meat store, but to a stone spiral staircase which led upwards.

At that moment they heard Wainwright shouting again, this time from inside the storehouse which they had just left. His voice became louder as he drew closer.

"He's searching for us. Quick, let's hide in here," Cora called to Gwendoline.

They huddled together in the gloom at the bottom of the stairwell and closed the door. They hardly dared breathe for fear Wainwright would hear them. From outside came the sound of him running about in the courtyard, then rattling the handle of the door into the main building.

"Gwendoline, where are you?" Wainwright seemed to be talking to himself, his tone switched from anger to pathetic entreaty. "Do not be afraid, my darling. This has all been a misunderstanding. Please let me explain." Miss Cope went stiff with fear.

There was a moment of eerie silence, followed by cursing and the sound of him kicking the locked door. He seemed angry again. Next came more footsteps and then rasping breaths only inches away from where Cora and Gwendoline cowered behind the door.

Gwendoline shrieked as the handle in front of them began to turn. They both put their weight against the door, gasping in a desperate effort to keep it shut, while Wainwright grunted as he strained to force it open.

The young women quickly realised he was too strong for them.

"Upstairs!" whispered Cora. Letting go of the door, they nearly fell over each other as they spun round and began to dash up the narrow spiral of steps. Behind them they heard Wainwright curse again as the door flung open and he pitched headlong onto the tiled floor.

The stone steps led up to a wooden landing where Cora and Gwendoline stopped to catch their breath. From below they could hear Wainwright dragging something behind the door. Then his voice echoed up the stairwell.

"We will not be disturbed now, Gwendoline," he shouted.

Gwendoline took hold of Cora's arm as they listened in terror. Instead of escaping Walter Wainwright, they were imprisoned by him. They heard him call up the staircase again. "Miss Blake, this has nothing to do with you. Come down now and you may go."

Cora felt Gwendoline's grip on her arm grow tighter. "Do not leave me, I beg you," she breathed.

Blake checked his watch for the umpteenth time. It was coming up to four o'clock and there was still no sign of Cora.

"I can wait no longer. I'm going to speak to Ramm," he announced to Edith. "If Cora arrives before I return, send her round to the police station."

Ramm's house in Queen Street was only a few hundred yards away and Nathaniel was there in a matter of minutes. The Inspector was surprised to see Blake again and realised there must have been an urgent development.

"Inspector, I am worried that Cora may have put herself in danger," Blake began. "I have discovered that she was planning to go with Miss Cope to the canal where Jervis's body was found. She and Jervis were close friends, apparently." He saw a look of dismay on Ramm's face.

“I have cycled along the towing path myself and seen nothing of them, although I think they must have been there,” Blake continued. “Cora has not returned and now I’m worried that something has happened to them.”

“How do you know they had been there?”

“Well, someone had laid flowers on the canal side and I imagine Miss Cope might have done that. Also I saw a person who said he had seen two young women on the towing path. The strange thing is, I now think it was Walter Wainwright.”

“Wainwright?” Ramm blurted out in alarm. “You say Wainwright was there?”

“Yes, I didn’t recognise him at the time because he was wearing one of those balaclava helmets, a great knitted thing that was too big for him. I could see hardly anything of his face. But thinking about it afterwards, I am sure it was his voice. I now realise he was trying to disguise it.”

“This could be serious, Mr Blake. Where exactly did you see him?”

“Right where Dr Jervis’s body was found. It looked like he was going to cut across the fields towards the asylum.”

Ramm shook his head. On the face of it, Miss Blake returning home late was hardly a police matter. But the mention of Walter Wainwright had disturbed him. He had spent the afternoon ruminating on what part the chemist may have played in the Jervis affair, especially after he had found ‘*WW*’ on the doctor’s list of creditors. He had called at both Wainwright’s house and his shop, but there was no sign of him. Now it appeared the man had been by the canal that afternoon and so had Miss Cope, one of Jervis’s women friends. Is that why he was there?

“Mr Blake, we must visit Miss Cope’s house,” said Ramm, grabbing his uniform cape from a peg in the hall. “If the young ladies are not there, I think we shall need to make our way to the asylum as soon as possible.”

Has Wainwright made fool of me? he thought. He was horrified to think he may have been deceived by someone he had trusted.

Chapter Twenty

Cora peered up into the tower that soared above them. Wooden steps, almost as steep as a ladder, led upwards to another platform and she could make out more landings going ever higher. At the centre of the tower was an empty shaft that rose all the way up to the very top. Somewhere up there, she thought, was the giant water tank.

It was a shadowy and forbidding space, the last of the day's light seeping through narrow arched windows which were cut into the brick walls at each floor level.

Gwendoline appeared bewildered. In contrast to her usual immaculate appearance, her dark hair was in disarray and when she put up her hand to tidy it she realised her hat was missing.

"I'm frightened what he will do next. He seems to have lost his senses," she whispered.

They both flinched as the sound of heavy footsteps echoed up the stone staircase, followed by Wainwright's voice. "If you wish to stay there, Gwendoline, then I shall have to come up to you."

Miss Cope turned to Cora in panic. "What shall we do?" she gasped.

"We must go up to the next floor," Cora replied. She turned and put her foot on the steps that rose almost vertically from the landing.

The climb was taxing, especially for Gwendoline who was impeded by her long dress and coat, but fear drove them on. By the time they reached the next landing their legs and arms were aching and Cora had splinters of wood in her hands from pulling herself up the steps.

She glanced down the central shaft in time to see the top of Wainwright's balding head as he emerged from the spiral staircase onto the platform below. She dodged back out of sight when she saw his face turn upwards.

Wainwright was breathing heavily after coming up the twisting stone steps. He was muttering to himself and sounded exasperated that his precious Gwendoline was not waiting for him.

Cora tried to think what they should do if Wainwright followed them up the wooden staircase. Could they fight him off? Or climb further into the darkness? They needed to raise the alarm before that happened, she thought. There were hundreds of people in the asylum, surely somone would hear them and do something?

"We have to shout," she said and immediately began to scream "Help". Gwendoline joined in, their cries echoing in the empty shaft. However, the tower's thick walls, thirty inches at their widest, soaked up the sound.

After a while they fell silent, gasping for breath, their throats raw from the effort. From below came a laugh. "Have you quite finished? No one will hear you, you know."

Cora and Gwendoline looked at each other feeling defeated. They had no time to think of what else to do because Wainwright had begun to stamp up the wooden steps towards them.

"Quick!" shouted Cora and pointed up the next flight of rough stairs.

The muscles in their legs burned from the effort, but they were both determined to secure precious minutes of safety from their pursuer.

When they reached the next landing they fell to the floor with fatigue. From below came the sound of Wainwright breathing heavily as he climbed to the top of the first wooden stairs. Minutes passed before he cried out again, his tone sounding distraught.

"Why is this happening? I so wanted to show you how much I cared, Gwendoline. But now you have spoiled it all. It was just the same when you fell for that man Jervis." When he continued, he seemed to be talking to himself. "At least the man's gone now. Then there was that nonsense with the *Lion* and that young fellow Finch. I had to put a stop to that, of course. Oh, when are you going to learn, my darling?"

Hearing his ramblings, the young women were gripped by new horrors.

"Oh heavens! He must have attacked James! He's a murderer!" Gwendoline whispered.

"And it sounds like he was the one who started the fire and hurt Oliver," added Cora, her voice breaking with emotion.

With Wainwright's voice droning below them, the gathering gloom only heightened the women's feeling that they were trapped in the tower. Cora realised that soon their prison would be in darkness. If he came after them again, they would have to find the energy to grope their way up another staircase. Cold and frightened, they sank down onto the rough planks and waited to see what the man would do next.

When they found Miss Cope's house, Ramm and Blake had been dismayed to hear that her aunt had no idea where her niece was. They dashed to the police station where Ramm had dispatched a constable to hire a two-horse carriage. He, Blake and two police constables had then set off for the County Asylum as fast as the horses could manage on the icy road.

By the time they arrived, the long winter evening was upon them, although the great buildings were aglow with the light of hundreds of electric bulbs. Ramm sent Constable Knowles to check the path across the fields to the canal and then asked the porter to summon Dr Gibson immediately.

When Dr Gibson bustled into the entrance hall, he looked unhappy at the intrusion and asked exactly what the trouble was.

The Inspector came straight to the point. "Two young women have gone missing. I want to mount a search because I believe they may be somewhere near the asylum and could be at risk."

"But…" was all Gibson managed to say before Ramm ploughed on. "I am also looking for a third person, Walter Wainwright, whom I want to speak to in connection with the death of Dr Jervis."

Blake was shocked to hear Wainwright might actually be a murder suspect. And to think he had accepted the man's word when he had seen him near the canal! Had he done something terrible to Cora?

"I can assure you, Inspector, these missing persons cannot be within the asylum. As you know, our doors are kept locked," Dr Gibson replied.

"Mr Wainwright's wife is a patient, is she not? Could he have been admitted as a visitor?"

"She is one of our private patients, yes, but even they are only allowed visitors on a Wednesday."

Ramm pressed on. "I want to search whatever buildings may be unsecured – when I was here last week I saw that not all of them are locked. I presume members of your staff can assist?"

"The inmates will be served supper soon…" Gibson paused as he saw Ramm's growing frustration. "But, I will see what we can arrange."

In the event, five staff joined Inspector Ramm, Blake and Constables Phillips and Knowles outside the asylum church. The volunteers, who included James Jervis's close friend, Arthur Forbes, had small hand lanterns similar to the police bullseye lamps that the other four were carrying.

"Check inside any building that is not locked. Keep a sharp eye out for anything that might show the young women have been there," ordered Ramm as he started to send the searchers in different directions.

Arthur Forbes spoke up. "Actually, I think there was someone in the villa this afternoon," he said. "It was some time after three o'clock. I was in the living room when I thought I heard someone on the stairs. When I came out there was no one there, but the front door had been left open."

"Nothing stolen, I take it," Ramm replied. Forbes shook his head, then looked at the Inspector earnestly. "Tell me Inspector, is this connected with what happened to Dr Jervis?"

"That may very well be the case, Dr Forbes," Ramm answered.

As the search began, Blake took out his pocket watch. By the light of his lamp he could see it was gone five o'clock, four hours since Cora had left home. "Where in heaven's name have you got to?" he said to himself.

One of the narrow windows gave Cora just enough light to see the fingers of the watch pinned inside her coat. Five o'clock. Her mother and father were certain to be worried, she thought. In fact, knowing Father, he would probably be searching for her already. Except she hadn't told them where she was going! She shook her head at her own stupidity.

Wainwright had gone quiet. Cora thought back to when she had seen him in his shop only a few days earlier. There had been no hint of his evil side, although he had certainly been curious about what had gone on at the canal. She wondered whether he still hoped they would give up and go back down to the floor below.

Or was he biding his time before coming after them? Another man in Cora's past had turned out to be a killer and she knew there was no way to predict what such a person might do.

Gwendoline was not moving and Cora feared she may have gone into fainting swoon as she had done when she had heard of Dr Jervis's death. Cora touched her arm to rouse her. "Miss Cope? We must be ready if something happens," she said softly.

"I'm sorry Miss Blake, but it has all been too much for me," she whimpered. "I cannot believe the horror of it all. To think a creature like Wainwright is responsible. I have barely spoken to him before and yet he is saying all these things about me and about James." Deflated, she added: "What can we do to save ourselves?"

Before Cora could answer they heard Wainwright stirring. Once more there was the sound of his heavy tread on the wooden steps as he started to make his way up the tower again.

The two leapt to their feet in panic and began to climb yet another flight of steps, straining their arms to pull themselves up by anything they could grasp. Once more the climb was punishingly hard and they were both on the verge of collapse when they gained the safety of the next landing. But Cora realised that Wainwright, a good thirty years older than themselves and much less agile, must be finding the vertical steps even harder. He was probably exhausted, too.

"Gwendoline, my darling, this has to stop. I never meant to harm you," he groaned. Then his tone became aggressive again. "Can you hear me?" he shouted. "You have got to see reason! This has got to end, one way or another." The young women winced at the muttered curses that followed.

Cora reckoned they were now more than half way up the mighty tower. It was becoming much colder and she could hear the wind whipping around the walls outside.

"We are going to run out of stairs soon. And anyway, it is almost too dark to see them," she whispered to Gwendoline. "But I think he's getting tired, too. We might be able to stop him if he tries to climb up again."

The truth was that Cora didn't want to run from Wainwright any more. Now she knew he must have started the fire at the *Lion*, she wanted revenge for Oliver.

Cora began to scrabble around the rough planks to find something she could use to defend herself. In the shadows she felt something cold and hard. She realised it was a piece of narrow metal pipe like those she had seen fastened to the walls. It felt about three feet long and, when she tried to pick it up, she found it so heavy she had to use both hands. If she could swing it, this would certainly stop Wainwright in his tracks, she thought.

But first, there was something else she wanted to do. With difficulty she hoisted the pipe onto her shoulder and rammed it at one of the windows, shattering the glass. Icy wind blasted through the hole as she leaned into it and started to scream once more. This time it was not just a cry for help, but a desperate wailing at the top of her voice. This might be her last chance to attract someone's attention.

As Arthur Forbes walked around the outside of the buildings, shining his lamp from side to side, his mind was on the two women they were looking for. Were they some of James's lady friends? Is that why they had come to the asylum? And what about the man? Ramm had not told him who he was, but was he another friend? Or had he been responsible for the attack? The lamp wavered as Forbes' hand began to shake. If this man was the murderer, he could not imagine what he might do if he found him.

He was pacing slowly across the inner courtyard, beside the square base of the water tower, when his foot snagged on something. By the light of his lantern he saw it was a woman's hat. He picked it up and examined it thoughtfully, wondering if one of the missing women had dropped it. On the other hand, it could have been lost by one of the nurses or a female attendant. It looked expensive though.

He decided he ought to tell Inspector Ramm about it and was turning to retrace his steps when he heard what sounded like shards of glass falling onto the frozen cobbles. Or was it ice cascading from the tower high above him?

A moment later he heard a curious sound. It could be the wind howling around the tower, he thought. Or – his senses were now alert – it could be a woman screaming. He craned his head back to take a better look at the huge black shape that rose more than a hundred feet into the night sky. He tried to see where the sound was coming from, but it was useless, it was too dark. He knew he had definitely heard something… and there it was again. A voice, not the wind, and wherever it was coming from, it was high up.

In all haste, he started to look for a way into the tower. He knew there was a butcher's store at the bottom, connected to the kitchens by a covered passageway, although the door to the main buildings would be locked. However, he remembered seeing another small doorway on the corner of the tower itself. He found it and tried the handle. It did not seem to be locked, but would not open. Oddly, it felt like something had been propped against the other side.

Forbes began to push the door with all his might, but could not move it. He needed help and, judging by those screams, he needed it quickly.

Dr Forbes was not the only one alerted by Cora's screams. Walter Wainwright had heard the window being broken and feared that someone outside might hear the cries. The situation was getting out of control. He started to force himself up the next flight of the steep steps. It was so dark he had to feel his way carefully to avoid missing a tread.

There was no sound from above and he surmised the two had decided not to climb any further. Had they given up their silly escapade? But perhaps his dream of life with Gwendoline was coming to an end, he thought.

As his head rose above the top of the steps, he screwed up his eyes as he tried to see where Miss Cope and Miss Blake were in the gloom. Were they huddled in a corner, awaiting their fate?

At that moment he heard a rustle of clothing and saw a shadow move in front of him. Then he felt a blinding pain as a heavy object hit the side of his head, cutting his ear and then crushing onto his shoulder. His legs almost gave way, but he managed to hang onto the edge of the platform. He heard the weapon clatter down to the floor below as he hauled himself up the last step and onto the landing. He cried out in pain and clutched at his ear which was dripping blood down the side of his face and onto his coat.

A shaft of light came through the broken window as the moon emerged from behind the scudding clouds. He could see Miss Cope sitting in the corner and Miss Blake standing beside her.

"What are you doing? Are you women crazy? You are as bad as my wife!" he screamed. "She's locked in this asylum, you know?"

Cora and Gwendoline gripped onto each other and then sank back against the cold rough bricks, as far away from Wainwright as they could manage. In the moonlight they saw his eyes were wide and wild.

Cora's voice came out of the shadows. "What did you do to Dr Jervis?"

"Jervis? He died in the canal, didn't he? Good riddance to him!" Wainwright retorted. "He charmed Gwendoline away from me, he kept my money, he even stole my place in the orchestra!"

As she listened, Gwendoline's hand closed around the long hatpin in her pocket.

"But you didn't need to hurt Oliver," Cora protested, her voice breaking with emotion.

"I couldn't bear the thought of any more stories in that newspaper!" Wainwright snapped. "Saying I was odious and that young reporter was nosing around Gwendoline. I had to stop him."

He paused as if recalling how clever he had been. "I was only going to burn down the door. Then I tried the handle and it was open, so I simply walked in and lit my chemicals inside. That's when I heard a typewriter upstairs…"

Cora gasped to hear the man boasting about his crime.

"You must believe me, I never intended harming the fellow. It was the *Lion* I wanted to stop. That's why I ran to raise the alarm."

"He could have died!" Cora wailed. She was sickened at the way Wainwright was trying to apologise. Then she was struck by another frightening thought. Why was he telling them all this? Was he was planning to do something to them, too? Then they would never be able to tell anyone else.

Chapter Twenty One

As Arthur Forbes turned away from the door and ran across the courtyard, he could hear no more screams. What had happened in the tower? Was it too late to save them?

He flung open the door to the storehouse where the electric lights had been turned on. He dodged around the tea chests and baskets to reach the far end. Once he was outside again he began to call for help. He ran on and almost collided with a man emerging from the tram shed. Forbes had seen him earlier with the Police Inspector.

"Quick!" Forbes cried breathlessly. "I think the women might be trapped in the water tower. I heard screams."

"What? That could be my daughter!" Blake shouted.

"The door's blocked and I couldn't move it on my own. We might need someone else."

At that moment Constable Knowles appeared, having heard the commotion.

"To the water tower! There's not a moment to lose!" Blake was close to panic.

Knowles took out his police whistle and began to it blow urgently. The three men set off towards the black shape that rose high above the roofs of the asylum.

When they reached the inner courtyard, Blake looked up at the threatening tower and then in desperation threw himself against the small door. He staggered back, winded by the effort.

Knowles let his whistle drop from his mouth. "We need a battering ram. I'll check the other buildings for something we can use," he said.

The constable, with Dr Forbes beside him, ran back to the storehouse while Blake stood staring at the tower, feeling frustrated and powerless. Minutes later they lumbered back with a hefty wooden bench about six feet long.

The three men thrust their improvised ram at the door and, after several blows, felt it start to give way. An asylum attendant arrived on the scene and added his weight to the struggle. With a sound of splintering wood, the door's hinges were wrenched from its frame and it tipped backwards. A wooden beam, which looked to have been braced against the back of the door, fell to one side.

Knowles shone his lamp into the darkness to reveal the narrow spiral staircase twisting upwards. Blake barged past him and was the first on the stone steps. He dreaded what he might find at the top.

The sound of the door being smashed open echoed up the hollow shaft in the centre of the tower. Six storeys above, Walter Wainwright was becoming desperate.

"Up the stairs, both of you!" he shouted.

"But there's nowhere…" Cora began.

"Stop arguing! Go up, I say!" Wainwright screamed.

The young women began to feel their way up the next set of wooden steps, legs and arms shaking with fear. Gwendoline went first, then Cora with Wainwright inches behind, roughly pushing at her stockinged legs each time she hesitated.

Then came a shout from somewhere far below.

"Cora! Cora are you there?" Blake was pounding up the spiral steps, followed by the others.

"Father!" she called weakly as she struggled upwards.

The prisoners and their captor stepped out onto the next landing just as an electric bulb on the wall glowed into life and the darkness was dissipated. Far below them, the male attendant had found a light switch inside the door. Cora groaned in despair as she looked around and saw there were no more stairs. Above their heads was the giant water tank. A spindly metal ladder led vertically into a round shaft that rose through the centre of the tank.

Wainwright looked at the ladder in surprise. He seemed unsure what to do next. Then things happened rapidly. Gwendoline sprang forward and threw herself at the man. She screamed as she plunged her hat pin viciously into his neck and then, in a frenzy of rage, stabbed him twice more. Clutching at his throat, he emitted an agonising gurgle as blood spurted through his fingers.

"Gwendoline…" he gasped, his eyes glassy as he tried to focus on Miss Cope. Her name was the last word he said. A moment later he staggered backwards and plunged down the steps to the landing below.

Chapter Twenty Two

Nathaniel Blake, breathing heavily, was the first up to the landing to find Walter Wainwright lying with a hat pin, perhaps six inches long, sticking out from his neck. Blood bubbled from his lips as he took his last breath and a fixed look came into his eyes.

Blake rushed towards the next flight of steps, fearful what he might find above. On the final platform, Miss Cope was sitting on the planks, moaning inconsolably. Cora was slumped against the wall, simply staring into space.

"Cora, my dear! Are you injured?" he said. She shook her head and allowed herself to be hugged, but said nothing. She was completely drained by the last hours and the fatal climax.

Arthur Forbes was the next up the steps and quickly checked Wainwright for any sign of life. Constable Knowles joined them and tried to take control of the situation. "Let me see what has happened. This is a police matter now," he announced.

Alerted by Knowles' whistle and the shouts of the search party, Inspector Ramm had arrived at the tower moments earlier and was now stamping up the spiral steps to the second floor level.

"What's going on up there? Are they safe?" he shouted as he peered up the central shaft. In the light of the sparse electric bulbs he could make out the wooden landings rising into the distance.

"Yes, Sir, the women are safe," Knowles' voice echoed down.

"And Wainwright?"

"Looks like he's dead. Fallen down the stairs with something sticking out of his neck."

The Inspector immediately started to clamber up the wooden

steps. He needed to study the scene himself. The rescue effort had turned into the investigation of another suspicious death.

When he reached Wainwright's body he took a careful look at his injuries and the elaborate hat pin covered in the man's blood. On the platform above, he found Miss Cope and Miss Blake in a state of shock.

"How did this happen to Wainwright?" he asked.

"That man's to blame for everything," murmured Gwendoline. Cora was unable to speak, still stunned by what had gone on.

"Who was first up here? Mr Blake? Did you see anything?"

Nathaniel shook his head.

Ramm gave a sigh. He saw there was little chance of finding answers while they were all in the tower. "Let's get you ladies out of this place. I shall need to speak to you both when you have recovered."

For the young women, descending the near vertical wooden steps took considerably longer than their hasty ascent. It was as if their legs would give way at any moment and they needed to rest on every landing, Cora kept upright by her father and Gwendoline attended to by Dr Forbes.

The operation to bring Wainwright down was even more troublesome. Eventually the body was wrapped in a sheet and lowered from floor to floor using ropes. When it was finally laid onto the icy cobbles of the courtyard, Ramm took another look at the injuries by the light of his bullseye lamp. "Stabbed just like Jervis. An irony indeed," he said to himself.

Cora and Gwendoline, bedraggled and exhausted from their ordeal, had been led to the nurses' sitting room to wait while another carriage was called. Ramm and Blake stood in the asylum entrance hall, deep in thought as they considered what had gone on over the last hours.

"So was Wainwright behind it all? I can barely believe it," said Blake.

"I very much want to hear what the young ladies have to say, Mr Blake. But Wainwright may well be to blame. It looks like the man has duped me good and proper," Ramm replied.

It was more than an hour later by the time Cora and Gwendoline returned home to worried loved ones. In Miss Cope's case, her aged aunt had been in a state of bewilderment since Inspector Ramm had appeared at the door asking for her niece. She was even more put out when Gwendoline arrived dishevelled and distressed after her mysterious absence.

For Cora's mother, it was yet another night to comfort her daughter after a disturbing adventure. Edith did not ask what had gone on, she knew Nathaniel would tell her later. She was simply relieved to see Cora home safe and was content to hug her until the crying subsided.

Chapter Twenty Three

Inspector Ramm's first act the following morning was to send Constable Phillips to bring Miss Cope and Miss Blake separately to the police station. A man had died in highly unusual circumstances and he needed to find out exactly how that had happened. If he was not satisfied with their explanation, then neither would the Coroner or the Chief Constable, both of whom he would have to speak to before the day was out.

When Miss Cope was brought into his office half an hour later, Ramm was struck by how quickly she seemed to have recovered from her ordeal. She had obviously taken care over her hair and appearance that morning. The young woman was confident too, answering his questions without hesitation.

"I must confess Inspector, I feel like a great weight has been lifted from my shoulders. I have been pursued by Mr Wainwright for months, not that I knew it was him."

"He admitted spying on you?"

"Indeed. It is embarrassing, but I think he was obsessed. That's what led him to take his revenge on Dr Jervis." Gwendoline proceeded to tell how Wainwright revealed his jealousy for Jervis, how he had killed the doctor and finally set fire to the *Leek Lion* office.

"So he definitely said that he had attacked Dr Jervis?" Ramm asked, who was discreetly making notes as the conversation progressed.

"He said he despised the doctor and wanted to get rid of him."

"You were a close friend of Dr Jervis, were you not?"

Gwendoline paused, colour showing on her cheeks beneath her face powder. "Yes. We played music together and we talked and we went for walks. I had not spoken to him for a number of weeks, though."

"You didn't send a postcard to Dr Jervis, asking him to meet you on the Monday night?"

Gwendoline became indignant. "Certainly not. Miss Blake showed me that and I did not write it. It must have been the work of the dreadful Mr Wainwright."

"Can you tell me how Mr Wainwright sustained his injuries?"

"Well, I pricked him with my hatpin when he set about me outside the asylum. Later, when we were in the tower and in fear of our lives, Miss Blake hit him on the head with a metal pipe. That didn't stop him, though.

"Then, when we were right at the top and there was nowhere else to go, he was raging mad again. I struggled with him, he put his hands around my neck, I pulled out the hatpin again and I stuck it in him to make him let go."

When Miss Blake came into the office a short while later, she appeared to be still affected by the previous night's events. Her eyes were puffy and red rimmed and she carried herself with the weariness of someone in need of many more hours of rest. It was obvious that, after the fire at the *Leek Lion* and the injury suffered by Oliver Finch, the confrontation with Walter Wainwright had been the final straw.

It was not just her demeanour that differed from Miss Cope. Ramm was surprised that, unlike her usual reliable self, Miss Blake could not recall in the same detail what Wainwright had said about Dr Jervis. However, she was sure he had confessed to starting the fire.

"So you were right about a newspaper article being the motive for the fire," said Ramm, hoping to coax more words from Cora.

"Yes, and then he tried to apologise!" Cora replied heatedly. "He said he used some sort of chemicals, but had not meant to hurt Oliver. That's why he went to raise the alarm."

Ramm's eyebrows shot up in surprise. So Wainwright himself had rung the fire station bell. The man was certainly unpredictable. He recalled that the chemist had been at the Oddfellows Meeting on Thursday night, but had left halfway through, giving him time to go to Market Street and set the *Lion* offices on fire.

"And what about his injuries?" he asked.

"I admit I hit him with a piece of pipe. I was trying to stop him. We were so frightened," said Cora. "As for the other thing…"

"When he was stabbed?" Ramm encouraged her.

"It all happened so quickly and there was so little light. One moment we were standing there, the next moment they were struggling. They both cried out, then he was holding his throat and fell down the stairs."

After Cora left, Ramm considered the women's testimonies. Wainwright had stalked Miss Cope for months, murdered her intimate friend, set fire to the newspaper office and then trapped her and Miss Blake in the water tower. In a final struggle, Miss Cope had stabbed him in self defence.

He was a little disappointed the chemist would not stand trial, but there seemed to be no doubt he was guilty. The man had the knowledge, the means and the motive for both the murder and the arson. And, in his ravings in the tower, he had confessed to his crimes. How he had managed to forge the postcard would remain a mystery, but it was highly likely he had spied on Jervis and Miss Cope beside the canal in the past.

Ramm also felt disappointed in himself. He had been foolish to allow himself to be deceived by Wainwright. He could not believe he had asked for help from the very person he should have been arresting.

"Perhaps I'm getting too old for this game," he said to himself with a sigh.

That afternoon, Ramm visited the *Lion* office to inform Finch who had started the fire. The editor was shocked to hear that the chemist, someone he had seen many times in the town, had been responsible for the destruction and the injury Oliver had suffered. He was equally baffled when Ramm told him that the seemingly inoffensive man had stalked Gwendoline Cope for months and had also murdered James Jervis.

Finch shook his head in disbelief, still coming to terms with the awful truth. Then he asked: "How much of this can I print?"

"Certainly we believe Wainwright was responsible for the murder and the arson. But please do not name Miss Cope, nor say precisely what went on with her and Miss Blake at the asylum," Ramm replied. "However, I'm sure you will find a way around it."

After all the distress of the last week, Finch knew he had a powerful story on his hands. Already the text of 'The Mystery of the Murderous Chemist' was forming in his mind. He would have no qualms about blackening the character of a man who had tried to kill his son.

Nathaniel Blake had spent most of the day reliving the terrifying scenes at the asylum and how close to death Cora may have been. The same thoughts had kept him awake through the night. Above all, he felt guilty.

He was in no mood to work and finally decided to close the studio early and call in on Finch on his way home. Although the building was still in a state of disarray and the stench of smoke lingered everywhere, the editor was busy at his typewriter.

"Wainwright, eh? Who would have thought it?" said Finch. When he saw Blake's expression, he added: "I gather Cora had a dreadful experience."

"And I allowed it to happen, FJ," Blake replied. "I should have persuaded her to stay at home. Then I didn't act quickly enough when I found out what she was actually doing with Miss Cope. I even believed what the ghastly Wainwright told me when I saw him by the canal, although I didn't know it was him at the time."

"It's easy to blame yourself, Nathaniel, but Cora has a mind of her own," said Finch.

"She's been in peril before, FJ, we both know that. But this time... when I couldn't get into that tower… I thought I had truly lost her." Blake shook his head at the memory of the desperate struggle to reach the young women.

"Thank God she wasn't harmed physically. But she was a victim all the same," he continued despondently.

"What has happened these last few days has been horrific, right from the moment the body was found under the ice. The murder, the fire, the state Oliver is in, the way Wainwright treated them. She might be scarred for life by this. It could take a miracle to bring her back to her old self."

Finch paused before he replied, seemingly lost in thought.

"Who knows, Nathaniel? There may be something around the corner to lift her spirits."

Blake looked up quizzically and was surprised to see that, for the first time since the fire, there was the trace of a smile on his friend's face.

It was nearing the end of the afternoon as Cora trudged towards the Cottage Hospital. She wondered whether she had the strength to face what might await her there.

When she had been summoned to see Inspector Ramm that morning, she had met Gwendoline Cope coming out of the police station. They had little to say to each other. Cora knew that what had happened in the tower would bind them in a way that went beyond words.

She opened the door into the small ward and saw Oliver was

still on the narrow bed where he had been for the last four days. He was staring upwards. Then he turned to look at her and his eyes opened wider.

"Oliver, do you remember me?" she asked, grasping his hand.

"Remember you?" He tried to laugh, but it turned into a cough. "Of course! How could I forget you?"

"But…" Cora began, searching for the right words. "You were so poorly and so… strange."

"The doctor says I was poisoned by some sort of gas. I still don't know what's been going on or how long I have been here. They wouldn't tell me. I'm just glad to see you, my darling."

They fixed each other with a gaze of longing and there were tears in their eyes.

The news of Oliver's improved condition helped to lighten the mood in the Blake house that supper time.

"It means so much to be able to talk to him again," Cora said, "although the doctor says we need to wait and see. It might take a long time for him to recover completely."

"FJ is going to have his work cut out without Oliver there to write half the newspaper. He will have to find someone to help him," Nathaniel mused.

For the first time in days, Cora dared to think about the future and her life with Oliver. At last there was a glimmer of hope, but she was not as happy as she thought she should be. Memories of what had happened with Miss Cope still weighed on her mind.

As soon as young William left the kitchen, Cora spoke up. "Father, can I ask you something?" Edith noticed a change in Cora's tone and cast her a concerned look.

"Certainly, my dear," her father replied.

"How did Dr Jervis die? I know he was in the ice, but was there anything else?"

Nathaniel's heart sank as he thought of the anguish she must be going through. "Oh Cora, I know the hurt is still fresh, but you must not torment yourself over that tragic affair."

"I need to know, Father!" she said with a steel that startled Nathaniel. He knew she would not rest until he gave her an answer.

"Inspector Ramm told me that the poor chap was stabbed, perhaps by someone with medical knowledge," he said.

"In the neck?"

"Why yes, I think that is what he said." Nathaniel was puzzled. How did she know that?

"Oh." Cora's voice shrank to a whisper. She looked across the room blankly, lost in her thoughts.

"Cora, please try to forget it," Nathaniel urged. "After a good night's sleep, things will start to look better in the morning."

But she knew her father was wrong. The ordeal was not over yet.

Chapter Twenty Four

As Inspector Ramm walked along Haywood Street towards the police station the following morning, he was puzzling as to how he should write his report on the tangled affairs that came to a head at the asylum. Although Walter Wainwright had apparently confessed to murder and arson, he could not be convicted because he was now dead. And a prosecution arising from Wainwright's strange death was unlikely. It looked like the investigation could be brought to a close, Ramm thought.

But his plans were thrown into confusion as soon as he opened the station's heavy front door.

"You have a visitor, Inspector," said Sergeant Reynolds, leaning across the reception counter and taking some pleasure in his superior's look of surprise. "It's Miss Blake."

Ramm frowned and glanced at the wall clock. "It's not yet eight o'clock!"

"She's been waiting for half an hour," Reynolds added.

When he reached his office, he saw that Cora appeared only slightly less tired than the previous day. Her eyes were no longer red, but there were had dark shadows beneath them. When she spoke, however, her voice showed something of her old resolve.

"Good morning, Inspector. I wanted to speak to you about Mr Wainwright," Cora began as soon as Ramm had settled into his chair.

"Indeed? Well I can assure you, Miss Blake, that after what you and Miss Cope told me yesterday, I am convinced that he was to blame for the fire at the *Lion* and, of course, the death of Dr Jervis. You have no need to worry about that."

Cora nodded and opened her mouth to speak, but Ramm, anxious to reassure her, carried on quickly.

"And if you are concerned about what happened to him in the water tower, I think it highly unlikely that any blame will be put on either of you."

Cora paused, apparently thinking how best to phrase her words.

"I've been thinking about it all night. What if Mr Wainwright didn't kill Dr Jervis?"

Ramm sat back in his chair, surprised to hear this.

"But you and Miss Cope said he admitted it," he said, his brow creased in exasperation.

"Mr Wainwright did say a lot of horrible things about Dr Jervis. But nothing about murdering him."

"Well, who said it, then?" Ramm asked, more forcefully than he intended, making Cora jump.

"It was Miss Cope. She said something like 'He attacked Dr Jervis. He's a murderer'."

"So what did Wainwright actually say?"

"I can't remember every word, Inspector. We were tired and so frightened. He said he was glad Dr Jervis was dead, but it seemed that he thought the doctor had drowned in the canal," Cora replied.

"That's not the impression Miss Cope gave me, I must say," said Ramm. He was disappointed at this new complication just when he thought the case was wrapped up.

"He did admit to starting the fire though? Or is that something else you no longer remember?" he continued.

"Oh no, I shall never forget that. He was almost proud of it."

Ramm went quiet. Miss Blake had put doubt in his own mind. Had he been too hasty in condemning Wainwright? But if it wasn't the chemist, who was the murderer? They might have to start the investigation all over again. That was unthinkable.

"Miss Blake, I very much appreciate you coming in to… clarify, shall we say… what you remembered. The whole thing must have been a terrible ordeal and I am sure it will take you some time to make sense of it all."

"But the stabbing…" Cora managed three words before Ramm cut her off.

"Honestly, we may never know the reason why Mr Wainwright behaved as he did. However, I am satisfied he was to blame for the crimes and for that reason, the cases will be closed."

Ramm felt guilty when he saw the dejected expression on Cora's face. He hated to turn the young woman away and cast aside her theories, but in truth, he thought it was for the best.

Cora nodded and hurried out.

Nathaniel was waiting anxiously when Cora arrived at the studio. Both he and Edith had been concerned when she had left the house so early, saying she needed to go to the police station.

"Inspector Ramm must have been surprised to see you this morning. What was so urgent?" he asked.

Cora hesitated before answering. "Oh, I wanted to tell him what I thought about Mr Wainwright," Cora replied.

"And did the Inspector think that was useful?"

"Apparently not." With that she turned away and began sorting through some postcards.

Whatever was going on, Nathaniel suspected it was more complicated than his daughter was admitting.

As the morning wore on, he tried to draw her into conversation, but received no more than the odd word in reply. Finally, when it was nearing midday, Cora called up the stairs to say she needed to go out. Before Nathaniel could ask where she was going, he heard the shop door slam shut.

Inspector Ramm had found it difficult to concentrate on his

paperwork for the rest of the morning, although he knew the Coroner and the Chief Constable were waiting for matters to be concluded.

Miss Blake's visit had disturbed him. What was she getting at? Why did she think Wainwright was not the murderer when she and Miss Cope were supposed to have heard him admit it?

He regretted the way he had reacted. Perhaps he should have let her finish? Perhaps he should delve a little further himself, just to be on the safe side?

He turned back to his papers, then threw down his pen and went to find Constable Phillips.

"Miss Cope is empployed in town, is she not? Did she tell you where?" he asked the officer.

"Yes, she told me she's at Miss Heath's, that fancy hat shop in the Market Place," Phillips replied.

Ramm returned to his office. He decided he would write another page, then stroll up to the Market Place. He wanted to hear again from Miss Cope exactly what had happened in the tower.

Gwendoline Cope seemed startled when Cora entered the hat shop. She looked around nervously just as she had done the first time Cora had gone there.

"I need to speak to you," said Cora, dispensing with the niceties of polite conversation.

"Oh? It might be rather awkward, Miss Blake. I am expecting Miss Heath back at any moment. Perhaps we could arrange another time…"

"It has to be now," Cora interrupted firmly.

Gwendoline took a moment to consider, then agreed. "Well, if you must. I hope you are recovered after that awful business on Sunday? I must say I still feel exhausted."

Cora ignored the comment, her face set hard.

"Why did you kill him?" she asked bluntly.

Gwendoline's expression was one of total surprise. "Kill? That awful Wainwright, do you mean? You know as well as I do that it was self defence. He was trying to do away with us."

"No he wasn't. He was just standing there and you threw yourself at him and stabbed him in the throat with your hat pin," Cora countered. "At first I thought you'd saved our lives. Then I started to remember exactly what happened."

Gwendoline's voice rose almost to a shriek. "He had killed James! The monster deserved it!" She reached for a posh handkerchief to press to her mouth, apparently about to cry.

Cora was unmoved. "Dr Jervis was stabbed, wasn't he? In the neck," she said, staring accusingly at Miss Cope.

"I know nothing about that," Gwendoline replied, shaking her head vigorously as if refusing to imagine the horrific scene.

"He was drawn to the canal by someone who sent him a postcard signed with a 'G'. That was you, wasn't it? Then you stabbed him, just like Mr Wainwright."

"No! No!" Gwendoline screamed, looking about wildly as if searching for help or an escape.

"What had he done to deserve that? I thought you said you loved him."

The word 'love' jolted Gwendoline from panic to the sort of vicious state Cora had seen when she set about Walter Wainwright.

"Love? James didn't know the meaning of the word! I worshipped him. I gave him everything he wanted. Everything! And then he cast me aside – just when I needed him the most!"

Although Cora had been steeling herself all morning for this confrontation, she was taken aback by the sheer hatred in Miss Cope's voice.

"I was desperate when I begged to see him that last evening. Desperate! But he just gave one of his smiles and said I needed to pull myself together. Said he couldn't get involved, didn't want to see me again… ever!"

"Did you use a hat pin, like you did on Mr Wainwright?"

"I never planned to do it, but when he was so, so horrible to me, all I could think about was hurting him." Gwendoline's voice trailed off as she seemed to focus on her memory of that night beside the canal.

"When he was lying there I panicked. I got some things out of his pockets to keep and... and I pushed him into the canal."

"And when we were in the tower you realised Mr Wainwright could take the blame," said Cora.

"You think you are so clever, don't you Miss Blake?" Gwendoline had snapped back to the present. "You don't know what you are talking about. James turned out to be a cad and Wainwright was fool to think I would ever consider him! They both deserved what they got!"

Cora was transfixed by the tall woman's malevolent gaze. She didn't notice Gwendoline's hand resting on a pair of dressmaker's shears on the counter.

Suddenly Miss Cope dived forwards, thrusting the point of the shears at Cora's neck. Cora cried out and was knocked backwards into the window display, toppling hats from their stands.

Gwendoline was towering over her and Cora was trying to squirm free when the shop door was flung open. Inspector Ramm threw himself at the attacker.

"Get out of the way!" Ramm gasped at Cora as he struggled to restrain Miss Cope who was still raging about the way Dr Jervis had betrayed her. After a desperate struggle with the woman, whose fury seemed to have given her unforeseen strength, he finally managed to put handcuffs on her.

A small crowd, including a distraught Miss Heath, had gathered outside the shop by the time a constable arrived to escort Miss Cope to the police station.

"Straight to the cells," said Ramm ordered as he wrapped a

handkerchief around a jagged wound on his wrist. "She's got a lot of explaining to do."

When the drama had subsided and the onlookers had begun to drift away, Inspector Ramm drew Cora to one side.

"Let me walk you back to your father's studio, Miss Blake," he said. "But first I must apologise for not taking more notice of you this morning. It appears you had a better idea of the culprit than I did."

Cora was hugging herself, shaking from both cold and shock.

"Really you should not have gone to see Miss Cope on your own. That woman is dangerous," said Ramm as they started across the Market Square towards Sheepmarket.

"I was beginning to think no one would believe me," said Cora. "I suppose I hadn't really thought what would happen if I came to the shop. But in the end she admitted she killed Dr Jervis."

"What gave you the idea it was her?"

"She had been acting oddly and saying strange things right from the start," Cora explained. "She was so quick to say Mr Wainwright was the murderer and so vicious when she attacked him.

"And when Father told me Dr Jervis was stabbed in the neck by someone with a medical knowledge, it all seemed to fit. I remembered Miss Cope saying she had books about nursing."

Ramm nodded appreciatively. Cora's powers of deduction were worthy of a detective, he thought.

"Of course, there was the hat pin. I must admit, that did make me wonder," he said.

"Yes, she was so quick at stabbing Mr Wainwright. As if she had done it before. It was horrible," Cora agreed, then added: "And I always thought that postcard had been written by a woman."

By now they had reached the Blake studio. Ramm opened the door and gave Cora a helping hand into the shop. Nathaniel, who had been worried where she had got to, hurried forward with a look of concern.

"Your daughter has had another adventure, Mr Blake," said Ramm. "But she has also done us a great service."

Ramm left Nathaniel to comfort and question his daughter. He knew he had a busy afternoon ahead unravelling the truth about the murderous Miss Cope.

Chapter Twenty Five

"I always thought that woman seemed peculiar." Ellen Simms was sitting with Cora in Pickford's Tea Room in St Edward Street. It was nearly two weeks after the dramatic scene at Miss Heath's milliner's shop.

"And you were so lucky that Inspector Ramm arrived just when he did. Otherwise…"

"Yes, I suppose it was foolish of me to go there on my own," Cora admitted.

"It was amazing you figured out that she killed the doctor."

"There were just so many things that made me suspicious. And when I saw the way she handled that long hat pin…"

The two were quiet for a while as they turned their attention to their tea and scones. It was Ellen who picked up the conversation again. "Are you still having nightmares about that water tower?" she asked gently.

"Not as often, thanks. And now Oliver is out of hospital, I have plenty of other things to think about."

"What about us going to London for the protest march? I don't suppose your parents are keen on that," Ellen asked a little wistfully, wondering whether her friend's suffragette activities would be coming to an end. "They are going to keep a close eye on you from now on," she teased.

"Well, that will be Oliver's job soon," Cora smiled. "Until then, there's still time for a little protesting. As long as I stay out of trouble!"

It was good to laugh again, she thought.

EPILOGUE

The Leek Lion

SATURDAY, JUNE 22ND 1907

MARRIAGE ANNOUNCEMENT

The marriage took place at St. Luke's Parish Church, Leek, on Saturday last of Miss Cora Elizabeth Blake, elder daughter of Mr. and Mrs. Nathaniel Blake of Portland Street, Leek, and Mr. Oliver Finch, only son of Mr. and Mrs. Fellowes Jeremiah Finch of Bath Street, Leek. The Vicar, the Rev. W. Beresford officiated. The bride was given in marriage by her father and attended by Miss Ellen Simms, a friend of the bride. After the ceremony a reception was held in the Assembly Rooms at the Swan with Two Necks, Leek.

The couple are to make their home in New Zealand.

NEW RECRUIT AT THE *LION*

Mr. Edward Croft has been appointed Senior Reporter at the *Leek Lion*. An experienced journalist, Mr. Croft was formerly Editor of the now defunct *Moorland Argus* which ceased publication in April.

VACANCY: Photographer's assistant. Candidate must have knowledge of photographic processes or be willing to learn. Duties to include printing of postcards, picture framing, processiong of photographic negatives, serving of customers, arrangement of window displays, handling of cash, occasional cleaning of premises. Must be of orderly habits, reliable and honest. Apply: Blake the Photographer, Sheepmarket, Leek.

FOR SALE: Shop premises, centrally located in Derby Street, Leek. Latterly operated as profitable chemist and druggist. All fixtures, fittings and stock included in sale. Ideal business opportunity awaits the right buyer. Apply: Bishton, Solicitor, 3 Church Lane, Leek.

Historical Notes

The plot and main characters of this book are fictitious, however the background to the action depicts genuine aspects of life in Leek and the Staffordshire Moorlands in Edwardian times. The descriptions of the County Asylum at Cheddleton give an idea of what the vast complex was like in 1907, less than a decade after it opened and before the site was masked by trees and shrubs. The institution went on to play a significant part in the community for over a century and employed hundreds of local people.

Readers may recognise many of the buildings which are mentioned, although some have been demolished or changed use. Chief amongst these, the County Asylum ultimately became St Edward's Hospital and finally closed in 2002. It is now the St Edward's Park residential estate and many original buildings have been converted to homes, including the water tower. Other locations which have been either lost or changed include:

Leek Railway Station: now site of Morrison's supermarket

Leek Police Station, Leonard Street: converted to apartments

Cattle Market: now site of the Smithfield shopping precinct

Leek Memorial Hospital, Stockwell Street: converted to apartments

Leek Fire Station, Stockwell Street: converted to a nightclub

Leek Town Hall, Market Street: demolished, now a car park

The *Leek Lion* office is fictional, although the real-life *Leek Times* had offices in Market Street in the late Victorian era.

Brunswick Methodist Church, Market Street: demolished, now a car park

Cruso's Yard, off Stockwell Street: demolished, now the entrance to Moorlands House

Wall Grange Station: now a private house

The Temperance Hall, Union Street: became the Majestic Cinema which burnt down in 1961, site is now part of Leek College

The following sources have been invaluable in my historical research:

The *Leek Times* newspaper files

Images of Edwardian Leek by Paul Anderton

A History of Psychiatry in North Staffordshire by Edward D Myers

History of St Edward's Hospital, Cheddleton by Max Chadwick and David Pearson

Local historian Brian Morris

Finally, my original inspiration for Nathaniel Blake was Leek's Edwardian photographer WH Nithsdale, although I know of no murder mysteries which Nithsdale and his daughter were involved in. Some of his photographs appear in the chapter headings of this book.